BESTSELLING AUTHOR

KAT T. MASEN

DEDICATION

For those still obsessed with the 80's.

OTHER Books by

KAT T. MASEN

The Dark Angel Series
Into the Darkness
Into the Light
Adriana
Julian

#Jerk

PLAYLIST

These are some of the songs that inspired me and made my characters come alive.

Heaven Is A Place On Earth by Belinda Carlisle
True Blue by Madonna
Love Shack by B-52's
Get Outta My Dreams, Get Into My Car by Billy Ocean
Broken Wings by Mr. Mister
The Flame by Cheap Trick
Eternal Flame by The Bangles
Total Eclipse Of The Heart by Bonnie Tyler
All Through The Night by Cyndi Lauper
Hungry Eyes by Eric Carmen
In These Arm's by Bon Jovi
I Want To Know What Love Is by Foreigner
Right Here Waiting For You by Richard Marx
Heaven by Bryan Adams

PROLOGUE

"*I*'M SORRY, YOU'RE INTO WHAT?"

I glance down at the rental application form, trying my best to make sense of what this guy just told me. Male, twenty-four, employed as a DJ at a popular night club in a seedy part of town.

"I'm into amateur sex. Filming hard-core amateur sex scenes. Will bringing girls here be a problem?" he questions, walking around the room, observing the prints on the wall as if this topic of conversation is no big deal.

I want to laugh. I *should* laugh. Is this guy for real?

"Kenny, is it?" I ask politely, without trying to ridicule him.

He cocks his head to the side and gives a nod, flashing his gold tooth like he just stepped out of a bad hip-hop video. "Women like to call me Ken."

I feed into my curiosity, which is usually a bad thing. "Why do women like to call you Ken?"

Shuffling closer, invading what I like to call my 'personal space,' he responds in his most seductive voice, "Because if I'm Ken, you can be Barbie, and yours can be the box I come in."

My throat closes, causing me to choke. That has to be the cheesiest line I have ever heard in my life! There is no way any woman would fall for this. Not unless they were drunk and desperately looking for a rebound. Even then—it's a far shot.

He rests his hand on his belt, lifting his baggy jeans that have fallen during his attempt to seduce me. His knock-off Calvin Klein's are purposely exposed, and I swear, with the thick gold chain draped around his neck, we've stepped back into the nineties when this was considered fashion. The logo on his shirt says FBI, with small writing below it that reads *Female Body Inspector.* Everything about this guy screams loser, and not the roommate I am hoping to find today.

Next.

I send him on his merry way, but not before he propositions me again by leaving his business card on my coffee table. *Wishful thinking, dude.*

Outside my doorway, another two applicants are waiting in the hall. After interviewing ten people today, I am praying that my next roommate is one of the guys left in the hallway.

I placed the advertisement only a week ago. My last roommate, Cherise, did a runner, leaving me with a pile of dishes and two weeks of unpaid rent. Apparently her boyfriend popped the question so she automatically took that as 'let's move in together.' Since then, I've been gun-shy about the whole finding-a-roommate thing. I had this theory—females were more likely to move in with a guy based on a spontaneous moment.

Men, they stood their ground for as long as they could. I figured it couldn't be too hard to live with a guy. I have years of experience with two older brothers. So they stink, and occasionally, if not always, leave a trail of mess behind them. The toilet seat is left up and count yourself lucky if you live with a male who actually knows how to aim. I'll take that over girly drama any day.

I open the door and call the next person in, my eyes glued to the clipboard that rests in my hands. Then, in walks blue eyes.

Blue eyes—or Liam, as his application form says—is an

absolute drop-dead stunner. His occupation says 'model.' *Well, duh.* Liam extends his hand and I shake it, noticing how soft, and large, his hands are. With my jaw permanently stuck to the ground, I attempt to compose myself and start the interview.

I clear my throat, trying to calm the nervous energy that so quickly escalated between my legs. "So Liam, tell me a little bit about yourself."

"Sure." He smiles warmly, and I can't help but be drawn to his full lips. They look so delicious and . . . *focus!* I cross my legs, ignoring my raging libido.

"I've got three sisters, all younger. I enjoy playing sports, my favorite sport being football."

Oh sweet Jesus.

The temperature in the room is stifling hot, and I scan the coffee table for the air-conditioner remote. It's nowhere in sight, so I'm forced to sit here in front of this beautiful man and pretend he has no effect on me whatsoever. All the while praying that my deodorant lives up to its slogan, protecting me from any sticky situation with round-the-clock fresh-smelling armpits.

His pose distracts me. Long, athletic legs with the perfect amount of muscle covered in loose shorts. If I tilted my head to the right, quite possibly, I could sneak a peek at the crown jewels.

He continues to speak, interrupting my plan. "I'm an aspiring model but during the week, I volunteer at an orphanage across town."

I'm swooning. I have never, *ever,* in my life swooned over a guy. I'm certain that an angel dropped this perfect man into my apartment with his piercing blue eyes, dashing smile, and gorgeous ripped body just to test me. He looks and sounds smart, and is everything a woman would want to wake up to each morning for the rest of her life.

But I'm roommate-hunting, not on some game show

looking for love.

My heart, mind, and body are torn into a great dividing wall.

I spent the last year saving every penny so I could afford to finish my degree in architecture. Distractions would deter me from reaching my goal. I'd be on edge all the time, trying to impress him or something. God forbid I wore my ratty T-shirt with the holes all over my back or leave my granny undies hanging in the bathroom. I know myself too well—I have to let him go.

But he is so pretty it hurts!

Move on.

Next.

I continue to make small talk then tell him I'll call him with an answer. Being the perfect gentleman, he extends his hand once again and a little too eager, I grab it and don't let go. The shake seems to go on forever until I reluctantly pull away. Liam walks out the door, allowing me a few minutes to pull myself together. *Why am I letting this guy go again?* Shake it off, Zoey. Eyes on the prize, not on his pants.

I call the next person to come in. The door creaks open and a young guy pops his head round the corner. I'm surprised by how young he looks—maybe twentyish—but it could be the SpongeBob T-shirt and old Chucks he's wearing. He is slightly on the chubby side, appearing self-conscious while he fans his body by airing the bottom of his shirt. He looks pretty ordinary with his dark hair and brown eyes hiding behind thick black glasses.

Placing his hand in his pocket, he pulls out his inhaler and takes a puff while I wait for him to get himself together.

Just admit it, he screams geek.

Perfect!

I motion for him to take a seat, and he sits down on the brown leather armchair and looks around the room uncomfortably, struggling to make eye contact.

"So, Andrew," I start, reading the details on his form. "Tell me a little bit about yourself."

"Uh, okay," he stutters nervously. "I'm twenty-four. Currently studying medicine. I work at a video store down at the mall while I finish my degree."

There is something unique about his accent. Not quite American, a hint of British or Australian if I'm not mistaken. I want to ask him, but he seems to be nervous and intimidated by this process. It isn't like a job interview. It's odd that a grown man would be nervous around me.

"Studying to be a doctor? Impressive," I tell him. "And your surname is Baldwin. Are you related to Alec, Stephen, Daniel, and what's the other one that starred in that movie as a stalker?"

He appears to relax a little, then releases a soft chuckle. "Can't say we're related but I think you're referring to Billy."

Of course he knows that. Sharon Stone is the epitome of sex goddess and every jerk-off fantasy. If you're a guy and haven't seen *Sliver,* you might as well be gay.

"Well, Andrew. Your application looks good and so far, you're the best applicant."

Just get this over and done with. Get Liam and his perfect everything out of your head. You didn't work your ass off so you could throw it away because of some guy that would make such beautiful babies. Andrew ticked all the boxes. He looked intelligent in a geeky kinda way, not a womanizer that would attract ladies to the apartment, *and most of all, I am not attracted to him one bit.*

I give him my best welcoming smile. "When can you move in?"

Adjusting his glasses above the bridge of his nose, he manages a small smile, extending his hand as we shake on our new agreement.

It would be the first time I lived with a man besides my dad and brothers, and the first time Andrew ever lived with a woman. After much deliberation, we agreed we needed to establish rules. And so, Zoey Richards and Andrew Baldwin vowed never to break the five cardinal rules of the roommate agreement:

Rule number 1:   Neither of us have 'maid' listed on our resume. It's every man/woman to clean up after themselves.

Rule number 2:   The toilet seat should *always* be left down.

Rule number 3:   No partners or lovers are to stay more than one night in a row. Otherwise rent is payable.

Rule number 4:   All disputes are to be settled old-school: rock, paper, scissors.

Rule number 5:   Nudity is not acceptable. In the event of any mishaps, it must never, ever, be spoken of again.

Just five simple rules we needed to stick to, and yes, I added the last one since I had a bad habit of getting drunk and sleeping naked on the couch.

A week later, Andrew Baldwin moved in, and I officially had a roomie.

CHAPTER One

Zoey

*O*H CRAP.

I look down at my tattered Rainbow Brite shirt. The guacamole sits right in the middle of my collarbone, producing a nice stain next to the ketchup spill from last week. Pulling my shirt towards my mouth, I run my tongue along the edge and carefully try to clean myself up.

Yeah, I'm a slob.

A slob that is lying across the couch on a Friday night watching reruns of *Friends.* The episode airing is hilarious; one of my all-time classic favorites. It's when the girls lose the apartment, forgetting Chandler's ever-so-elusive job title. I'm in stitches, accidentally spitting a corn chip that goes flying across the room. I should probably go pick it up, yet continue to lie here ignoring the mess surrounding me.

It's the best way to unwind after a horrendous week in the office. It's surprising that I made it through the week without strangling my boss. Another reminder that my job sucked, and I was the moron putting up with his shit. Cue the violins; I only have myself to blame, and sitting beside a bag of jumbo corn chips I found at Costco is living proof.

Sadly, the jumbo bag of corn chips was the highlight of my week. I literally jumped with excitement when I came across them stacked up on the shelf. I also resorted to taking a selfie with the chips and went on to post it online, hash-tagging the pic like an attention-craving social media whore.

Pathetic in all forms.

And that says everything about how uneventful my life had become.

Since Friday night is supposed to be the time to let loose and party, I thought why not skip dinner and head straight to the corn chips and guacamole—and it's not a party without some beers. I'm even wearing my fluorescent-pink hoop earrings with my hair crimped just for fun.

Party of one. Just little old me.

Throughout the ads, I begin to channel surf when I hear the rattle of the door followed by the sound of keys. The door opens wide and my roommate, Drew, walks in carrying a grocery bag. With his spare hand, he shuts the door behind him and throws the keys onto the nightstand that sits near the entrance.

I'm not surprised that Drew is still dressed in his scrubs since he practically lived at the hospital. On top, he wears a grey hoody with matching grey Nikes. My eyes move back to his grocery bag, praying that he picked up some shampoo since I used the last of his bottle this morning. All I see is carrots and a bunch of green stuff. *Ugh.*

"You know, that shirt doesn't have much life left in it. Another spill and I think it's time to part ways," Drew happily points out while blocking my view of the TV.

"Oh, hello roomie! Nice to see you. How was your day, Zoey? Fine thanks, Drew," I commentate.

"Hi Zo, how was your day?" he humors me.

I don't even give him a chance to sit down, and rant about my shitty day at work that began when my asshole boss walked into the office with a chip on his shoulder. I refer to

that chip on his shoulder as his stay-at-home wife, who I believe is having an affair with the electrician. *There's only so many bulbs that need replacing.*

"So then he says to me, 'I sent you that email yesterday Zoey, to be acted on today,' and I'm like, it was to order paper for the photocopier. The receptionist does that. I'm supposed to be your right hand, learning about architecture and studying blueprints, not fetching paper." I let out a huff, barely catching my breath. "Anyway, how was your day?"

"A woman died on the table today. Complications with a breast augmentation done by some backyard surgeon."

His face remains placid, and I struggle to comprehend how someone can watch that happen and then carry on as if it's an ordinary day. Plus, I'm a douchebag for rambling on about my problems.

I twist my body and sit up straight. "I'm sorry. God, I sound like an idiot with my first-world problems."

"I like your first-world problems. But seriously Zo, get rid of the shirt. And what's with the pink earrings?" He grimaces.

Drew liked to joke around, but this is taking it too far. Shirt jokes were not well received. This wasn't the first time we'd had this conversation and it wouldn't be the last.

"Do you know how long I've had this shirt? And if I get rid of this shirt, you get rid of your SpongeBob shirt."

"You owned it before you had a pair of tits. Your auntie gave it to you on your thirteenth birthday. You almost lost the shirt in your move back in two thousand and you cried for a week till you found it buried in a box labelled *fragile*," he says all in one breath. "And the answer is no. SpongeBob stays."

"Okay, Mr. Know-It-All," I sneer. "My point is that it's still in great condition and this stain would easily come out."

Truth be told, this shirt had weeks' left, a couple of months tops. The last time I ran it through the wash,

Rainbow Brite lost her dress, leaving only the outline of her head. The holes keep getting bigger and that ketchup stain is a reminder that the fabric is so fragile that even the best of stain removers wouldn't work. This shirt is my comfort zone, and I have a terrible habit of holding on to things of the past.

Like my ex, Jess.

Don't think about that dirt bag now.

"There's holes all over the back. And Zo . . . I think your nipples are showing."

I look down in horror. *Bullshit.* In fear of losing my shirt at this very moment, I stretch my arms and remove it, standing in the living room, only wearing my white-laced bra.

"Happy? I'll soak it now."

His eyes wander to my breasts, and he does that thing with his lips where he bites the corner. Boy did it annoy the shit out of me! The same bite that supposedly got women into his bed at the drop of a hat. "Hey, just looking out for your shirt."

I mumble something about him being a dick on the way to the bathroom. Placing my shirt in the sink, I run the hot water and let it soak with some stain remover, praying for a miracle before heading to my room and opening my wardrobe.

As usual, my wardrobe is full yet I have nothing to wear. Rephrase—nothing that fits.

The right-hand side is jam-packed with designer dresses and skirts that no longer zip up, and the few hangers on the left-hand side hold a couple of new pieces that I was forced to buy. Otherwise, I would be wearing only my birthday suit every day.

I tug the grey tank off the hanger and quickly put it on. The full-length mirror is positioned next to the wardrobe and stupid me stops to examine myself. I take a deep breath to

control the anxiety that seeps its way through when I see how much weight I've gained.

For some reason, I have no idea how to stop the vicious cycle I fell into of eating and sitting on the couch. My gym membership continues to be debited from my account, yet I hadn't stepped foot in a gym in over a year. The motivation, willpower, and drive for success in all areas in my life disappeared into thin air.

Turning to the side, the extra skin across my belly sits comfortably on my sweatpants. *Muffin top.* And is it wrong that the word 'muffin' just makes me hungrier? If Drew wasn't my roomie, I would probably smash this mirror to pieces with how angry I am at myself for getting to this point. But I knew better than to be destructive and I head back to the living room, ignoring my inner demons.

I plonk myself back on the couch with the remote in hand. It's not long before a delicious aroma enters the living room and I breathe in the exotic spices that make my stomach growl in anticipation. Drew is humming away, some tune to a song that sounds familiar. We didn't exactly see eye to eye with music. Drew liked modern funk or whatever the crap they play in clubs is, and I'm all about the eighties. Madonna was—and always will be—the goddess of music.

"Whatcha cooking?" I yell out.

"Do you really want to know?"

I probably don't. Another thing we didn't see eye to eye on: food.

Drew is a health nut and is always trying some new diet that involved food claiming to be the next best thing for your body. We were forever arguing over the food I purchased, and Drew was the biggest nagger when it came to what food you put in your mouth. He drove me insane. A far cry from the guy who walked into my apartment four years ago.

Andrew Baldwin, the chubby geek that I chose as a roomie over Mr. Blue Eyes.

Back then, Andrew was your typical university student living on pizza and Ramen noodles, struggling to get his medical degree. After moving in, he made the decision to go on a health kick given the demanding hours he would soon have to commit to in the medical field. He admitted that he struggled with many things in his life, and his weight was one of them. At that time I couldn't relate, thinking I was invincible. Being twenty-five with a banging body, I thought I was one of those lucky women.

Ha! What a delusional idiot I turned out to be.

Andrew started hitting the gym every day and eating like a rabbit, while I threw myself into a destructive relationship. Over time he transformed his body and I had to admit, he looked *good*. He was no longer that geek who walked into my apartment that day. Spending that much time in the gym toned his body and it felt like overnight his abs came out of nowhere. For a while I thought he had some compulsive gym disorder, but he was just motivated and didn't stop till he achieved the results he was after. The cocky bastard knew he looked good and so began the shirtless parade through the apartment every day.

Watching him transform didn't bug me the slightest bit. If anything, I was proud that he made changes to better his situation. Aside from the weight loss, he cut his hair shorter and started wearing contacts. He threw out all his clothes and went on this shopping spree, purchasing trendier pieces since he was hitting the club scene every spare moment he got.

Women began throwing themselves at him, and soon, he referred to himself as 'Drew.' Of course I went along with it, being a supportive friend. He was living the life: a rocking body, a career beginning to take off, and gorgeous women begging to be in his bed. He knew how to play the 'Doctor' card when it came to luring women to his room.

I'll be the first to admit that seeing him transform should have motivated me, but instead, I went the opposite

direction.

Throwing myself into a relationship that was toxic.

Jess was your typical tattooed bad boy. A chain-smoking, Harley-Davidson-driving bad boy.

He was every daddy's worse nightmare. My own dad warned me on several occasions that I could do better than him. That his little girl deserved the world, and Jess was a deadbeat living paycheck to paycheck with a drinking problem. It just took me so long to figure that out.

We dated for a year and half, breaking up a dozen times because of his jealous antics. It's easy to look back now and realize how destructive our relationship was, but in the midst of it all, I thought I was going to marry him.

We vacationed at some beautiful resorts, and had fun most of the time, but Jess's drinking problem spiraled out of control. It was brought to my attention by Drew one day, yet I ignored him, thinking he was pissed off because Jess spent so much time at our apartment. When Jess got drunk, Drew was his target. The thought of me living with a male drove him insane.

To think I nearly moved out to live with him in his rundown shack shows how pathetic I was. I guess you could say that it was a blessing that I found my ex-best friend, Callie, blowing him in the back of his workshop.

Reiterate—ex-best friend.

I lost my sense of strong, independent Zoey, and turned into the devil, cursing revenge on their lame asses. I was on a warpath to make their lives a living hell, and in the meantime, all that did was put me in a depressive funk that could only be cured by eating more.

My love life dwindled after that and not because I didn't get any offers, but because I just couldn't be bothered anymore. I had joined the anti-men bandwagon. They were all the same. At least in my eyes they were.

"Since you didn't reply, I'll take it you're not interested?"

Drew yells back from the kitchen.

"Pass," I shout back, digging into my corn chips.

He emerges ten minutes later with a plate of green crap. Settling on the couch beside me, he devours his meal, making these odd sounds. It smelled good but boy did it look like a pile of mush.

"Geez, you sound like you're having an orgasm."

"Kale does that to you." He moans on purpose, closing his eyes as he runs his tongue along his top lip.

"Honestly, where is the fun-loving Andrew that would fight for the last slice of Hawaiian pizza? Remember pizza wars? When we would battle for the last slice?"

"I believe that is buried along with that name. C'mon Zo, you know I hate being called Andrew."

I wasn't about to get into that argument again. Drew struggled with talking about his past every time I got all Dr. Phil on him. It's a *man* thing. Something I wish I could do because I had no problem dragging up the past. A *woman* thing.

Fumbling with the remote and skipping past all the Friday-night rubbish on TV, I stop at some wedding dress show until Drew warns me to keep surfing.

"The last time you watched this, you cried for an hour, saying you would end up a spinster collecting cats."

"It was that time of the month," I mumble with a mouthful of corn chips.

He removes the remote from my hands and settles on some travel show. Although I let out an annoyed huff, crossing my arms like a spoiled child, I end up enjoying watching the hosts trek through Asia and explore different cultures. Another reminder that my life had become so stagnant. Yet that push, that drive, my mojo, had no desire to go experience life outside of this apartment and my office.

"So, what are you doing this weekend?" I ask, swiftly

changing the subject before my head explodes.

"I'm going to the beach down the coast with a couple of guys. I think it would be good for you to join us."

"Why? You know I hate the sun. It's a freckle funeral in this heat."

"Because you need to get out. Ever since you broke up with what's-his-face you've been down in the dumps, eating rubbish, and watching reruns. You're young, Zo, how many other single girls at twenty-nine do you see doing the same thing?"

"They don't because they're all engaged or married."

"Exactly."

"I don't need a man. I'm fine."

"When you can say that to me without pulling that ridiculous face, I'll believe you. And as for tomorrow, go find your bikini because I'll be dragging you out of bed at six am."

"SIX!" I cry out.

Fuck. My bikini would cover only one boob. I hadn't worn it since my ill-fated trip to Fiji with Jess. Back then I was a B cup. These Ds had no chance of staying put.

"I'm not going," I say firmly.

Turning to face me, he extends his hand. "Rock, paper, scissors?"

"Argh, you're so annoying," I moan, following his move.

We both clench our fists and shake three times. At the same time, we release our hands, both pulling out rock. We repeat the game and when Drew pulls out rock again, I throw my scissors hand into the air in frustration.

"Okay. You win," I complain, sinking deeper into the couch with my arms folded.

Drew pulls my wrist towards him, reading the time on my watch. "Shit. I've got to start getting ready."

"Hot date?"

He winks. *Man whore.*

Since Drew is so anal about cleaning, he couldn't leave without washing the dishes and tidying the kitchen. The dishwasher starts to run and he heads to the bathroom to take a shower, but not before accusing me of leaving corn chips all over the floor and ordering me to vacuum it up.

Housework is so mundane, so I do just a quick vacuum before shoving it back into the small storage cupboard without wrapping the cord around it properly. *I'll pay the price for that later once Drew finds it.*

Feeling lonely and bored, I walk to his room to find him out of the shower and changing into his clothes. Already wearing his skinny black jeans, he pulls a white tank over his head before grabbing his ironed shirt off the hanger.

"Ooh, that's your I'll-definitely-get-laid shirt," I tease, throwing myself on his bed while I fiddle with his iPod.

"I like to think every shirt is my definitely-get-laid shirt."

"Bets that you're bringing home a blonde," I tell him.

"Nah," he says casually. "How about two brunettes?"

I look up at him in shock. "A threesome?"

"Relax." He smiles. "I save those nights for when you're on work trips."

Without even thinking, I throw his pillow at him.

"What's that for?!" he yells, annoyed that the pillow touched his perfectly styled hair.

"For being a man whore. I liked it better when you were a geek that couldn't get laid and probably jerked off watching Princess Leia in Star Wars."

Who was I kidding, Drew being a man whore had its perks. Like how in the mornings the women were always trying to impress him by wearing his shirt and cooking him breakfast in the kitchen. At first, I was taken aback and slightly threatened, but soon realized there were advantages to his sleeping around. These chicks would cook enough for

an army. My favorite one-night stand was Jacinta. She cooked a mean omelet that I craved for weeks. I even asked Drew to bring her back but it was a big fat no. Something about her being clingy and being a dud in the bedroom. Such an arrogant asshole.

Drew takes a bottle of aftershave and sprays it on himself. The scent smothers the room and I inhale it, closing my eyes, enjoying the masculinity of the fragrance. Okay, maybe for a split second I am craving the touch of a man. *God, it's been forever. You're on the verge of becoming a nun. A pizza-eating, sweatpants-wearing nun.*

"How do I look?" he asks, turning around to face me.

Despite our platonic relationship, I'd be a fool not to see how good he looked. The maroon-checked shirt enhances his tan from his last vacation to Cancun. His dark brown hair is slicked to the side with a slight spike and his face is freshly shaven, showing off his masculine jawline. I notice that he has put in his contacts, his normal reading glasses sitting on his bedside table.

"Good. For a man whore," I add.

He moves towards me, leaning down to kiss my forehead. "I love you too."

With that said, he grabs his wallet, keys, and cell and tells me to behave.

The door shuts and I'm alone. *Again.*

Behave. Impossible to get into trouble when you're on your own and let out the biggest yawn at only nine o'clock.

Back in my room, I change into my nightie after brushing my teeth and applying my face cream. Pulling back the comforter, I climb into bed and make myself comfortable. The lamp sitting on my bedside table is turned on, so I pull my drawer open and take out my Kindle that so conveniently sits next to a pair of handcuffs I got as a gag gift at a bachelorette night. I put my iPod on shuffle and adjust the volume to low. The first song to play is Madonna's "True

Blue," and as I softly sing along to the lyrics, my head lies on the pillow, eyes staring widely at the ceiling.

True love . . . does that even exist?

I used to be a believer, but being burnt once was enough to make me a pessimist. Yet, I continue to lie here, dreaming that somehow, someway it'll happen to me. Find that great love that will rock me to my core. A man that will sweep me off my feet and love every part of me. The good, the bad, the ugly.

Alone, and in bed, the Kindle switches on and I begin to read a new release that my online book club is raving about. A book about a jerk. A very hot jerk according to the ladies. Somewhere during the seventh chapter, my eyes struggle to stay open and once again, I fall asleep to the only thing that keeps me company at night.

My fictional boyfriends.

CHAPTER Two

Drew

A WIDE SMILE SPREADS ACROSS my face as a warm sensation envelops my cock. I must be dreaming; one of those fantastic dreams where a girl's sucking you off like it's her last meal on earth. My arms stretch above my head and I let out a longwinded moan, forcing my eyes to open. *This is some fucking good head.*

The mess of brown hair surrounds my groin, and instantly, my eyes flash open wide and my body stills in fear while I take in the situation. *Oh fuck.* Quickly, I close my eyes, hoping it's all just a terrible dream. One that will go away once I open them again.

Her name is *Michelle* something. It only took one flirtatious glance across the dancefloor for me to realize that I needed to take her home. Long lean legs that had a nice bronze tan, and full tits that *begged* to be played with. The details were blurry; lots of shots and some dirty talk led to her being in my bed.

We stumbled back to the apartment where I told her to keep her trap shut if she wanted me to fuck her. Great, she cooperated. But then it happened. On our second round somewhere during the night, she started to blow me, and since the both of us were completely out of it, I ignored the fact that she was talking to my cock. *Baby talk.* Like I said, we both had a lot to drink, and just when I think I can move past that, she begins to giggle as she strokes my shaft.

"Who's the cutest little peewee in the room?" She giggles childishly.

And there it is again.

No man, and I repeat, no man wants their cock to be referred to as "little peewee." Especially since I knew I wasn't *little,* and I don't think peewee is the appropriate terminology for anyone above the age of four. Shit! How do I get out of this? My cock starts to feel flaccid, but I want to let her down gently without causing a scene.

My head moves towards the clock on my nightstand. *Seven am.* I told Zoey we would leave for the beach at seven. To her convenience, she hadn't knocked on the door to wake me up. No fucking surprises. *It is now or never . . .*

"Uh, Michelle." I gently tug on her hair, hoping I used the correct name. "As much as I would love for you to continue, I promised some friends I had to be somewhere."

Lifting her head, the mess of brown hair surrounds her pretty face. The bright-red lipstick that was perfectly applied last night is smeared across her lips, and beneath her vibrant blue eyes are traces of leftover mascara. Jesus, not the best sight. What the hell was I thinking?

You weren't thinking. You wanted to get laid.

She bows her head, giggling once again, continuing to latch onto my cock. "Surely a couple of minutes won't hurt?"

Of course a couple of minutes wouldn't hurt. But how could I blow under these circumstances? Her mouth envelops my cock once again, and with her childish noises gone, I shut my eyes tight, trying to remember my night with that French woman, Bijou. Now she was *all* woman. Mid-forties, mature, and knew how to get me off . . . *and quick.*

The next minute is spent with my mind on Bijou's beautiful tight pussy, drowning out the squeals of Michelle

till the pressure mounts and I can't hold it in any longer, blowing all over her manicured hands.

With a satisfied grin, she says, "See? A couple of minutes didn't hurt."

She looks proud. Accomplished, even. I didn't have the heart to say anything. I just wanted her gone and out of my life. Forced to open my eyes again, I manage a fake smile as she rolls to the side and puts my shirt on. *Oh no, not my favorite shirt. SpongeBob doesn't deserve this!*

"How about some breakfast before I go? Is French toast okay?" she asks coyly, standing beside the bed, tugging on the bottom of my shirt and trying to act all cute.

"Yeah, sure," I mutter.

She leaves the room and I jump out of bed, gathering my clothes for a quick shower. I needed to wash last night and this morning off me. This is probably why I should stop bringing random women home.

The door to the bathroom is shut and all I can hear is Zoey singing some godawful tune that used to annoy me when I was younger. About a love shack or something ridiculous. Her taste in music is appalling. It seriously wouldn't hurt her to turn on the radio and listen to something modern occasionally.

"Uh huh . . . yeah yeah!"

"Zoey!" I bang on the door.

Nothing.

"Baby . . ."

I bang on the door again, calling her name loudly. The water stops, so I wait for her to open the door, shuffling my feet impatiently. The door opens and she's wrapped a towel around her body. Her blonde hair is dripping wet against her back, her skin barely dry.

"*What?*" She scowls.

"You need to help me," I beg her, peering down the hall in

a panic.

Latching onto my arm with a forceful grip, she pulls me into the bathroom and shuts the door behind her. "What have you done now?"

I can barely make out Zoey's silhouette with steam lingering in the air. No wonder our bill is so high. The amount of hot water she uses is ridiculous. Quickly moving to the window, I click on the latch and lift it open, allowing the hot air to escape so the both of us can breathe a little.

"You need to get Michelle out of here."

"Who's Michelle?"

"The girl I brought home last night."

"The one that called your dick a 'little peewee'?" she asks, trying to keep a straight face.

"You heard that?"

"Hard not to," she chuckles.

"It's not little. Now please help me?"

"Okay, whatever." She continues to laugh while brushing her hair, complete disregard for the severity of the situation. "You owe me."

"Anything you want. Just please say we need to go out, that we have plans."

"We do have plans," she reminds me, waving her bikini in front of my face. "Okay fine. Can I finish getting changed or does your little peewee need to use the toilet?"

My teeth clench, followed by a low rumbling growl escaping my throat. *This isn't a fucking joke.* My anger combined with anxiety threatens my ability to think clearly.

But you have no choice; you need Zoey to fix the mess you created.

Leaving her to complete her bathroom rituals, I retreat back to my room for some momentary silence. The second she is out, I have a quick shower before changing into my board-shorts and shirt. I brush my teeth and slowly make

my way to the kitchen where the only sounds are their voices chatting animatedly.

"Hey there, roomie!" Zoey greets me with a mouthful of French toast.

Fucking traitor! It's always about food with Zoey. Never mind my needs. I had to admit it smells delicious, but Michelle wearing my favorite T-shirt near the butter and oil is giving me a coronary.

"You have to try Michelle's French toast; it's to die for," Zoey exaggerates as usual, the maple syrup dripping down the side of her mouth. She slides her tongue to the side, and carefully licks it up, flashing me a mischievous smile. *Grub.*

"Ah, I promised the guys we would be at the beach before lunch and it's a two-hour drive."

"Zoey, call me Mickey. That's what my friends call me," Michelle tells her.

In another annoying move, Zoey sings the lyrics to "Hey Mickey" much to Michelle's amusement. Definitely not mine.

"Every time," Michelle laughs. "It never gets old."

Are these two fucking kidding me?! What the hell did I walk into? My head turns to the door, retracing my steps. Didn't I just ask Zoey to help me get rid of Michelle?

Michelle serves the French toast on a plate, placing it on the table. I politely thank her and scarf the thing down, hoping to get out of here without any drama. Zoey has tuned out, fiddling with her cell and taking a photo of the French toast which, no doubt, will make it online somewhere. So much for helping a roomie out. I kick her under the table, catching her attention. With a slight yelp, she shoots me an annoyed look.

"Oh, look at the time. You're right, Drew. You know how I stop a million times to use the restroom," she lies convincingly. "That time of the month. Can't stop Aunt Flow when she's painting the town red."

Jesus, did she have to add that last bit?

Michelle takes the final bite of her toast, then walks over to sink to wash her plate. She walks back around and puts her arms around me. "I'll just have a shower, then I'm out of here."

Phew.

She disappears to the bathroom, and once again, I use the opportunity to kick Zoey under the table.

"What the hell was that for?!"

"Don't start making friends with her. I don't want her back here. And really Zo . . . did you have to play your menstrual-cycle card?"

"God, for someone with a small peewee you sure have a strong kick."

The closest thing to me is a banana peel. I take it and aim straight for her face, smacking her in the forehead with the soggy peel.

"Gross! Grow up, Drew. The last time we had a food fight I won and you cleaned up the mess. I'm going to get ready. Better go pack my super heavy-duty tampons," she adds, walking past me to leave the room.

I shake my head, bothered that she brought it up again. I didn't need to know these things. "I'll be downstairs packing the car. Make sure she leaves."

Inside the garage, I load the car with the essentials we needed for the beach; towels, cooler with water and snacks, sunscreen, and of course, my surfboard. With my surfboard strapped securely to the roof of the car, the sound of Zoey's voice travels down the communal stairwell.

"Ready?" I turn to Zoey, cringing as I see Michelle standing beside her.

She nods, but not before Michelle hugs her goodbye. When they let go, my eyes narrow, infuriated, staring Zoey down as she walks to the passenger side to enter the car.

"Don't forget to add me on Facebook," Zoey yells back to

Michelle.

Oh no, she didn't just say that.

Michelle moves towards me, placing her body in flush with mine. My arms stiffen; trying not to encourage any further intimacy on my behalf.

"When can I see you again?"

I kiss her on the cheek, a friendly gesture keeping it placid between us. "I'll call you."

"You'd better, Drew Baldwin." She blows me a kiss before disappearing from my sight.

I tighten my grip on the steering wheel, arching my head to the left to relieve the built-up tension in my neck. The moment we reversed out of that garage, I had no problem unleashing my thoughts on how she asked Michelle to add her as a friend on Facebook.

For the past thirty minutes, Zoey had been jabbering away about some book she started reading last night, but not before changing the radio to some oldies station that was having an eighties marathon. Again, her taste in music is awful. It's like some time machine landed on Earth and transported her back to the eighties, freezing her in that era.

With her phone placed strategically in her hand like a microphone, she sings loudly along to the song.

"That is the most ridiculous song," I complain. "Get outta my dreams get into my car? Really?"

"You've never wanted a hot girl to get outta your dreams and into your car? How about to touch your bumper?"

"If by bumper you mean cock, then yes," I admit.

"Honestly Drew, no respect for the classics. License to Drive was *the* best movie ever. I loved the Coreys," she informs me, bopping her head along to the music. The song ends, much to my pleasure, until Boy George plays and an excited Zoey sings at the top of her voice, off key, something about a chameleon.

With the visor pulled down, she grabs her Lipsmacker, applying it carefully. Zoey had the habit of applying that stuff a million times a day, and she only used the stuffed that apparently tasted like different beverages. Even her lip balm was full of sugar and junk.

"Anyway, so this damn book you're going on about . . ."

"Oh yeah! So the guy is like THE biggest jerk ever and get this . . . he is pierced," she narrates excitedly. "Then he screws this chick in the alleyway and she gets knocked up. After one night . . . can you believe that?"

"Zo, it's fiction. Anything is possible, but yes, I do believe it. Medically speaking— "

"Hold the medical, scientific mumbo-jumbo. Don't kill my buzz."

"Fine," I mutter under my breath.

I swear Zoey could be a royal pain in the ass sometimes. For the most part we got along, but she is plain old stubborn, living in this imaginary bubble filled with pizza and book boyfriends. Not that I had much spare time with my hectic schedule. I did enjoy reading when I got a chance to. The past few years had me focusing on studying so textbooks became my life. Yet every now and then, I love to pick up a Stephen King novel and immerse myself in his stories. *No one was pierced in that type of novel.*

"Are we there yet?" she asks for the tenth time.

I shake my head. "Another hour."

"Hour!" she yells, crossing her arms like a petulant child. "Fine. I'm going back to sleep."

With her head leaning against the window, my eyes remain focused as we drive up the windy part of the road. My beaten-up old car barely makes it, choking as I place it into gear. *Please don't break down now.*

Betty is my 1954 Volkswagen Beetle. Trunk in the front, all power in the back. Lately, she's been stalling, and I've been too busy with work to get under the hood and see what's

happening. I knew by taking this drive that there was a chance Betty wouldn't make it. It was a chance I was willing to take. My biggest concern was the snorer sitting right next to me.

To set the record straight, Zoey is my roommate, or in her lame terms, 'roomie.'

It was four years ago that I first laid eyes on her.

There is no doubt that Zoey is a beautiful woman. On the short side, with strawberry-blond hair and pale delicate skin. Over the years she went through a dozen hairstyles, but even then, it's her deep pools of green eyes that were like these magical orbs. They had this eerie way of transcending you to a different place. Stupid, I know. At the beginning she would reprimand me for staring at her, calling me a creepy geek that needed to get laid. Over time, I got used to being around her without gawking at her like she was a Penthouse pin-up girl on my bedroom wall.

As for her personality, Zoey Richards is a lot to handle. Feisty, stubborn, and extremely lazy. To be honest, I hadn't really been around women. I was twenty-four when I first met her and still a virgin.

Call me pathetic.

Women scared me. I was uncomfortable, being slightly overweight, and my priorities were to study medicine. Girls didn't throw themselves at me, and I didn't have the balls to try anything on them. I had no clue all those years what I was missing out on. Never having a sister or a mother around, I wasn't sure how to act around women. My dad once told me that women were like badly tuned engines—unpredictable, temperamental, and extremely capricious. This was coming from the man that was burned by a woman—my mother—and since then had a string of one-night stands to avoid being hurt again.

Nevertheless, his words stuck in my head, much like that terrible Billy Ocean song.

I guess you could say Zoey is all that and more. She *was* ambitious and smart, and talked her way out of anything. I told her once she should have studied to be a lawyer, but of course, her passion remained with architecture. A career that had nothing to do with talking.

It was early last year that she began dating this loser, Jess, or who her friends dubbed 'Bad Boy Jess.' Miss Ambitious lost sight of everything, falling head over heels for this guy. I get it; she thought she was in love and it would end in a happily ever after.

The guy was clearly using her, living almost rent-free with us, and when I brought up Roomie Rule Number Three, she was quick to defend him and paid his share in rent. I wasn't fucking stupid; she was normally a thrifty saver, just waiting for the day when she could design and afford her dream home. This fucker was eating into her bank account, and into someone else's pussy.

Her work and studies took a big hit, and she almost abandoned her goals so she could party with him on the weekends at out-of-town exotic locations. His drinking was out of hand, and as a result, Zoey would come home drunk more times than I could count.

Then it happened; the cat was let out of the bag.

Bad Boy Jess was getting it on with Miss Jugs—aka, her best friend Callie.

I had never, *ever,* in my life witnessed a more disastrous breakup. I'm talking endless tears, belongings thrown off the balcony, and the burning of all photos of the two of them. Ballads would be blasted on repeat. The fact that I knew of the artist Tiffany and could sing all the lyrics to "Could've Been" says a lot about how badly this all went down.

It was extreme, and a huge wake-up call that I was not ready to settle down with a woman. Relationships were complicated. I had my whole life to worry about that after I finished my internship. Again, Dad's words rung true in my head. Women were nothing but a complicated species that

walked on this earth to make our lives miserable.

They were only good for one thing, and even then, some had no clue.

Zoey was hurting really badly, and being a guy, I wasn't sure how to help her. Several nights I had spent sleeping beside her in bed, just trying to console her. At first she blamed herself and all the things she should have done for him, but that soon turned into hatred, and finally, she accepted that he was at fault and no matter what she did, he was a fucking dickhead.

Thank fucking god she came to that realization, because I couldn't stand hearing any more about it being her fault. The guy was a deadbeat.

Eventually, she moved on, but never really was herself. She dated a few guys after that, but nothing quite as serious. She deferred her studies and just prodded along, working as an assistant to her boss. She stopped partying and buying expensive clothes and shoes, and just stayed at home like a hermit of some sort reading romance novels.

And she ate pizza almost every night.

One time, the delivery guy cracked a joke about moving in since he was practically at the apartment every day. I thought it was funny. Zoey, on the other hand, lashed out at the both of us, putting on some drama-filled show before slamming the door to her room.

She blamed PMS.

She *always* blamed PMS.

Every day she would ridicule my healthy eating habits. I knew deep down inside it was killing her that she had gained the extra weight. And something I had learned about women was Golden Rule Number One: Never comment on their weight.

As time went on, Zoey accepted the fact that she was no longer fitting into her expensive outfits. I knew firsthand what it was like to be uncomfortable in your own skin, but one day, I realized I couldn't go on being unhappy. It wasn't an overnight miracle. In fact, it took two years to change my eating habits and achieve an image that gave me confidence.

You see, Zoey, is not only my roomie, she is like a sister to me. And when someone that close to you is feeling down, you do everything you can to pick them up. Hence, this trip to the beach that I organized.

A bunch of the guys were tagging along and meeting us there. She knew of them and got along well with Rob, a guy from my gym. It was the confidence boost she needed. A little one-on-one flirting for her to get back to her normal self again.

I see the beach ahead and nudge her slightly. She lets out a loud snore followed by a snort, then opens her eyes in a daze.

"Are we there yet?" This time, she is less enthused.

"Yes," I answer, turning into the parking lot.

I park the car, lucky to arrive early before the beach became busy.

It's a popular spot with nice big waves and a park area for picnics. Exiting the car, I stretch my arms and legs and take in the view. It's gorgeous, and with the sun already piercing my skin, it is going to be one hell of a hot day.

"It's hot," Zoey complains immediately after stepping out of the car. Squinting, she rummages in her purse and emerges with a pair of oversized white sunglasses.

"C'mon vampire, put on your sunscreen and let's unload."

She pokes her tongue out as she begins to lather her skin with cream. Handing me the bottle, she turns to me. "Back and shoulders, please. I don't want to leave today looking like a lobster."

Pulling her T-shirt off, she reveals a teeny tiny white bikini top. It has a pattern of pineapples all over it. She had this obsession with pineapples. Apparently they were good luck or some bullshit story like that.

Her tits look *huge* in them.

I obviously wasn't the only one to notice; a bunch of guys walking in front of us almost trip over our stuff because they are too busy staring. My eyes wander back to her tattoo that sits just above her bikini line. She inked herself with a *My Little Pony* image one night on a bender. A stupid mistake. I wasn't a fan of tatts, unlike Zoey. She made it clear on several occasions that she only dated guys who had tattoos and drove a nice car.

I pull the bottle out of her hands and rub the cream all over her back, irritated at her choice of attire. Honestly, one wrong move and her tits would be all out for show.

"Ow!" she yelps. "Easy with the cream."

"Sorry," I mumble, patting her back hard when I'm done.

We settle for a spot with close proximity to the sand and picnic area. Moments later, Rob and another friend, Isaac, arrive in his newly purchased convertible.

"Drew," he howls with the top down.

Jesus, what a dick. It's like Rob went through a midlife crisis at the age of twenty-eight. He had a job at some posh real estate agency and used his clients as a reason to purchase this unaffordable car. What does Zoey call it again? A penis extension. She doesn't seem to comment though, instead looking rather pleased when he drives past.

"Oh, you didn't tell me Rob from your gym was coming. And in his new penis-mobile." She smiles instantly, posing comfortably with her hand resting on her hip.

"Would that have made you complain less?"

"That depends. What food did you pack for me?"

"You don't want to know."

She squats towards the ground, opening the cooler and rummaging through the ice. "Oh, c'mon Drew!" She raises her arms in frustration. "It's the beach, for crying out loud. It's beer-and-chips kinda eating."

"How about cucumber juice and carrot sticks?"

"I'm not talking to you for the rest of the day. In fact, I think I will go help Rob unload his *nice* car."

She throws her T-shirt onto our pile of stuff, skipping over to Rob like a teenage girl with a crush. Jesus Christ, her tits were bouncing like crazy, and again, prompted every dick to look at her, including Rob, his eyes bulging like an over-excited cartoon character.

The both of them begin talking, followed by laughing, and with that all sorted, I pack my gear and get ready to hit the waves. The three of them, including Isaac, walk over and drop their stuff beside mine.

"We're going for a swim. Back soon." She winks, linking her arm into Rob's as they turn towards the beach.

Isaac grabs his board and I follow his lead, leaving our belongings as we walk through the hot sand.

The water is refreshing, cooling my heated skin as we swim out pass the shallow water and families frolicking in the waves. The water begins to rock and I get ready to ride the wave, noticing Zoey in the corner of my eye, waving her arms with Rob smiling beside her. They seem to be having fun, so I ignore them, focusing on the strong current moving my body. The wave moves towards me, and I'm on high, riding my board till the wave dies off. Isaac is only a short distance away, swimming towards me when the ocean calms. His fast strokes bring him closer to me, and I can see that his face is panicked as he tries to communicate.

"Dude, Zoey looks like she's in trouble." He motions for me to look at the beach.

My eyes scan the body of water where I saw them last. *Nothing.* When Isaac points to the beach again, I only see legs peeking through a crowd. It could be anyone, but then Rob is jumping about and waving his arms frantically, and he becomes my primary focus. Abandoning my board, I swim as fast as I can till I'm at the shoreline. With barely any

breath, I race over, shoving people out of the way. Zoey is lying on the ground, unconscious. Her face ghost-white and lips a shade of dark grey.

"Where's the lifeguard?!" I yell, glancing around me in sheer panic.

A stranger respond's instantly, "They aren't on duty yet."

"Then fucking call 911!"

I call her name, but she doesn't respond. Studying medicine should help me at a time like this, yet terror-stricken nerves swamp my body, causing the shakes. I need to clear my head so I remember the basic steps. *C'mon Drew . . . you fucking know this! This is basic everyday knowledge. Calm the fuck down and don't let her die!*

"She got caught in a rip tide . . . I got scared . . . I didn't know what to do," Rob stutters in a rush, pacing beside me with his hands frantically running through his hair.

Three . . . two . . . one

Nothing.

"C'mon Zo. I was lying about the carrot sticks. Wake up please," I beg softly.

My heart is racing a million miles a minute. I'm thinking about how if anything happened to her, I wouldn't know what to do with myself. *Get your shit together! Follow the CPR steps again . . .*

I place my lips onto hers, blowing into her mouth, desperately trying to resuscitate her, all the while praying she could hear my thoughts. *Fucking wake up, Zo . . . I wouldn't know what to do without you. I need you.*

Everything I've ever complained about, I want back. Her annoying quirks, like singing Madonna off-key in the shower, dropping crumbs on the sofa, and her loud snoring. Her hair pins scattered all over the apartment. The way she would lie in my bed and talk to me for hours about her day or some random TV show she landed on during channel surfing.

Her obsession with fictional characters.

I want it all back. Every bit of her back.

I can't fucking lose her!

Pressing my lips against hers once again, I beg the Lord above to bring her back to me. They feel warm. *Full of blood.* They are soft . . . they have life. I pull away slowly, and see the green orbs staring back at me.

The second they do . . . my heart falls back into place.

"Drew," she mouths, barely above a whisper.

"I'm here, Zo."

I know she can see me; she's spoken my name.

Her eyes dart back and forth, the panic building when she realizes everyone is watching her. A second later, I abruptly turn her over to her side, the fluid projecting from her mouth.

She's alive.

CHAPTER *Three*

HIS VOICE IS ALL AROUND me.

    Begging me to look at him.

Praying for me to come alive.

Telling me he can't live without me.

And I try to reach out to him, but he's not anywhere within reach.

Then it happens.

A warm feeling graces my lips.

And it feels nice.

Really nice.

I don't want it to stop. It comforts me; it fills me with peace and serenity, racing through my veins and warming my flaky cold skin. I want to savor this moment. Stay like this forever, where everything feels just right . . . almost *perfect.*

Then out of nowhere, the sensation stops. The bitter cold harshly knocks me back and forth, followed by the terrifying feeling of the unknown. My eyes open wide, and there he is— *Drew.*

I call his name and he smiles back at me.

He is right by my side. He is real. I'm not dreaming this. *I'm alive.*

This euphoria, this short-lived relief, disappears. With my chest heaving and my breaths short and quick, my lungs cave in a panic and there is a rush to move me. I don't know what's happening. The voices are muffled; my chest is regurgitating some sort of fluid. I'm terrified . . . *what is happening to me?* The fits of panic pump heavily through my weak limbs as I lie here . . . wherever I am.

"Drew . . . Drew . . ." I call his name, my voice raspy and strained. I reach out for his hand and he holds onto it, observing me with sorrowful eyes.

"I'm here, Zo. I won't let get of you. I promise."

There are people surrounding me—strangers. Dressed in blue uniforms, a man and a woman check my limbs and begin speaking to me. Several questions are asked, but I can only manage to answer a few, lying here like I'm in a freak show while the crowds watch in anticipation. I remember now what happened. Rob was telling me a joke, I was flirting and trying to show off, then all of a sudden I lost control. The waves forced me under, and then my body was pulled beneath the surface with such strong force.

The paramedics tell Drew I'm fine, but as a precaution, to take me to the hospital. Drew's shoulders are slumped and his face is full of worry. His eyes appear bloodshot; his normally tanned skinned looks pale and cold. *Just like mine.*

"I'm sorry," I mouth, over and over again.

The paramedics pack up their equipment as people start to disperse. As soon as they leave, Drew diverts his attention back onto me, scooping my body up in his arms and carrying me to the car with Rob and Isaac following close behind. My head remains close to his chest, closing my eyes to control the tears that want to escape. He has a few words with the guys, then places me carefully in the car.

Luckily, we didn't have to wait long at the hospital. They ran some tests and let me go, advising me that everything was clear but that if I wasn't feeling well, to make sure I saw my doctor immediately.

On the drive home, the weight of today exhausts me. I rest my head against the window pane and close my eyes again, not wanting to talk about what happened or how foolish I was to be so careless in the water. All because I was trying to impress Rob. Because my confidence was shattered, and just once, I wanted to feel wanted by another man.

I doze off for most of the ride home, opening my eyes when we are parked in front of our apartment. Drew rushes to my door and opens it, reaching out his hand.

Offering a weak smile, I tell him, "I can walk."

"It's three flights of stairs."

"I know. Remember? I'm the silly one that thought it would be a good idea to rent this apartment, thinking the view was spectacular."

"And how many times do you sit on the balcony?"

I manage to laugh, but it's followed by a violent cough. Drew is watching me, worried, and to rest his paranoia, I latch onto his arm for support. Okay, three flights of stairs could be compared to walking up Mount Everest. With no energy, I feel weak and ready to sleep again, unprepared for the physical toll today took on my body.

We enter the apartment, and immediately, I want to lay on the sofa and rest my eyes and my body. Drew suggests I take a long shower and get changed, just to remove all the sand off me.

In the shower, the hot water relaxes my tense muscles, and the struggle to keep my eyes open becomes too hard. There is a knock on the door and Drew asks me if I am okay. I yell back and shut off the water, dry myself, then change into my tee and boxers. My hair is soaking wet so I run the hairdryer for a few minutes, still leaving it slightly damp.

As soon as I open the door fully dressed, Drew is standing at the entrance, blocking my way. With his arms folded, he presses his lips together, almost biting his tongue. He must have taken out his contacts; he's wearing his glasses, his eyes narrowing underneath his lenses.

"You weren't singing," he thunders.

"I'm tired."

"Well, if you were singing then I wouldn't have panicked for the last fifteen minutes."

He motions with his hands in frustration. "I was this close to breaking the lock to see if you were okay."

"I don't lock the door, you goose. Besides, if you came in, you wouldn't have seen anything you haven't seen before."

"That's different," he mumbles awkwardly, scratching his stubble and avoiding my gaze.

I shake my head at his awkward demeanor. "Oh yeah . . . shaving my vagina is *totally* different."

"Can we not talk about that again? I made you some soup."

"Sure, I'll stop the vagina talk as long as there's some pizza on the side."

"Continue with the vagina talk . . ."

Crap. He called my bluff. I didn't care for vagina talk either.

I slowly make my way to the kitchen, not wanting to admit that I'm starving and Drew's soup smells like heaven. After devouring two bowls, heaven was an understatement. Perhaps I had been eating way too much pizza.

"What's in this again?" I ask with slight hesitation.

"I never told you. Some things are best left a mystery."

Great. Some healthy concoction that will probably give me the runs. *Pizza doesn't give you the runs, unless, of course, you ordered from that dodgy wannabe Italian chef around the corner from the apartment.*

We both sit at the table silently, finishing our bowls without saying a word to each other. The kitchen is small but large enough to fit a round table in the center with four chairs. The apartment was built sometime in the sixties, and still had this retro feel to it. I loved the charmed it oozed but Drew often complained it wasn't modern enough. Since he enjoyed cooking, he had every right to complain about the rundown stove with only two burners that worked and the oven that could barely fit a roast. Again, this was the beauty of pizza. It gets delivered to your door with no cleanup necessary.

Drew stands up and collects the dishes, then walks over to the sink and runs the tap. The gentle fall of the water makes me yawn, and he is quick to notice that my head has almost fallen onto the table.

"You look tired. Let's get you to bed."

I wasn't about to argue. He walks me to my room, and as soon as I'm under the covers, the battle to keep my eyes open is too much.

"Stay with me . . . till I fall asleep," I beg softly.

Drew lies beside me on the bed and rests with his arm propped up, stroking my hair out of the way. It feels nice. It feels like home. When the exhaustion creeps in, I begin to sob.

"I thought I was going to die."

He pulls me into an embrace and kisses the top of my forehead, my heavy sobs buried into his chest. The emotional trauma of almost drowning has finally caught up with me. Although there are parts that remain hazy, the terror I felt when I lost control and got caught it the rip tide start to invade my memory, leaving me shaking as my sobs echo throughout the room.

"I was terrified, Zo, but you pulled through. You're here. That's all that matters now."

In between my cries, I softly murmur, "Thank you . . . for

making me come alive again. For everything you do for me . . . *Pineapples.*"

"Pineapples?"

"*The pineapples . . . on my bikini. It's good luck . . . Maybe that's why I'm still here.*"

My eyelids become too heavy and sleep is imminent. With the warmth of Drew's body beside me, I bury myself into his chest, never wanting to let go. His lips brush against my forehead, the sentiment not lost on me even in my exhausted state. Soon, I fall into a blissful and dreamless sleep.

When I wake up, it feels like I've been hit by a truck. It's dark outside and the moon is hiding behind the clouds, shadowing the walls in my room. There's a struggle to move, and I barely manage to twist my body to see the time. It's after eight. Had I really slept that long?

What does it matter anyway? It's not like I have anywhere to be.

My bed is empty, and for a split second, I'm imagining things. But soon after, the aches and pains seep throughout every muscle in my body, becoming difficult to ignore. *You nearly drowned. How could you forget that?!*

Tilting my heard towards my nightstand, I stare deeply at the gold pineapple ornament sitting beside by lamp. I had this thing—about luck—and pineapples were supposed to bring luck.

When I was nineteen, I took my first trip to New York City with a couple of girlfriends. We ate at a small restaurant in Chinatown that was oddly decorated with gold pineapple ornaments. Curious, I asked the lady serving us, "Why all the pineapples?" I remember her exact words: *"Pineapples bring you wealth, luck, and fortune."*

With an aged face and grey hair, her wise words always stuck with me. That, and she looked like the female version of Mr. Miyagi, even sporting a slight beard.

When it came time to crack the fortune cookies, my cookie

was not so fortunate. *Something about a storm ahead.* I remember sinking into my chair, jealous that all the girls got messages about love and happiness, when Mrs. Miyagi came and handed me one of the gold pineapples. She told me to never let it go, and to keep it somewhere safe.

And I did, beside my bed.

I don't know what saved me today, but the pineapple appeared more golden than before. I would keep this theory to myself, since Drew didn't share the same beliefs as me.

The apartment is dead quiet. Nothing unusual for a Saturday night, since Drew worked three weekends in a month. I get onto my feet, a little unsteadily, and make my way down the hall to the living room. There is a faint light flickering against the walls; it's the TV, which happens to be switched on.

The moment that Drew lays eyes on me, he jumps to his feet, helping me onto the couch. "Hey, how you feeling?"

"I'm okay. Just a little sore," I offer, not wanting to worry him further.

I grab the small pillow and place it on my lap, hugging it as we watch some thriller playing on TV. Drew knows that movies involving possessed children freak me out, and switches the channel to a more laid-back program.

We watch in silence until Drew disappears into the kitchen, returning with some painkillers and water. Standing over me, he extends his hand and I reluctantly take the pills. I hated taking medication, especially when the pills were the size of a crater. Something about them terrified me. It usually took multiple tries to swallow, even when I cut them in half. What idiot invents pills so big anyway?

"C'mon Zo, just swallow. Don't overthink it."

"Such a guy thing to say," I say, deadpan, before throwing them towards the back of my throat, following with a huge gulp of water. It fails on the first attempt, forcing me to drink

41

more water and attempt round two.

"See, not so hard. Excellent gag reflex," he compliments.

A trickle of water escapes the corner of my lips. I smack his arm, then wipe my chin.

"Don't ever make jokes mid-swallow."

"I'll remember that for next time."

"Uh huh, whatever. What time are you heading out?"

Drew smiles, looking pleased. "I'm not."

"It's Saturday night. You always go out—"

"*Not tonight.*"

I fall into silence, staring at the TV. Today's events had really taken it out of me. Apart from the physical state, my mental state was confused. There was no reason I should have survived. Everyone knows how rough the sea can get and I was being plain stupid. I wasn't a religious person either; never went to church since my parents dragged me at a young age. There was no rhyme or reason for why I was given a second chance.

But I sat here, breathing, all the while thinking that I couldn't waste a single moment living this sheltered life because some guy cheated on me. It wasn't just the cheating. It was everything he made me feel about myself—insecure and unwanted.

Before Jess, Zoey Richards ruled the world. I was this close to accomplishing everything I had worked so hard for. Women envied me, men wanted to be with me. The world was supposedly my oyster, yet I chose the rotten one. They teach you everything at college. Everything but how to stay away from the bad oyster.

"Let's go out," I say out loud, throwing the cushion aside and ignoring the slight head spin.

"Zo, you need to rest."

"No, I've rested all day. C'mon, even just for an hour?" I beg.

He looks at me oddly. "Are you okay?"

He places his hand on my forehead, but I shake it off instantly.

"I'm fine, Drew. I just . . ." I stop mid-sentence. If there is anyone I trust more than my life, it's Drew. No matter what, he has been my rock through it all. Seen me at my peak, seen me hit rock bottom. "What have I been doing for the past year? Nothing. I let that creep get to me and bring me down. What's the purpose of me surviving?"

"Because you're young and have your whole life ahead of you."

"A life of sitting on the couch unhappy?"

"Zo, you can't blame anyone for that. Life happens. Shit happens. How we react and how we move forward determines what type of life we live. Maybe this is a good thing. Pull you out of this funk you've been living in."

"Maybe. I guess I can only blame myself."

A lie. Of course I could blame Jess. The hottest guy to walk into my life and treat me like a fucking queen, till one day I told him I wouldn't have a threesome with him and this chick on our vacation. All of a sudden, our relationship went pear-shaped.

I never told Drew that part of the story. It was bad enough that Jess would ridicule my sexual acts for never being quite what he wanted, or because I didn't perform like he expected. He fed off my insecurity, and I was the stupid idiot who believed him.

The day that I busted Callie giving him a blowjob was the end. It cut me like a knife, and to think that I didn't feel I was worth it was ridiculous. But of course, I let my insecurities get the better of me, and throwing myself into the dating scene was a lot harder than everyone made it out to be. I wasn't Drew; I no longer exuded confidence that lured the prey in and bingo, you've got yourself someone new. *Men were jerks.* They were untrustworthy jerks with wandering dicks.

With my persuasive voice, I ask the question again, "So, are you up for a walk?"

"Alright. But promise me you'll tell me if it's too much?"

"Yes, roomie."

On this late summer's night, the air is warm with a gentle breeze that laces my skin with goosebumps. Wearing only a light blouse and denim shorts, I cross my arms, blocking my chest from the cool air.

With the city lights as a perfect backdrop, we stop off at a busy ice-cream shop not too far from the apartment. There is a small queue waiting to be served, forcing us to wait in line.

The shop is decorated in 1970s decor, Elvis portraits hanging on almost every wall. In the corner sits a jukebox. An older woman is standing in front of it, pressing the buttons and browsing through the catalogue. Placing her hand in the pocket of her skinny blue jeans, she produces a coin and slots it into the jukebox. A U2 song plays; the woman looks very nostalgic until a man joins her. Their body language says it all; it's a relationship on the rocks, and judging by the way the man's eyes wander as a younger woman strolls past, I'm guessing it's your classic trust issue.

The song choice isn't helping my already depressed mood, and thankfully, the line moves quickly and we're out of there in a flash, continuing our stroll through the streets.

"Sometimes I forget how beautiful this city is," Drew says wistfully, staring into the sky as he walks alongside me. "You know, growing up in Australia is completely different. Especially in a rural town."

"Do the kangaroos just hop around your front yard?"

"Out where we lived, yes. But not in the city," he laughs.

"See, I've been misinformed. My understanding was they

just hopped around everywhere and sometimes you hitched a ride with them to the local store to pick up a jar of Vegemite."

"They're not donkeys, Zo. You never hitch a ride with a kangaroo."

"Do you miss being there?"

We stop at the intersection and wait for the light to turn green. "From what I remember. Dad and I left when I was ten. Most of my growing up was done here, in the States."

"You know, if you had a thicker Aussie accent . . . you would score *more* chicks," I tell him jokingly.

"Are you saying I don't score enough now?"

"I'm saying you haven't scored the right one," I point out.

"The right one? I've scored some pretty good ones."

"True. But your Mrs. Right. Your damsel in distress. Where is she? All I'm saying is that maybe you should use your Aussie background to your advantage. Slap the accent on then bam, she'll be coming round the mountain."

"I worry about you," he laughs, again. "Honestly Zo, you read way too much fiction."

He had a point. I loved to read. Books had become my life since I had no one. Although I enjoyed reading romance, I didn't limit myself to only that genre. For me it was the escape. The feeling of being transported somewhere else and pretending to be someone else, if only just for that one moment.

"There's so much more I want to do and see," I say to myself out loud, switching the subject without even thinking.

"Like what?"

"I don't know. Travel . . . explore the world."

"You're afraid of flying," he reminds me.

"I could take a boat?"

"Where exactly would you take a boat to?"

"I don't know. To London?"

He grins, licking the top of his ice cream cone. The strawberry looks so good, and I instantly regret getting my vanilla groove on. "That's a long haul, if there even is one."

"I'm only afraid of flying by myself. With friends I'm okay."

"Maybe we should plan a trip together?" he suggests.

"You and me?"

"Yes. Why not?"

This time, I laugh. "Everyone would think we are a couple."

"Why would everything think that? Males and females can be friends and travel. I've got a ton of friends that backpack through Europe together. It's what our generation does."

"I'm just saying people will think that, so don't get all awkward when they ask questions or make like we're such a cute couple." I tilt my cone and lick the ice cream in a clockwise motion to avoid it dripping on my hands.

"I wouldn't be awkward . . . I'll prove it."

He takes my hand and places it in his. This isn't the first time we've held hands while walking, but to prove him wrong, I wait in anticipation. Around me, most people are busy doing their own thing until we almost run into an old lady.

"I'm so sorry!" I apologize, almost dropping my cone on the pavement.

"It's okay, my dear. Don't want to let go of your boyfriend's hand. I understand." She smiles dearly.

Drew's face drops. With a widening smirk, I watch him with my I-told-you-so face. I loved every opportunity to prove Mr. Know-It-All wrong. Drew is very competitive, so I knew there is no chance he would let this one go without getting worked up.

Mimicking the old lady without being rude, "Oh, how dare I let get of my boyfriend's hand."

"You're a bitch when you're right," he grits, dropping my hand and shoving his own into his pocket.

"See, you're awkward. I personally don't care. Do whatever the hell you want and—"

My words are eaten up as his lips press firmly on mine. In complete and utter shock, I continue to stand still, frozen, eyes wide open as I try to comprehend what the hell is happening. I'm not a person that kisses with their eyes open. In fact, I don't understand that at all, but when your roomie of four years is Frenching you like it's high school, you stand in complete and utter shock.

I close my eyes quickly, fearing he will open his and an awkward glance will pass between us. *Too late.* He slips his tongue, gently grazing mine.

What the hell is happening!

Drew pulls away, and I leave my eyes closed, uncertain of what to do. I can't believe he kissed me. What does this mean? And why the hell did it feel good? Who would have thought the former geek could kiss like that! *No, don't read any more into it. You haven't had a boyfriend in like forever and you just miss the touch of a man.*

"You can open your eyes now," he says in a normal voice.

"But if I do it'll be awkward."

"You said you didn't care."

I open my eyes quickly. "Yeah! About holding hands. Not tongue wrestling."

My cheeks flush, the embarrassment far from over. Looking straight into his eyes, I ask the burning question, *"What was that?"*

With a confident pose, he responds, "A kiss."

"Well, duh . . . but . . . now . . ."

"Now what? We carry on, Zo. Point is, I'm not awkward.

C'mon, I've seen you shave your pus—"

"Oh my god!" I shout loud enough that people turn to see the commotion. "Twice in one day that *incident* is brought up. We were never, *ever,* supposed to bring that up again."

"You brought it up first. Look, nothing will change between us. I promise you that."

Eyeing him dubiously, I try to downplay what just happened. "Okay, you're right. A kiss is nothing. But hey, nice roll of the tongue. You got the moves, dude."

We both laugh in unison, yet inside, my body has gone into overdrive. That kiss could have sent me into an orgasmic meltdown, but as his roomie, I'm brushing it off and telling an awkward joke that I heard on the radio.

It's cringeworthy, but anything to forget that my lips still taste like him.

Strawberry mixed with Drew.

Fuck.

What did we just do?

CHAPTER *Four*

Drew

F**UCK.**
Everything's changed.

It was supposed to be a joke. You know, something you did to prove a point and laugh about it afterwards, then life goes on. I just wanted to shut her up since she thinks she's always right.

Just once—I wanted to be right.

I hated fucking losing, but this little stunt of mine backfired . . . *big time.*

How does a man like myself, who has spent years studying medicine, act on a whim and change everything between us? And her lips tasted so . . . fuck, I can't even go there. I've kissed women—many women.

Yet no one—nobody—in the space of ten seconds, had kissed me in a way that left me breathless. Geez, that sounds so fucking corny.

It was the French vanilla ice cream mixed with her Coca-Cola Lipsmacker. *You love French vanilla. Don't mistake this situation, thinking her lips always taste like that.* Might as well blame my dick getting hard on that as well . . . *Just don't go there.*

After she told me this lame joke about a monkey, we agreed to make our way back home, which suited me fine. I was worried that her body was still recovering from today's events and didn't want her to push herself.

The walk back felt longer than usual, but she appeared to let the kiss go, and the whole way home, we talked about random things like we normally did.

Well, she talked. Rambled. And boy could she talk. I think I just nodded and listened, like I usually did. Thank god, because bringing up that bathroom incident left me with a walking hard-on.

It was all her fault, the whole thing. I still remember it like it happened yesterday. It was a year ago, and with a mouthful of pizza, she told me she was going to her room. Obviously, I misheard.

My mind is all over the place. Melinda, this hot, older exotic dancer, just propositioned me via text. All I need to do is take a quick shower and get over to her place with a pack of rubbers.

I clean the kitchen, quickly discarding the pizza box that lies on the countertop since Zoey can't be bothered. Zoey mumbles with a mouthful of pizza that she's heading to her room and grabs a bottle of soda as she walks away. With the kitchen tidied, I head to the bathroom and open the door.

"Holy fuck, Drew, get the hell out of here!" Zoey yells, her high-pitched voice piercing my sensitive ears.

In a state of disbelief, I continue to stand frigid on the spot. Zoey is sitting on the edge of the bath with her leg up and spread open, armed with a razor and some cream. I can't look away . . . I mean her pussy is staring me in the face . . .

It's shaved.

It's pink.

It's so . . .

Her legs close abruptly. She grabs the towel hanging on the towel rack and places it over her legs in a frantic rush. Then, she throws my toothbrush at me.

Unfortunately, it lands in the toilet.

"Fucking hell, Drew, why aren't you listening to me? Get the hell out! Stop staring at me!"

"I'm sorry, you said you were going to your room!" I yell back at her. "You were carrying a soda, for Christ's sake."

For some unknown reason, the soda is sitting on the bathroom vanity. This is not my fault. How was I to know that she would drink soda in the bathroom while shaving her pussy? Oh my god, Drew . . . fucking stop using that word with Zoey's name attached.

"I said 'the bathroom'!" She holds the towel with her hand and scrambles to push me out of the room.

"Jesus Christ, Zo. Why the fuck are you shaving your—"

Pointing her finger directly at me, her face is bright red, the shade complimenting her bright-green eyes filled with anger. "Don't say it . . . don't ever say what you saw, you got me?"

I nod and almost tumble out of the room like an awkward teenage boy.

Revert to Rule Number Five. The clause about accidental nudity. It was there to serve a purpose. I just never thought it'd be for something like this.

I struggled for weeks after that incident, banging every girl I could to get that image out of my mind. Equally as affected, Zo took a trip to her parents' beach house and returned a couple of weeks later. Thank god everything between us went back to normal, but every now and then, the image pops up, much to my discontent. I mean, don't get me wrong, she had a great looking pus . . . *genital area.*

Yet, I was a fool to kiss her tonight. Something odd

happened in the past twenty-four hours. The thought of losing her almost killed me, and having her sob into my chest as I held on to her tight drudged up questions that shouldn't be asked. *We were roomies.* There is a code of conduct that is attached to that label. We aren't allowed to think of each other in any way aside from friends, let alone entertain sexual thoughts.

And I'll be damned if I break the code. *I don't break rules.* They are in place for a reason. To prevent shit from happening. To avoid life being all fucked up because somewhere along the line you thought with your dick instead of your head.

Again, what the hell was I thinking? I need to get away tonight, for my own sanity, yet I don't want to leave her in case something happens.

As much as she tries to convince me she is okay, she looks exhausted from the close call this morning. Her normally pale skin looks even whiter, and the dull green in her eyes looks tired and lifeless. Even with the warm humid air, she appears cold, her teeth slightly chattering. A sign that she needs a good rest to recover.

The sound of Zoey clicking her fingers interrupts my thoughts.

"Earth to Mars."

"Huh, what?" I ask, confused.

"We're home."

She opens the door, throwing her keys onto the nightstand. It misses, and she turns back to watch them fall to the ground, yet continues to walk away. I swear to god this woman is going to drive me fucking insane with her disregard for a clean environment. Walking right behind her, I pick them up off the ground and place them on the nightstand where they belong.

Twisting her arms, she removes her jacket and carelessly dumps it on the sofa. She wore a white top with a hot-pink

bra underneath. *God, it looks fucking sexy.* I shake my head trying to remove my unnatural thoughts. *She's like a sister . . . stop it right now.*

"You up for a movie?" She plonks herself on the sofa, waiting for my response.

"Yeah, sure. But nothing girly."

"Oh c'mon," she pouts. "We haven't watched *Dirty Dancing* in ages."

"No, my choice."

"Fine." She sulks.

"How about the *Wedding Singer?*"

She smiles. I know she loved this fucking movie because of all the eighties shit, and this was the only one I could tolerate because of Adam Sandler's comedic acting.

"But no singing," I warn her.

"Deal."

I grab the remote and scan through the movies until I find it. The credits start as I take a seat beside her. She grabs the blanket and squishes in right beside me. It's nothing out of the ordinary, but all of a sudden I feel conscious of her being so close. Her legs are draped over mine, and why have I never noticed how soft her skin looks? *My hands have nowhere to rest.* Stretching my arms, I place them behind my head, which had to be better than on her legs.

"Do you think stuff like this happens? You know, people expressing their undying love by playing a guitar on a crowded plane?" she wonders out loud.

"You're asking me? You know I'm never been in love, Zo."

"I don't believe you. When you were dating that girl, Kim, you seemed like you were. Even though it was only for a month. You used to gush over her."

"I did not gush."

"Sure you did. You were gushing all the time. It was kinda cute."

"Don't confuse the length of a relationship with love. We dated for two months. She was nice, but there was no future for us," I remind her, my eyes fixated on the screen.

She seems to let the subject go and shifts her focus back onto the movie. It is just what we both needed. A good ole laugh to shake off what happened tonight. That is, until she excitedly squeezes my thigh when her favorite scene comes on. The one when the leads kiss for the first time.

On cue, I stiffen up. *Did she know that my thigh had some connection to my cock? Fuck, it's on the same route . . . and way too close for me to ignore.*

"Why are you being all weird . . . and stiff?" she notices, her face wary of my mannerisms.

I loosen my shoulders, trying not to look too obvious, but Zoey is extremely observant. *Just breathe . . . don't show any fear.* She's like a wild animal; they can smell fear a mile away.

"Just feeling restless. You know, it's a Saturday night and all," I blurt out, hoping it will get her off my back.

She pauses the movie and stands up, placing her hands on her hips. Oh shit . . . here we go. The vein on her forehead looks like it's ready to pop. Her dull green eyes suddenly spark . . . with rage.

"I get it. You'd rather be elsewhere," she huffs. "Why on earth would you want to spend Saturday night with your friend who almost died today when there's some fresh pussy waiting to be fucked!"

"No, it's not like that—"

"I'm going to bed. Goodnight Drew," she says without looking my way as she heads out of the room. *What the fuck was that?!* I want to follow her down the hall, but obviously something is bothering her, and I was too on edge. We were forever arguing about things, forever at war but this . . . this is so out of left field.

Minutes later, I find myself staring blankly at the TV,

wondering what the hell was wrong with her. It's like almost instantly she snapped, and why? I had no idea.

The clock on the wall says it's just after eleven. For the club scene, it's just the beginning of the night, but my head wasn't in the right frame of mind to go out and have fun. On top of that, I had called the hospital and told them my roommate had to be resuscitated today. They told me as long as someone covered my shift, I could have the night off. While Zoey was sleeping, I had called around, begging everyone to swap with me. It's the worst night to have to switch, given that everyone cherished their rare weekends off. Finally, one of the other interns, John, agreed on the condition that I did his nightshift. *Great.* I agreed only because I thought being here for Zoey was important.

Boy was I wrong.

CHAPTER *Five*

Zoey

ON SUNDAY MORNING, I'M GLAD to wake up and find the apartment empty. Last night turned out to be one of those nights I would rather forget. *Make that the whole day.*

After Drew's eagerness to head out and party mid-movie, I'd lost my cool and threw a girl tantrum. So I was irritable and exhausted. And just maybe I had acted like a spoiled little brat because I didn't get my way. You would think that spending time with your roomie on the day she *almost* lost her life wouldn't be too much trouble, but hey, what would I know?

Drew never came to my room to smooth things out. I wasn't surprised one bit; he had left the apartment to probably drown his frustrations in someone's vagina.

Typical.

As for me, I was wide awake with nowhere to go. I had cleaned my room after a sudden burst of energy, throwing my earphones on and mellowing out with some New Kids on the Block. It was either that or go for my ballads, but I didn't need a reminder of my tragic love life.

Upon cleaning my room, I found one of those miniature vodka bottles someone gave me at a party and downed it in one go, ignoring the persistent burn it made on its way down my throat. The perfect end to a day that screamed disaster.

And so here I lie, at some godawful hour on a Sunday morning, with the sounds of birds' incessant chirping invading my room. The sun lit up my walls, forcing me to open my eyes. The vodka—although a small quantity—was enough to give me a slight headache.

After yesterday's near-death experience, something inside me was triggered. I didn't want to be the fat girl eating pizza on a Friday night by myself. I didn't want to fetch paper for my boss. And most importantly, I wanted to feel the touch of a man again. The *love* of a man. I wanted to close my eyes each night next to a man whispering sweet promises in my ear of the beautiful life we will embark on together.

Romance—that's what I craved. To feel worthy. And just because *I am* only human, maybe some kinky sex on the side. A man that made me feel like a goddess in the bedroom.

Maybe this happening was a good thing. A much needed wake-up call that Zoey Richards was wasting her life away. I just needed a plan. Plans were better executed with some music. Leaning across to my nightstand, I fumble for my iPod and scroll through my playlist. Katrina and the Waves—perfect. I *should* be walking on sunshine, considering that I survived.

I text my friend from work, Mia, to see if she's up for a run. This out-of-character text prompts her to call me immediately.

"Are you okay? Is this an SOS message because you're in danger?" she panics over the receiver. "I've got 911 on speed dial."

"No, I'm fine, but I could use the run."

We agree to meet at the park around the corner in twenty minutes. Buried in the back of my closet are my shorts and

a sports tank I bought after my New Year's resolution of losing weight and getting fit. The tags still attached to the garments were another reminder that New Year's resolutions were a waste of time. Stretching my arms, I pull the tank over my head and it is *snug,* and that is being generous with my words. My boobs look like water balloons ready to burst, and my tights, they give me massive camel toe. Sitting on the edge of my bed, I slip my feet into my joggers and grab a hair tie, throwing my hair back into a tight ponytail. No doubt, this time tomorrow, I will be sitting in the same spot, regretting my mission to become thin and fit.

The park is located a block away from the apartment. I attempt to throw myself into the deep end by running as soon as my feet touch the pavement, but by the time I hit the end of the street, I can barely breathe and am certain that I'm having a heart attack. Resting against the street lamp, a couple stops by and asks me if I'm okay. How embarrassing! I simply smile and manage to cough out the words 'major stitch.'

There are a few benches where some people sit with their dogs, and a small playground for children which is deserted. Beside the water fountain, Mia is already stretching her limbs. I stroll over and wave hello.

"Hey Zoey, nice getup," she laughs.

"Can you see my camel toe?"

"I'm trying not to." She cringes. "So what the hell is going on with you?"

I motion for her to start walking alongside me as I tell her the events of the past twenty-four hours, minus the kiss with Drew. If she knew, she would make it a bigger deal than what it was, and considering it meant absolutely *nothing,* the topic is officially closed. Buried. Beneath six feet of dirt and a pile of crap.

Mia is that annoying friend that believes in finding soulmates and leaving things up to fate. The one person that updates her social media with inspirational posts on love to the point that it's nauseating. She was always on my back about finding true love, similar to what she has with our IT geek, Troy. Granted, Troy is a nice guy. He didn't exactly have lines of women knocking on his door, and considering that they worked with each other eight hours each day, five days a week, it was bound to happen.

"Shit, Zoey, I'm so sorry. You should have called me. I could have—"

"Nothing, Mia," I interrupt. "It's fine now. Drew stayed with me all day and I'm fine."

"But you almost died."

"Almost," I reiterate. "But I didn't."

"You're so lucky Drew was there. It's like he is your guardian angel or something."

I stop mid-step, following with a loose laugh. "Guardian angel? He's my roomie. Trust me, Drew ain't no angel."

Mia doesn't appear offended, and instead, nudges me along. We walk a couple more blocks till we reach a popular cafe that serves *the* best Nutella donut shakes, a new fad rocking the foodie groups. It takes every part of me to resist the urge and settle for a green tea. It also doesn't help when everyone else orders them, the shakes sitting deliciously on their tables as they take selfies.

Genius doesn't even describe the person that thought, 'Hey, let's shove a straw in the middle of a donut and plonk it on top of a milkshake made of Nutella.'

But I need willpower.

Strength.

Resistance.

We settle for a small table down the back and chat about Mia's birthday, which happens to fall the day before her upcoming wedding.

"Thirty is *so* old," she moans.

"No it's not . . . it's the new twenties. I read that online somewhere."

"What I would give to be twenty-one again."

"You and me both. I would have eaten less pizza." I sigh, sinking into my chair. The hard plastic back makes it difficult to get comfortable. "Then I wouldn't have camel toe."

"I would have taken that junior art position I was offered in France." Mia sits back, stirring her tea before taking a sip. Her hair is cut just above her shoulders and almost falls into her cup. Frustrated, she grabs a hair tie from around her wrist and ties it back.

"I wouldn't have stayed so long with my ex. I would be able to afford the deposit on the block of land I wanted to buy near the beach if I didn't blow it all on him."

"Ouch." She winces. "That's gotta hurt."

"Still paying the price."

We sit in silence for a moment and I get to thinking about how easily I allowed that relationship to destroy everything I worked so hard for. I came from a united family; Mom and Dad were still married. I didn't have a fucked-up childhood or 'man issues' that would lead me down the wrong path. For a long time prior to Jess, I was independent. Men were great to have around, but I never truly grasped how women lost their identities all because of one man that had entered their life. From the moment that I met Jess—at the backyard party of a mutual friend—something about me changed. He had this hold over me. You could say I was obsessed, and my need to please him was greater than I thought I was capable of.

"So, I need your RSVP for the wedding," Mia reminds me.

"Well duh, of course I'm going."

"I know that, silly, but are you taking someone?"

"I'll probably take Drew since he owes me big time for yesterday morning. You know how much I hate going to these things alone. Weddings make single people look pathetic and needy."

Mia nods her head in agreement. "Alright, I'll RSVP the two of you."

I take a sip of my tea and Mia tugs on my arm, almost spilling the hot liquid all over my chest.

"Is that Drew?"

Turning my head to where she is looking, I see Drew walk into the cafe with some cute brunette. They are both dressed in scrubs, nothing unusual, and as they stand at the counter ordering a drink, he places his hand on the small of her back. A lump forms in my throat and I swallow cautiously, not able to grasp why this is bothering me so much. *I don't want him to see me.* Obviously, he is busy finding some new chick to get his hands on like the fucking ass he is.

"What did you say?" Mia asks, raising her eyebrow at me.

Shit! Did I say that out loud?

"Uh, this green tea tastes like ass, would rather have a donut shake."

"I don't know what ass tastes like, but okay."

Her comic relief prompts me to relax, and with a small giggle, I shake off how much that gesture bothered me. It's Drew. *Man whore Drew.*

"So aren't you going to go over and say hi?"

"Nah," I say casually. "He looks like he is trying to get his groove on. Don't want to break his swagger."

Mia's shoulders shake as she laughs quietly. Trying not to stare, I force myself to turn away and focus on Mia. In the corner of my eye, I watch Drew and the mystery girl leave the cafe, instantly letting out a breath of air that I'd been anxiously holding in. *What the hell was that?* You've seen Drew with many women. You've even been home while he screws them in his bed. Why this sudden jealous streak?

"Okay, let's head back. This time, we're running," Mia tells me.

By the time I reach the apartment, I'm sure that I'll collapse from exhaustion. Mia had been running every day to achieve that perfect wedding body. I hadn't been running since back in my early twenties. Even then, it was only because I was checking out the marathon runners in their tiny shorts.

Jumping straight into the shower, I linger long enough that my skin begins to prune. The water is heavenly, and I use that fancy shampoo that Drew must have purchased yesterday. It smells like a rainforest and coconuts combined. I could eat it. That would be weird, right? Or not. They invented soda-flavored Lipsmackers; they were somewhat edible.

I should get into the business of inventing everyday products you can clean with and eat. *Seriously?* My brain is over stimulated. *Probably from 'accidentally' swallowing some shampoo.*

With my shower finished, and my brain ready to explode with random thoughts, I head back to my room to change. On a whim, I dress in a navy summer dress with spaghetti straps paired with my white wedges. I can't even remember the last time I had worn them. It was about time I abandoned my weekend sweats. They had sweatpants cancer: holes. The ones that started somewhere near your thigh, and before you know it, your asshole is completely exposed.

After a day spent roaming around the city window shopping, I wander back to the apartment around five, armed with a bag of groceries. I had texted my mom to ask for the recipe for her lasagna, and much like everyone else, she called me instantly, worried something was wrong.

"Honey, you haven't cooked since you moved in with Drew. What's wrong?" she panics over the phone.

"Relax, Mom. Nothing. Okay? I just felt like a home-cooked meal," I lie.

"Why don't you come up for the weekend? Daddy and I will

pay for your fares."

"I've got money, Mom."

Having no life and staying home meant that I had rebuilt the nest egg that I had so carelessly thrown away during my relationship with Jess. It wasn't enough to buy into real estate, but slowly, it is growing.

"Listen, I have to go. I'll call you later. Okay, Mom?"

I hung up the phone, annoyed at my mom. Not only did she frustrate me, she made me feel like a pathetic nobody that everybody felt sorry for. Poor Zoey, can't cook. Poor Zoey, she's as fat as a pig. Alright, maybe not the last comment, but I knew everyone thought it. They just didn't say it out loud. Or to my face.

That's it. No more feeling sorry for poor Zoey.

Inside our kitchen, I lay out all the ingredients on the countertop and start prepping just like Mom said. Sometimes I wonder why I don't do this more often. I am pretty sure there must be some law against feeding your kids pizza every day.

With the lasagna in the oven and the timer on, I wait patiently at the table, reading Drew's medical textbook which was left on the countertop. I'm engrossed in the chapter about heart surgery when the voices enter the apartment. *Voices . . .* shit, is someone else here?

There is no time to think—or escape.

"Hey, you're home. And what's that smell? You're cooking?" Drew states, shocked.

Behind him is the same brunette I saw him with today. I wipe my hands on the apron and offer a fake smile. Fake, because something about her, about them being together, just didn't sit right.

"Yep, where else would I be?"

"And you're wearing a dress?"

"So? It was nice out."

"You went out? On a Sunday?" He scratches his head, pausing, then continues to watch me with inquiring eyes. "And are you reading my textbook?"

"What's with the fifty questions?" I push past him and cordially reach out my hand. "Hi, I'm Zoey."

"Hey, I'm Kristy." She smiles, shaking my hand in return.

The timer goes off, and I move towards the oven. With my mitts on, I open the door and see my perfectly cooked lasagna sitting inside. The creamy béchamel sauce looks to die for, bubbling at the surface, just the way my mom makes it.

Taking it out, I place it on the cooling rack and pull out a plate. Then, I realize they are still watching me. Drew is in shock; his face couldn't be any more transparent. I turn around to be polite and offer him a plate. "You guys want some?"

They both decline, having eaten not long ago.

Whatever.

With my plate in hand, I make small talk for a couple of minutes before retreating to my room and eagerly shutting the door behind me, careful not to slam it and display my anger. The nerve of him to bring her back! Did he not care about me at all? Who cares that Zoey almost drowned . . . let's just carry on!

Okay, that's selfish. I could audition for a Broadway play with an act like that.

I'm hungry, and with the lasagna cooled down, I devour the plate, licking my lips in delight. Seconds would have been great, but I decide against it, not wanting to disturb their *alone time* in the living room.

No, they're probably screwing in his room. Argh! I pick up a sneaker off the floor and throw it at the wall, creating a loud bang. *Do you really think that will stop them?*

Minutes pass and nothing. No sounds, no giggling of any sort. Bored, I sit at my desk and scroll through my emails, then browse some travel sites just for fun. My neck and eyes become sore from staring at the screen for a long time. Leaning down towards my ankles, I unstrap my sandals and toss them in the corner. What's missing is some tunes. When I press the shuffle button on my iPod, "Eye of the Tiger" blares through my speakers, and just like always, I play my air guitar, singing along.

My sweats tease me, hanging over the small armchair. It is late, and while attempting to remove my dress, the zipper gets caught midway down my back. Letting out a frustrated groan, I feel hands against my back, causing me to yelp as I turn around in shock. Drew is standing in the middle of my room. He carefully unzips my dress, then walks to my iPod and turns down the volume slightly.

"Fucking hell, you scared the shit out of me!" I shout at him.

"Well, you didn't hear me knocking. What was I supposed to do? We're ordering pizza. What do you want?"

"I'll pass," I say casually. "Besides, I cooked. Remember?"

"You'll pass? I know you cooked but you never pass on pizza." He stands before me, rubbing his five o'clock shadow with curiosity. "Remember that time we went to All-You-Can-Eat Pete's? You had four plates of Pete's ribs, including the side of lobster, and still ordered pizza on the cab ride home."

"It was that time of the month."

Checkmate, Drew. He hated menstrual talk. His body shudders when I mention it. I didn't want to invite any more questions.

"Alright. We need to talk. Something's up and you're acting really weird, Zo. Kristy has a shift that starts in two hours and mine starts in four so we'll talk then, but seriously, what flavor?"

"Hawaiian." I sigh.

He leaves my room without another word while I sit on my bed, sulking. *I am weak.* Day one of my new life and

everyone thinks I've gone cuckoo.

Was there even a point in trying?

And who was I trying for?

Me? Or for a man that hadn't walked into my life yet?

CHAPTER Six

Drew

I COULDN'T STAND IT ANYMORE. Zoey was acting all weird, and trying to read her mind was like reading a Chinese novel upside down. Wearing a dress on a Sunday . . . not to mention an apron on top. It was like I'd walked into the 1950s and all I needed her to say was, "Honey, dinner's on the table."

Being the stubborn woman that she is, she refused to acknowledge that something was wrong, carrying on pretending everything was normal between us. I called bullshit the second I saw her, but Kristy was beside me, and I didn't want to have a heated argument with Zoey in front of her.

Kristy had kept me occupied for most of the day, and despite what one may think, she wasn't interested in me. Having broken up with her boyfriend only a week ago, she confided in me that he was abusive, emotionally and physically, and she really needed to find herself. I respected that. Hanging out with her was easy. Kristy was pretty laid-back despite the traumatic events she had endured.

Normally, Zoey would chill with the girls I brought back, yet this time she retreated to her room. I let her be, hanging out in the living room with Kristy, watching reruns on MTV.

When her stomach growled, she suggested that maybe we order some pizza. Miss Moody declined the offer to have some, but in the end, she caved. I made it my business to get to the bottom of this the second that Kristy left for her shift.

I tap on Zoey's door, wanting an end to this saga. She doesn't answer, so I open the door anyway, but not without warning her that I'm coming in. She's sprawled across her bed in her sweats with that book she was talking about, not a single movement to acknowledge that I've entered the room.

"Alright, what's going on, Zo? All day you've been acting weird. Ever since last night when you stormed out of—"

She drops the book onto the comforter and turns to face me. Her eyes are doing that thing where it looks like the pools of green are circling rapidly like a cyclone. Her lips tighten as she bites her tongue, warning me that I should have probably never walked in here and opened my mouth. *Smart move, you idiot.*

"I didn't storm out. I was pissed with you that you thought it was more important to go find some pussy then hang out with me."

And there it is . . . the truth comes out like the rain after the crack of thunder. Stunned at her choice of words, I sit on the edge of her bed, trying to find the right thing to say. Talking to women can sometimes be like walking on eggshells while carrying barbells. *Choose your words carefully . . . do not anger the beast.*

"It wasn't like that . . . it's hard to explain," I fumble incoherently.

"Really? That's the best you can come up with? We've known each other for, like, what? Four years. I've seen you vomit on yourself. I've even rubbed your belly when you had that bout of stomach flu," she quips. "And the best you can tell me is it's hard to explain?"

"Okay, the kiss made it awkward," I confess.

70

Her hands toy with the cover of her book until a sheepish—annoying—smile, sweeps across her face. At first it's small giggles, but soon her laughs erupt into a coughing fit. "Of course it was awkward. How long did it take you to realize that?"

"Alright, whatever. Can we move on from what happened?"

"Sure. But just admit I was right?"

"I'll admit you had a strong point."

"Admit I was right." She moves closer to the edge of the bed where I sit, settling on her knees as she rubs her hands in delight. She's watching me intently and I can't stop grinning, knowing full well that Zoey would lose if she attempted to arm wrestle . . . *again.* But hey, let's humor her into thinking she has a chance.

"And what if I don't? Whatcha gonna do, Richards?" I tease.

"Try me," she warns with a smirk.

I don't say anything. What could this girl possibly do? Zo is tiny compared to me, plus she's a girl. I stretch my arm, propping it up in position and ready to wrestle when she grabs my forearm and twists the skin until it burns.

"Ow! What the fuck? Let go!" I bark.

"Admit I was right?"

"Fine, you were right."

With a satisfied smile, she lets go. The little bitch left red marks on my skin and the burn is still stinging like crazy. I rub the skin on my arm to soothe the pain.

Raising my voice at her again, irritated by the persistent sting, "Fucking hell, that hurt!"

I'm still reeling in pain while she turns her attention back to her 'Jerk' book, acting as if nothing happened. I sit on the edge of her bed in silence until she utters, "So what time does your shift start?"

"Got to leave in an hour. And listen," I tell her, "Kristy just broke up with her boyfriend and let's just say he makes Jess look like an angel. I'm not there to hook up with her, she just needed someone."

She puts the book down and focuses her attention back on me. Her face softens, the compassion evident in the way her eyes glaze over over. "Is she alright? I mean, you know. Does she need any help?"

"To be honest? She puts on a good front and I can't divulge the rest."

It was last Wednesday when I had learned of Kristy's relationship with her boyfriend of five years. I was grabbing some supplies off the shelf when I accidentally knocked into her side. She instantly recoiled and winced in pain. At first she said she was fine, but I had seen enough in the hospital to realize something was wrong. She eventually showed me the extent of her injuries, and boy did I see red. She admitted to her family that he had been abusing her and finally put a restraining order on him. I'm glad she finally sought help, but she wasn't the first person I had encountered who was suffering in silence. They all had their own stories to tell and their reasons for why they stuck it out so long.

This was one of the pitfalls of working in the hospital. Emotionally, I had to harden up. It was a tough job, but one that I had fought so hard for. I just never expected it to be this difficult. I considered myself a good listener, yet when it came to offering advice, I wasn't a psychologist. I knew only what I knew and what I thought was the right thing to do.

"Drew," Zoey says softly,"I admire you for following your dream. I can't even begin to imagine how difficult your line of work is."

Difficult is an understatement. I could have chosen any career path, but deep inside I knew that I chose this path because of what happened to my mother. My parents divorced when I was only three, and my mother died shortly after. She had suffered from a nasty virus, and because she

lived in a rural town in Australia, they didn't have the resources to medically attend to her, sending her home with a fever that they thought painkillers could manage. I was only four when it happened, and because I had been back and forth between my dad's and my mom's, my memories of her were foggy. To me she was just a woman that cared for me on the weekends. It was my dad who raised me.

"You do what you have to do, Zo."

"I know but you could have chosen to do anything. I understand how great the reward is, but why choose a career that defines who you are as a person?" she questions seriously.

"I just want to help people," I half admit. "As much as Dad wanted me to be a mechanic, I felt like I needed to be someone who made an impact in people's lives. Helped them. Maybe because I felt so helpless in my own life back then and all I wanted was to feel important. Like I mattered."

"Whatever you choose to do, you would matter to someone," she tells me.

"Well, growing up, I felt the opposite."

She shifts her body closer to mine and places her hand on my arm. The warmth of her touch comforts me; it always had a way of doing that. "I get it, you only had your dad, plus you were awkward looking."

I turn to face her, amused by her comment. "Gee, thanks for the uplifting compliment, Zo."

"But you turned out hot. Just like Tom Cruise."

"You're comparing me to *Tom Cruise?*"

"Brad Pitt, George Clooney, you name it. They all had their I-wouldn't-touch-them-with-a-ten-foot-pole awkward phases."

"And I guess you never had that? You've just been a goddess your whole life?"

She shakes her head and jumps off the bed, moving

towards her shelf where she pulls out an album. It's fluorescent pink with stickers scattered all over the cover. Placing it in front of me, she opens a page. The pages look worn and fragile, the background tinged with yellow. The binder is barely holding the album together, the spiraling metal bent out of shape. There is a photo of her with a couple of girls. She is dressed in a cheerleading outfit.

"You were a cheerleader?" I ask, eyes fixated on the photo.

She looked gorgeous. *Well, she is gorgeous.* The kinda girl I would have fantasized about in high school yet never gone near for fear of being laughed at and given a wedgie by the cool crowd.

"Uh huh. In senior year."

"You looked hot for a sixteen-year-old," I admit.

"Oh, just you wait a second." She flips the pages back, showing me a different photo.

Taken aback by the difference, I zoom in closer to look properly. It looks nothing like her. In the photo she is wearing some granny jumper with patterns of roses all over it and awful, mustard-colored baggy jeans. Her face is covered in zits, and behind her smile are braces.

I pull a face, not intentionally wanting to offend her. *"You look . . ."*

"Awkward? Hideous?" She laughs. "I've never shown this photo to any guy. It's like my worst nightmare. Secret-business-type stuff that I should burn but don't want to regret letting go of the memory."

"I'm flattered I got to see your pic that will give me nightmares," I joke.

She punches my arm softly, laughing along with me. We both relax on the bed, chatting with ease about our high school memories. With Zoey rambling in my ear about some fashion faux pas in her senior year, I turn the page back to the first photo she showed me of her in the cheer-squad dress. The uniform was royal blue and yellow, tight, and

typical of a cute cheerleading outfit. There are four girls in the photo, Zoey standing proudly in the middle, perfectly posing with her hand resting on her hip. Her blond tendrils are tightly curled, sitting just above her waist. The green in her eyes captures the moment, sparkling, with her lips curled into a cute smile.

She was beautiful.

And if life had a different way of working out, just one moment with a girl like her would have completely changed everything. Given me the much needed confidence boost during the years when I thought Andrew Baldwin didn't deserve to be here.

The year when Lacey Everson, the homecoming queen, blatantly said to my face that I was a worthless geek who should go home, turn the car on, and close the garage door behind me.

A motherless waste of space with a poor loser of a father.

Her words—still engrained in my memory to this day.

This is what the popular girls did. Beat the not-so-cool boys down for their own pleasure. And I was definitely not in the cool crowd.

The memory disturbs me, sending this chilled moment into the shadow of a dark cloud. Zoey is still chatting away at record speed, and with my head wanting an escape, I listen and catch the end of her conversation.

"As much as I would love to stay and chat, I need to go get ready for work." I stand up and stretch my arms, my shirt pulling up, exposing my skin. "Zo, are we all good now?"

Her eyes are lingering on my stomach, watching me with an odd stare. She doesn't realize that she's biting her lip until she catches me watching her, immediately covering her embarrassment by over-smiling and distracting herself by playing with her hair.

"Yes." She grins, disguising the red face. "Sorry for my bitch fit."

"Sorry for my awkwardness and for accidentally getting a boner when we kissed."

She scowls then tilts her head back, laughing painfully and holding on to her stomach, trying to control the outburst. "See, I had no idea. Must be the little peewee," she babbles in baby talk.

I seriously want to pull my pants down to prove her wrong, but then it would be equal to the shaving incident. *There goes my stupid brain for bringing that image up again.*

"I know what you're thinking, Baldwin. Don't you dare. This weekend has already scarred me and I don't need your baby wang to throw me over the edge," she warns me.

I give up. Upon exiting the room, I hear my name again as she scurries behind me. I turn around, stopping her fast in her tracks. She fiddles with the ends of her hair. Her signature move when she's nervous or needed a favor from me.

"Totally forgot. So you know how I saved you yesterday? I need a favor."

"Don't you mean I saved *you?*" I remind her.

"Yeah, sure, you saved my life, uh huh, super nice of you. But hello, Mickey would still be here if it wasn't for me, and imagine the peewee talk."

Zoey batts her eyelashes, pretending to be innocent and sweet. *This is the look of pure evil.* I hated when Zo had something to hold over me. It never ended well.

Taking a deep breath, my voice tightens as I bellow, "*What do you want?*"

"I need a date for Mia's wedding."

"When?"

Responding promptly, "Two Saturdays from now."

Argh. I hated weddings. I don't think any man likes them. Maybe the groom. But that's because it guarantees him pussy for life. They dragged on all day, plus I had to put on

a suit. Hmm, a suit eh? *Suits attract women. Weddings were swarming with single women.* Maybe, just maybe, this wasn't such a bad idea.

"Will there be any hot single ladies there?" I query, folding my arms in anticipation.

Zoey's face quickly drops. Her eyes, shifting towards the mint-green painted wall, ignoring my presence. A moment later, she glances my way, then follows with a perky—albeit fake—smile. "Mia is one of five girls, so chances are, yes."

I wink. Leaning in, I kiss her forehead. "You got yourself a date, Richards."

CHAPTER *Seven*

Zoey

*S*UNDAY NIGHT BLUES.

    When a case of the Mondays is just around the corner.

After Drew left to go to work, I finally finished my book and was suffering from *the* worst book hangover in history. It's like the life had been sucked out of me. I dreaded nearing the end, when I knew the story would be all over. So they got their happily ever after. *Where's mine?* Three fucking days that these characters had consumed me. People often commented on how invested I became in the books I read. Telling me that if I devoted this much time into my love life, I would be married with three kids by now.

People—meaning my mother.

She never understood my love of reading. At an early age, I would lock myself in my room and finish an entire *Babysitter's Club* book in an hour, then bug my mom to take me back to the store to buy another one. In the car ride to the store, she would complain about how I should be outside riding my bike like the rest of the girls my age.

The rest of the girls my age were hiding behind trees,

making out with boys, and competing over who had the biggest hickey. I thought that was gross, until I turned fourteen. The world suddenly became a different place, filled with cute boys and even cuter college men.

And sure, I did invest a lot of time into reading. Books had a way of transporting me to another world when my own was so boring and mundane.

Yet here I sat—completely numb.

Happy, but numb. Because I had no clue what to do now. *Start a new book . . . move on. This happens to you every time.*

I even used social media to contact the author, telling her how much I loved the book, needed a pierced 'Jerk' in my life, and to hurry up and write her next book because I was having massive withdrawals.

My eyes stare at the clock on the wall, watching the hands tick past at what seems like a very slow pace. There is nothing left to do except scroll through my iPad and play a game of online poker. Something I did occasionally when I was *that* bored. My disinterest in the game urged me to go all in, angering the rest of the online gamers. Apart from one guy, Derek Smith. He had the balls to ask me what I was wearing. When I responded, "A red wig and a clown suit," he suddenly went offline.

Derek Smith doesn't know what he's missing.

A couple more games, then I retreat to YouTube, watching episodes of *Family Ties.*

Michel J. Fox—what a heartthrob. After two episodes, I settle on watching *Back to the Future* until I remember how annoying Biff is, shutting down my iPad to refrain from swearing and possibly throwing it against the wall.

Bored and alone, I wander across the hall to see if my neighbor, Gigi, is home. I tap on the door, not surprised to hear the sounds of Gloria Gaynor's "I'll Be There" blasting through the small apartment. There is no chance that Gigi

will hear me with the music loud, so I grab the spare key on top of her porchlight and open the door. I yell out down the hall as she dances past and stops mid-step.

"Hi Doll!"

She doesn't stop for long, dancing barefoot back into the living room.

Gigi had been living in this apartment complex before I moved in. She never revealed her age, but a couple of references here and there led me to believe she is well into her sixties. Having been married five times, Gigi is your original hopeless romantic. Much like Mia, she was a firm believer that fate would serve you your soulmate on a silver platter. Fate worked in mysterious ways, since Gigi lived alone and is currently single.

I was around to meet Husband Number Five, but unfortunately, he died of a stroke a few years back. Since then, Gigi said she was done with marriage, and instead, adopted stray cats. Patti, Diana, and Gloria had moved in and Gigi had never been happier.

One pussy away from turning into a crazy cat lady.

Gigi loved to read, much like me. Her apartment is scattered with several bookcases, housing everything from classic novels to trashy Hollywood romances. She read at lightning speed, and if ever I needed something new, she would recommend something from her ever-growing library.

In her spare time, she enjoyed writing—mainly poetry. During the week, she worked at the local thrift store. That sums Gigi up in a nutshell. That, and she's a complete nutcase. *A lovable nutcase.*

I take a seat inside her living room, making myself comfortable on the soft, brown leather sofa. Every time I sat down on it, I would inhale the scent of the worn leather until Patti would smother me, jumping on my lap and purring. She is such an attention whore, climbing on top off me whenever she got the chance.

Gigi turns the music down and offers me a drink. A Long Island Iced Tea, because she liked to get buzzed on Sunday night.

She prances in front of me, placing the tea down on the table beside the sofa. "Why the sad face, doll?"

I recap my weekend, again leaving out the bit about Drew and the kiss. I just couldn't bring that up, especially to the people who knew the both of us. Gigi loved Drew, but she would be the first one to tell me to be careful. Roomies had this special code; you broke it, you were pretty much screwed. Don't play with fate or karma, because they didn't play nice.

Gigi lifts my left hand and trails her fingers along the crease. *Great . . . this is where she tells me I'm going to meet the man of my dreams and have three kids.*

Her hands are covered in rings, my favorite being an oval turquoise ring she picked up on her travels with a gypsy and a bunch of carnie folk. Flowing past her knees is a purple dress. She is rarely seen wearing any other color, amethyst being her birthstone.

Her long grey hair sits just above her waist, styled in a tight plait. She closes her eyes briefly, then releases a deep breath, humming some unknown tune.

"There's something troubling you," she tells me. "A man."

"Well, I don't exactly care for the *seafood buffet* if you know what I mean." I laugh at my own joke. Gigi is smiling at my humor; having known me for so long, she is accustomed to my awkward jokes.

"You've got to get your groove back. Stella did, and now so can you," she says, continuing to trace my hands. Her frown worries me. Can she really predict the future? Am I dying? I have cancer, don't I?

Calm the hell down, Zoey!

"I'm trying, Gigi. I really am this time." Patti jumps off my lap, abandoning my need for affection. *It's all about her.* "But

it's like everyone is shocked when I try to change. 'Predictable Zoey eating pizza. Predictable Zoey in her sweats,'" I complain, slumping further into the sofa.

"So? Who cares about everyone? This is your life, doll. One that you're letting slip away. Did you speak to your boss about that promotion yet?"

"No," I sulk.

"Tomorrow's a new day. A new Zoey. I read your horoscope today and it said exactly that."

Okay, so I said Gigi was a nutcase—throw in *cuckoo* as well. Did I mention that her apartment is covered in candles and crystals, and she reads her horoscope like it was the Bible?

She enjoyed travelling, returning with more junk and clutter each time. Her last trip was to India. One look at her bedroom and you would think that you entered the Taj Mahal.

Oh, and my horoscopes. God forbid she forgot to read mine and inform me of how my life will suddenly take a positive turn overnight.

If I had a dollar for every time I heard that.

"Did it say that I would meet some hot guy that would give me multiple orgasms because of his pierced cock?" I humor her.

She laughs and passes me the newspaper. To be polite, I skim my star sign, only to be let down. *Well that blows.* Perhaps Drew was right; I needed to stop comparing my life to the books I read. Fictional boyfriends were great on paper but they weren't going to keep me warm at night.

"You know, you're right." I stand up, embracing the sudden confidence, imagining myself as He-Man standing on top of Castle Grayskull, telling everyone that I have the power. "Tomorrow is a new day, and first thing in the morning, I'll march into my boss's office and ask for that promotion."

I shuffle nervously at my desk, trying to muster up the courage to ask my boss for that overdue promotion that was promised late last year. It is silly of me to be so insecure and tense, considering he had praised me on my work several times, even mentioning often how my talent is being underutilized. That, and I had been with the company for a solid five years. Either you considered that dedication, or work in reverse, a poor decision on my behalf. *Only time will tell.*

In an attempt to boost my confidence, I wore my charcoal tunic dress with a white collared shirt, and paired it with my patent leather Mary Janes. My hair had been washed and styled into a tight bun, neatly pulled back from my face. Makeup isn't my strong point, never spending much time on learning since I couldn't be bothered. I did, however, apply a thin layer of foundation and a few strokes of mascara. Drew had this thing about women and makeup, often complaining about how cheap it sometimes looked and how most women looked better off without it.

And why am I thinking about what Drew thinks? Focus!

For extra luck, I wore my gold pineapple earrings. Gigi had bought them for me during her travels to Asia last year. Now, all I need to do is walk into Mr. Becker's office and deliver my speech. One that I had practiced numerous times in my head and in the shower.

"Zoey." My name is called, and I swivel my chair around to see Mr. Becker standing beside my desk.

Mr. Becker had inherited the business from his late father, but is a well-known architect with the reputation of a shark. Luckily for me, he also had a soft side to him, taking me on board, knowing my passion for architecture and keen interest to further my career. But much like a hormonal pregnant woman, he had his mood swings, hence the paper incident last week. Today, he is dressed in his favorite brown suit, which is a sign that he is in a pleasant and giving mood.

I bet he got laid by his wandering wife!

"I'm heading out today to visit a potential site where an investor is looking at building some condos. I would really like it if you could make it out there around three." His face shows no emotion.

With an overenthusiastic smile, I respond excitedly at being given the opportunity. "Sure, I'll be there. I was actually hoping to have a chat with you sometime today."

"Anything urgent? I have back-to-back meetings, then my wife wants to catch up for lunch."

"It can wait," I say, instantly scolding myself for letting the opportunity pass once again.

"Great. I'll see you at three."

He disappears around the corner and out of sight. My disappointment is short-lived, as the excitement of being on site with a potential new project takes over. Turning back around to face my computer, I let out a small squeal, excitedly tapping my feet under the desk. I didn't know what it meant, but I took it as a positive sign that things were progressing in my career.

I had to share this news with Drew, grabbing my cell and immediately texting him. Given that he worked the nightshift last night, I didn't expect him to respond at all.

> That's my girl!
>
> Why is our shampoo almost finished? Did you 'accidentally' eat it?
>
> I should stop buying coconut-scented products
>
> Pick some up on the way home please
>
> And toilet paper

Huh, what an odd request. I could have sworn we had several rolls stored underneath the bathroom vanity. My fingers type fast, asking him to check again.

The bubble appears on my screen, and I wait impatiently

for his response, clicking my pen at a fast speed.

> I may, or may not have, used the last 3 rolls to squash a spider I found in the shower.

I burst out laughing, my cell slipping out of my hands and falling onto the floor. Panicked, I reach down and check my screen. *Phew.* The glass appears intact—thank god.

Drew is terrified of spiders. If you ask him, he'll tell you that he's not, and his desire to eliminate them from the world is only because they're annoying. He doesn't realize that his face turns pale white, and his scramble to find anything to squash the poor lil' fellas, ticks all the boxes of being a scared little wuss.

I, on the other hand, had no problem with them. In fact, I wouldn't even flinch when one would crawl across the floor. Drew is armed with bug spray and a biohazard suit in less than five seconds.

The sound of my inbox dings, so I focus my attention back onto my computer, answering my pending emails. I'm in the middle of responding to a client when a distressed Mia sits on my desk, twisting a piece of paper in her hand.

"What's wrong?" I ask her.

"I'm going to be Mrs. Bono in a few days."

"Yes . . . you are." I hesitate, unsure of where this conversation is heading.

"Mrs. Bono. People will call me Mrs. Boner."

I laugh, snorting accidentally in the process. "Who the hell is going to call you Mrs. Boner?"

"People are mean, Zoey, they'll call you whatever they please."

"Okay, so say they do. You love Troy. I don't see what the problem is."

"My dress didn't fit right at the fitting last night," she adds, fiddling with that piece of paper like a hyena on crack. "*Do you know how much that dress costs?*"

86

"You have several days left. Surely the tailor could—"

"Don't you see?" she raises her voice. "It must be a sign!"

Cold feet. I thought it was a myth, but Mia's pale face, barely brushed hair, and bloodshot eyes were a sign that the so-called myth was actually a condition.

"Mia," I say calmly, "it's okay to be stressed out about the wedding. Remember how much you love Troy. You always go on about how he is Mr. Perfect and came at the right time in your life. You're just experiencing the normal cold feet. Once Saturday is over, you'll be glad to be Mrs. Boner."

She giggles, her shoulders relaxing as she lets out a long sigh. She lets go of the piece of paper, dumping it in the trash. "He picks his nose and shows me his boogers. Trust me—he ain't that perfect."

"Thank god!" I exhale. "All this time I've been looking for the perfect man and wondering why I couldn't find him. Now I know he just doesn't exist!"

"Did you ask Drew to be your date?"

Quickly correcting her, "Plus one. Not date."

"Same thing. And?"

"Of course he said yes. He owes me big time. Besides, if there's anyone I want to keep me company on the night, it's him. At least someone who understands my humor."

Mia traces her finger along the edge of my desk. "You two are a great fit."

"Yeah, a just-friends fit," I remind her.

"But you know the best relationships come from being friends first. It would be so easy," she carries on. "You both know each other inside and out, and you already live together. Your biggest dilemma would be whose room you would sleep in every night."

"You're crazy. It'll never be like that between us." I reiterate, "He is my roomie. End of story."

With the thought planted in my head, I start to think

about what it would be like for two roommates to get together. I guess it would be easy from a living perspective. You could have sex whenever and wherever you wanted. No boundaries. No one else to answer to. And it would be kinda hot to sleep in a man's bed but still have your own space across the hall. Oh my god! I am going to kill Mia for making me even think about this!

Think about a naked, hairy fat man running across a meadow.

Phew . . . forgotten.

We continue to chat for a few more minutes before work consumes us both. To ease her fears about the wedding, I suggest we have a quick drink tonight at a local bar to unwind.

Three o'clock rolls around quickly, and the site foreman, along with Mr. Becker, show me around the vacant block of land before settling on a spot so we can open the blueprints. The site has so much potential; my brain is exploding with ideas. Even Mr. Becker looks pleased with my enthusiasm, suggesting I attend the next meeting. With a successful day behind me, I am eagerly looking forward to unwinding with a few drinks.

At the bar, Mia orders us two martinis as we settle for a spot on the upper deck. The view of the city is spectacular on this beautiful summer's night. The sky is a shade of pale pink, a sign that tomorrow will be another warm summer's day. For a Monday night, the bar is unusually crowded. Many people are dressed in their corporate attire, most likely unwinding after a stressful day at work.

After our first glass, both of us relax and chat about the wedding. Usually wedding talk bored me, but Mia's concern over her traditional Asian family being in the same room as Troy's Greek parents is pure entertainment. Somewhere during Mia's rant about wearing something old and blue, I feel a gentle tap on my shoulder.

"Zoey?"

The voice sounds familiar, and I turn around to be met by Noah, a guy I had a brief fling with a couple of times after I broke up with Jess. Yes, he was my *rebound* guy.

"Noah? Oh my god, how are you?" I'm shocked to see him. I jump up and give him a quick hug. He doesn't have to answer; he looks *damn* good. Wearing a grey V-neck tee and dark jeans, his body looks even better than I remembered it. My eyes move towards his forearm where a new tattoo sits. I can't quite make out the design—something tribal by the looks of it.

Leaning forward with a gentle brush against my ear, he whispers, "Great, but even better now that you're here."

Oh.

What. A. Line. Noah always knew exactly what to say. He was *the* perfect gentleman, coming into my life at just the right time. Gigi told me that a great rebound guy would help me move forward, but warned me that you don't go falling in love with said person.

Noah was great. Just what I needed after Jess's indiscretion. Attractive with slight cockiness, attentive to my needs, and he was a fantastic lover. I mean knock-your-socks-off, barely-crawl-out-of-bed type of fantastic lover.

"May I sit down?" he asks politely.

How does he manage to make that sound sexy?

I nod. Mia looks pleased, taking a cheeky sip from her glass until it's finished. She briefly announces that she will grab another drink before quickly disappearing, leaving us alone.

"So, what have you been up to?" I ask, continuing the small talk so I don't blurt out, *Come back to my place and fuck me like I'm the last woman on Earth.*

"Not much. Just got back from Hawaii."

"Land of the pineapple," I laugh. "New tatt?"

I lean forward to take a closer look, and also as an excuse

to grab his arm. His muscles are defined, but not so chunky that he looks like a walking ad for a steroid company.

"You like it? I tossed and turned about the design." His sexy smile and flirtatious eye-gestures are difficult to ignore. I need to get laid—now. Here. The restroom! *Argh,* I shouldn't have watched that documentary with Drew about what diseases lingered in public toilets.

"You look good, Zoey. It's been a while." His smooth voice hints that tonight may end well. For the both of us.

Although I look like shit, I welcome the compliment because I'm weak and hadn't been flattered in such a long time. There's something about flirting with a hot guy that is a nice ego booster on this already positive Monday.

"You too. You seeing anyone?" I blurt out.

Stupid no filter! That sounded so desperate!

He leans in closer and smiles with a cocky grin. His tongue sits patiently at the corner of his mouth, teasing me relentlessly. "No, and I hope you aren't either."

Oh.

There comes a point in your life when a dry spell is no longer a dry spell—more like a century drought. This is that point, and Noah is awakening the ravaging beast inside of me that so desperately needs to feel a man's body pressed against my skin. That, or even to have the smell of a man on my sheets.

"Zoey . . . Zoey," he calls my name.

I shake my head and refocus on the gorgeous Noah.

"So how about it?"

Confused and embarrassed for zoning out while he asked me a question, I ask coyly, "How about what?"

He laughs on cue. "I've been crashing on a friend's couch. Can we head back to your place?"

With a giddy smile, I tell him to give me a second. My cell is peeping through the top of my purse. I pull it out and type

a message to Drew.

Code Red.

I don't wait for a response and quickly shove the cell back into my purse. Noah gently traces the tips of my fingers, watching me with playful eyes. My body is telling me it's the right thing to do; *go have fun and be a single twenty-nine-year-old woman.* Sweats, pizza, and wallowing in self-pity are things of the past. I've been needing to get back in the game, and Noah is the perfect excuse to do so.

Mia strolls at a snail's pace back to our table. I'm quick to tell her we're heading off, grabbing my purse in a frenzy. Offering me a cheeky wink, she says goodbye as Noah and I follow closely behind her.

I didn't know where tonight would end, but I knew this: It is *definitely* my lucky day.

CHAPTER Eight

Drew

WORKING IN THE HOSPITAL IS never predictable. One minute you're filling out paperwork, and the next, you're assisting in saving someone's life.

Some days I wondered what it would be like to work in an office, nine to five, with a set lunchbreak and less pressure. Then, I'll have one of those days where something I do makes a difference. *Saves a life.* Those are the times that everything I have worked so hard for—the blood, sweat and endless hours of studying—are brought to light. There is so much more I need to learn before I'm a qualified surgeon, but that doesn't stop me in the slightest bit.

However, this week's schedule is wearing me down. With one intern on vacation and another two struck down with the flu, we are spreading ourselves really thin. Almost every shift this week is rostered to be a double.

The hospital is understaffed in general. It isn't as big as the main hospital in the city, given that it is in a seedy part of town. However, poverty and lack of healthcare made the waits even longer and stretched the resources. Tonight was one of those nights, not having even stopped to grab something to eat. Somewhere during the night my energy levels fell low, forcing me to stop at the vending machine to grab a protein bar just to get me through the rest of the night.

Taking a seat on the uncomfortable plastic armchair near reception, I pull my cell out of my pocket to check any calls I might have missed. Earlier on, I had felt it vibrate in my pocket. Usually I ignored my cell at work, but something compelled me to check the message. I enter my passcode and the text appears on my front screen. It's from Zoey.

Code Red.

My eyes do a double take, staring at the illuminated screen in shock. *Code Red?* I hadn't received a Code Red text in . . . *forever.* My eyes read over the message again. It definitely says Code Red. I shove the cell back in my pocket, ignoring the text, praying that it will magically disappear.

It has been a long fucking day with the hospital inundated with some sort of stomach virus that's plaguing the city. The last thing I need is my roomie sending me texts because she's about to get fucking laid, especially since we were messaging earlier about her good news. Is this how she celebrates?

I close my eyes and try to get some sort of grip on why Zoey's text is angering me. *Code Red had me seeing red.*

We came up with Code Red when I first brought a girl back home and Zoey walked in on the chick unzipping my pants on the couch. It was agreed that we needed to set boundaries and forewarn each other to avoid situations like this. It's never been an issue before, and it shouldn't have been now. I just didn't think Zoey would send me a text like that. And why is it bothering me so much?

The stark-white wall beside me looks like a perfect target to smash my fist into, because the frustration and unknown feelings are consuming me. I'm *not* that guy. The one with a chip on his shoulder, carrying the jealously gene that destroys relationships. But the thought of another man touching Zo is just . . . unbearable.

Get over it; she's dated and fucked men before.

The roomie code . . . remember the roomie code.

One of the shift supervisors approaches me. "Hey Drew. John called in sick. Any chance you can cover his shift?"

"Sure," I agree, exhausted.

I accepted the second shift just to get my mind off it, but only an hour into the shift, my thoughts won't settle and I find it impossible to focus. Why would she do this? It was unlike her to bring someone home—a stranger. She hadn't mentioned that she was seeing anyone, so I could only assume it was some guy she picked up. It could be Rob. That was even worse! The guy is a fucking dick. *Yet you had no problem setting them up a week ago.*

Luckily, it quiets down, and the hospital agrees to send me home.

Hopping onto the next bus, I ride it home until it approaches my stop. It's still two blocks till our apartment, and with the very little energy left in me, I run all the way home, only to be greeted by an empty apartment. *What the fuck did I expect to do if they were here anyway?* I throw my keys onto the table, walking through the small hall, flicking all the light switches on.

My immediate plan is to race to the bathroom and remove all the condoms, just in case they do turn up. No glove, no love. Brilliant!

Inside the bathroom, I open the bottom drawer to find an almost empty packet. *Oh yeah . . . I forgot about how I used them up.* After dumping what's left into the trash and covering it with an empty bottle of shampoo, I lie on the couch, drifting away into a restless sleep when the sounds of keys tapping against the lock wake me.

Behind the door, Zoey's giggles echo through the common hall. The door opens wide, forcing me to sit up, and all I see is a pair of hands all over Zoey's ass.

And her lips are glued to some jerk's face.

I clear my throat, mostly to release the grunt that wanted

to escape.

"Drew?" She acts surprised to see me, letting him go while she adjusts her dress.

Crossing my arms, I sit up on the couch, not budging. I wasn't going to fucking leave now, but I also didn't want to sit here while she took him back to her room and fucking screwed him. I needed a plan . . . *think fast.*

"Yeah, I wasn't feeling well so I was hoping we could stay in," I mumble, coughing slightly.

Her face immediately drops. "Did you get my text?"

"Text? Sorry, I must have fallen asleep. What did it say?"

"Never mind," she responds, disappointed.

With her hands pressed against his chest, she pushes the guy out the door. In the hall, I hear mumbling followed by more laughter. When the door opens minutes later, Zoey walks back into the apartment alone, locking the door behind her. She throws her purse onto the hall table and sits on the couch beside me, letting out an annoyed huff. Kicking her heels off, she places her feet on the couch and begins to rub them.

Her constant exhales, her disappointed face, and the way her body slumps towards the cushions tell me one thing: She is annoyed that I stopped anything happening between her and the jerk. Well, high-five to me! It still doesn't erase the fact that she is disappointed that she didn't fuck that loser. Something I have no control over.

The thought, morbid and twisted in my overtired mind, only enhances the jealously.

"You need anything?" she asks quietly, as if she knew that my body would explode at any moment due to my erratic heart rate.

Blunt and without any consideration, I fire back, "Who was that guy?"

"That guy? Don't you remember Noah? My rebound after

Jess," she chuckles innocently as if this is some big fucking joke. "Remember how my friend, Audrey, knew him through a friend? Apparently he is dubbed 'Mr. Rebound.'

"That was Noah?"

Of course I remember the guy. He was some loser she met after she broke up with Jess. *A rebound.* She fooled around with him a couple of times, but then admitted she still loved Jess, so there was no chance for Noah.

That, and apparently Noah Mason had a reputation for finding vulnerable women.

"Weirdest thing ever. I ran into him today at a bar while having a few drinks with Mia. He looks good, doesn't he?"

"Am I supposed to answer that?"

"I swear, for someone who works in a hospital, you are such a grumpy bum when you're sick." She places her hand on my forehead, pretending to know what she is checking. It's comical, to say the least. And coming from someone with a medical background.

"I'm not sic—" Shit, I nearly blew my cover. I hide it with another cough. "So what did your text say?"

With a conceited grin, she divulges, "It was a Code Red. Yeah, I know. I haven't done that in a while, but I really need to get back in the game. I am this close to joining the nunnery."

"You don't need to do anything, Zo. What's wrong with being single? Sex isn't everything," I play it off. "Besides, lots of people masturbate and it's perfectly healthy. In fact, studies have shown that people who masturbate daily have longer and happier lifespans than those that don't."

"Says the man who has a revolving door in his bedroom." She rolls her eyes. "And you're trying to sell masturbation to me over the touch of a man?"

"Yes." I act confidently. "But it's different for a male. The whole sex thing. It doesn't matter how many women we sleep with."

"No it's not, Drew. Women equally have that urge. That need to get down and dirty as much as a man. It's just not as widely accepted for women to feel that way without being called a tramp."

"You don't need a guy to validate yourself." I sound like a fucking hypocrite, given that I was trying to push her onto Rob that day at the beach. *But that was different.* And it was before I thought I was going to lose her. Things have changed. Jesus fucking Christ, would you listen to yourself! What is all this 'feelings' bullshit going on in my head?!

She pulls her hair out of the bun, the waves cascading down her back. It smells like shampoo, and I want to reach out and run my hands through it before my head does a reality check.

You can't just touch her hair. That's an intimate gesture . . . one that roomies shouldn't do.

"So how about I fix us something to eat and we watch a movie?" she says with more enthusiasm, dropping the subject completely.

"No pizza."

"I can make grilled cheese sandwiches and soup. Sick people food."

"You haven't made that in ages." I smile.

"Well, I must like you or something."

She wanders off to the kitchen, and the sounds of the pots clanging bounce off the walls. I quickly grab my cell, ready to turn it off, not wanting to be interrupted tonight. With the TV turned on, some news program plays until Zoey returns with a plate and bowl on a tray. She places it on my lap, then heads back to the kitchen, returning with a glass of water.

"My god, this smells so good, Zoey."

"Thanks, roomie. What are you going to do one day when I'm married with kids? I'll have to build a makeshift room in my garage for you to live in like a third wheel. Like in *Full House.* You can be Uncle Jesse . . . the hot one."

I stop mid-bite. "That's not going to happen."

"Excuse me?"

"I mean . . ." I clear my throat. "You'll never settle down. You're not exactly a kid-person."

In a sudden and unexpected move, she slams the bowl onto the coffee table, creating a bang. Wild eyes stare directly at me, breathlessly waiting for some sort of apology. My comment, merely innocent, was not intended to cause Zoey to lash out.

"I am so a kid-person," she answers in defense, crossing her arms under her heaving breasts. *Stop fucking staring at them.*

"You have the memory of a goldfish," I scoff in a deadpan voice. "Remember when you dragged me to your cousin's birthday and her kids made you go on that bouncy castle thing and one kid threw up? You were the first to run out, leaving all the kids crying."

"Wow, so I don't react well to vomit."

"And the next birthday after that, when the same cousin made you take care of the baby for like ten minutes and you forgot, leaving it in the pram in the front yard?"

"So what! It couldn't go anywhere. It was wearing a seatbelt." She brushes off like it was no big deal. "Just because I don't ramble on like other women, or have had a *few* incidents, doesn't mean I don't want kids. I just haven't found the right person that gets my ovaries all riled up. You know, that one guy that makes my ovaries yell, 'Yippee!'"

"Okay . . ." I say, unsure of where to go from here. "Medically speaking, ovaries do no such thing."

"It's a metaphor! Of course they don't do that," she responds heatedly. "Honestly, you are such a guy. You have no clue sometimes when it comes to women."

Zoey had been really crabby lately. I couldn't go one conversation with her that didn't end up in a fight. Okay, so maybe I shouldn't have said she would never settle down. I just didn't want her to . . . *yet.* There, I said it. I admitted that her being with another guy right now felt like a stab in my fucking heart.

She grabs the bowl again but remains disgruntled, exhaling at regular intervals, purposely letting out grunts to show me she's annoyed. I know this conversation is far from over, but I'm a man. I don't want to pull all that emotional bullshit out of her, so I change the subject to something more lighthearted.

"So, the wedding. It's black-tie formal?" I sway the conversation.

"Yeah," she answers, disinterested.

And that was the end of our night.

Saved by the bell; my pager goes off with an emergency at the hospital. Although I'm exhausted, I take it willingly, wanting to escape the mess that has unfolded. I quickly finish dinner, then explain that work paged. Zoey doesn't appear surprised, and instead, disappears to her room without saying goodbye.

It has been the shift from hell. A pile up on the interstate with multiple injuries. Ten hours later, I am released from duty and finally able to head back home to get some much needed sleep.

Seeing our apartment has never felt so good, until I walk into the kitchen, oblivious that there would be an unknown male inside making coffee. His back is facing me, and just when I'm about to fucking hit him, he turns around and I see that it's Noah.

"Oh, hey. Drew, right?" Noah extends his hand as a courteous gesture. I don't know why I shake it. Maybe the lack of sleep, or my blurred vision from the numerous cups of coffee I attempted to hold down last night.

"It's me, Noah."

Code Red guy.

My grip tightens on his, but like a handshake of death, I pull away, clenching my fist to curb the rage building up inside of me. The fucking nerve of her to bring him back here after last night! Did my being fake sick mean nothing to her? Or the conversation we had afterwards? And what about the rubbers? *She better not have fucked him bareback.*

The temperature in the room rises at a rapid rate, my lungs barely able to hold the air I need to breathe. I could kill him here, now, with my fucking bare hands. Nobody would know.

"Oh, good morning, roomie. You remember Noah, right?" Zoey strolls casually into the kitchen without a worry in the world. She's awfully cheery and has that glow. *Yeah, the kinda glow the ladies get after multiple orgasms.*

"Uh, yeah . . ." I manage.

The two of them gather at the coffee machine, laughing quietly. My eyes move towards her torso, covered in *his* shirt. When she stretches on her tiptoes to grab a mug from the top cupboard, her sheer black panties are slightly exposed.

Fuck.

My teeth clench, straining the words, *"Can I speak to you for a second?"*

She kisses Noah on the cheek, then follows me down the hall, overly pleased with the situation.

"You brought him back here?" I fume, clutching for coherence as my brain seethes in pure and utter rage.

"Yeah. Is that a problem? I told you. Code Red."

"No. You didn't get my permission!"

Fuck, wrong choice of words.

"Permission?" she laughs. "I'm sorry. You're my roomie. Not my boyfriend. And I don't recall you seeking *my* permission when you brought Kristy back, or even Michelle."

"I didn't sleep with Kristy. I hope you are being safe," I

101

scold her.

"Um, okay Dad. Thanks for the lecture. I think I know not to sleep with a guy without being protected, and you know what?" She points her finger at me, her tone bitter and laced with resentment. "I'm sick of your double standards. Lately, it's been all about you. Drew can do this, sleep with whoever he pleases, *whenever* he pleases. But Zoey . . . no. God forbid I have a life outside of this apartment. It's almost like . . . like . . ." She trails off without finishing her sentence.

"Like what?"

"You're controlling and jealous," she admits. "There. I said it."

Quick to defend my actions, I growl, "I am no such thing . . . why . . . why would you say that?"

"I don't know, Drew. Something is changing between us. I don't know what it is and I'm not sure I like it." She faces the floor then looks back at me with her deep green eyes, warning me of what's about to come. "Last night, Noah gave me exactly what I wanted. What I needed. I don't feel ashamed for that and you shouldn't make me feel that way either."

I've said it before. I am not a violent person, but the thought of my fist against his face is so tempting that I have to mentally restrain myself from harming him. As for Zoey, I have no fucking words right now. I mumble something and escape to my room, throwing myself onto the bed. The tiredness is overwhelming, but not as much as the anger towards Zoey for bringing that douche home. What the fuck is she thinking? Oh that's right . . . she's not thinking! A thousand names run through my head, but nothing I should be saying or voicing an opinion on. *Don't be that guy that calls her a name you know you'll regret.*

Everything she said rang true. I am turning into this guy that has double standards. That wants to control the situation. And the jealously is becoming difficult to ignore, all because of the threat of losing her. The mere thought of

them being outside my bedroom door with his hands all over her is enough to drive me insane. What could I do? Nothing. *You are helpless. Helpless, unless you admit to yourself that you want Zoey Richards to be more than your roomie.*

The thinking, stress, and deliberation are all too much.

Somewhere in my admission to myself, I doze off, and in my dreams, I see her face.

It's beautiful, glowing, and she's smiling back at me with adoration.

She's calling my name.

She's begging me to touch her. Begging to feel me deep inside her.

In my dreams, she is mine.

CHAPTER *Nine*

Zoey

DREW HAD BEEN ACTING WEIRD all week. Our relationship was strained ever since that morning when Noah stayed over and our heated argument that followed. Since then, he had been avoiding me, and when we were in the same room, he didn't talk much, retreating to his room any chance he could. It's almost like he was jealous that I had another man over, but then that would be very hypocritical of him and made no sense to me whatsoever. I narrowed it down to male PMS. That, and he was exhausted from his double shifts at the hospital.

Thankfully, he wasn't around much, and on his minimal time off, he sent me a text saying that he was driving to his dad's place and spending a couple of nights there.

It was better that way. I needed my alone time and Drew needed some quality time with his dad, who had been complaining that he never saw his son anymore.

Noah proved to be just what I needed for that night, and that night only. I didn't see myself pursuing a relationship with him, and I wasn't one to maintain a fuckbuddy. Just to make it clear, I made sure that he was aware of my intentions. Silly me. Tell me what guy would have said no to a *one-night fling*. We had fun that night, he gave me an orgasm, and it scratched that itch that needed a good ole scratching.

The week had gone by fast, and working on that new project took up most of my time. Mr. Becker was in a good mood, showing me the ropes and spending the time to train me in new areas of the business. I welcomed the learning experience, hoping this was the foot in the door that I needed. With a positive outcome, I enquired into furthering my study, just for that additional advantage, and to make myself more marketable should my career lead me in a different path.

Zoey Richards is finally making a comeback!

The excitement of throwing myself into the deep end was both thrilling and exhausting. Most nights I stayed back, working late, wanting to prove myself to Mr. Becker. At night, I would chill in the apartment with a glass of wine and read over my notes for the day. The peace and quiet was exactly what I needed, and not having Drew around gave me exactly that.

I did, however, make sure he was still going to attend the wedding as my plus one. He wasn't the type to make empty promises, and towards the end of the week, everything between us reverted back to normal. *Just like it always did.* He had driven back from his dad's house and was in a much better mood. As usual, he talked endlessly about the cars he helped his dad fix in his shop and was quick to point out how his dad was disappointed that he hadn't given Betty the attention she needed, and as a result of that, her engine was on its way out. I didn't care for car talk, yet I politely indulged in the conversation so as not to cause any further conflict between us.

On Saturday morning, I wake up early to do my hair and makeup. I had spent the night watching this tutorial on YouTube on how to brighten my eyes and sat at my dresser

carefully stroking the eyeshadow like the clip showed me. They made it look so easy. My clumsy hand had me removing the eyeshadow several times and starting all over. By the fifth time, I looked decent enough and not like a two-dollar hooker auditioning for a beauty pageant.

For most formal occasions, I leave my hair out. Today, I decide to do something a little different by styling my hair into a fancy side bun. Yes, *another* tutorial. With my hair and makeup done, I stare back at myself in the mirror. Not bad. The eyeshadow has definitely brought out the green in my eyes, and with my hair neatly placed in a bun, my neckline is exposed, showing my pale skin.

Inside my jewelry box lies a pearl necklace my mom gave me that used to belong to her. It was an heirloom—a beautiful classic piece that would go perfect against my navy dress. I carefully place the necklace on, then further accessorize with some small diamond earrings.

Since Mia's wedding starts at midday and the reception isn't until five, I chose two outfits to wear. A subtle dress for the church, and what I like to call my 'party dress' for the reception. Something about low plunging backs at the church didn't seem appropriate.

I walk out to the living room where Drew is fiddling with his cufflinks. Letting out a whistle, he looks up, and instantly, something in his eyes changes. They soften, yet there's something else I can't quite figure out. His stare lingers, making me slightly uncomfortable. My gaze moves towards the floor, and when I look up again, he is still staring at me with a beautiful smile across his face. My heart starts to beat erratically and my breathing hitches slightly until I realize it's the butterflies swirling around in my stomach making me so nervous.

Butterflies—I hadn't felt them in forever.

Ignore them. They have been hiding in captivity and are merely desperate for attention.

Drew looks incredibly handsome. His dark charcoal suit

is tailored perfectly to his physique, and underneath he wears a simple, white, collared shirt with a slight sheen. The top button is undone, as Drew hated to wear ties. With his hair slicked to the side, he wears his contacts along with a freshly shaven face.

He looks ridiculously yummy. Wait . . . *did you just call your roomie 'yummy'?*

"Zoey," he murmurs, leaving me almost breathless by the call of my name.

I move in closer and lift his arm, helping him with his cufflink. The battle to keep my eyes fixated on this task proves difficult as the heavenly smell of his masculine scent invades my senses. I fumble like a child with placing his cufflink firmly in position. What is it about men's cologne that makes your whole body flutter in delight? I just want to devour him.

Get a grip!

"You clean up good, Baldwin," I say with ease, beaming as his face mirrors mine.

"You look beautiful," he responds, eyes still fixated on mine. "Nice pearl necklace."

"Was that a dirty joke?"

"Do you want it to be?" he switches his voice to a husky tone, his eyebrow raised, poking fun at my question.

"Funny," I chuckle lightly. "Wait till you see my next dress. It doesn't leave much to the imagination."

"You wouldn't believe how *dirty* my imagination can get, Richards." He glances back at me with a wicked smile and does that thing with his lips again, but for some reason, it doesn't bother me. *Quite the opposite.* Every roll, flick, and slither of his tongue against his lips has me drawn to him.

What the hell? Ignore that, Zoey. Shake it off! It's like some vortex trying to suck you in.

Nervously, and trying to control my stutter, I ask him,

"Ready to go, plus one?"

Drew opens the front door and politely waits for me to pass. "After you. *Mademoiselle.*"

Mia looks gorgeous in her satin gown that hugs her figure nicely. It had long sleeves and a low back with a million buttons. The sheer fabric sat beautifully against her Asian complexion. According to Mia, it took a year for Troy's aunties in Greece to make this dress. I can see now why Mia was so paranoid about gaining some pounds. There was no room for any weight fluctuation.

I had been to several weddings but never one this long. With Troy's Greek background, the mass is performed in Greek and English. Two hours feels like an eternity, and reiterates the fact that I should never marry a Greek man.

Eloping to Vegas with Elvis waiting at the altar. That is my perfect wedding.

I spend most of the two hours taking in the beautiful architecture. The church is a hundred years old and the whole building is still in its original condition. The pitched ceilings are made out of old oak wood with hanging pendant lights to brighten up the space. The main area is adorned in gold—plenty of it. Yet even with its age, everything is pristine.

Mia and Troy have added their own personal touch with lilac satin draped along each pew, and fresh lilies intricately tied to each row. Beside me, Drew twitches his nose from the scent of the flowers. Occasionally, he suffered from hay fever, and given the amount of flowers, I wouldn't be surprised if my plus one bailed the reception. Jesus, the priest needs to hurry up! Oh my god Zoey don't say that in church!

I'm going to hell.

When a final applause erupts, I welcome the end with an overenthusiastic clap. Mia walks down the aisle with Troy as the guests smile in adoration. I can see the weight lifted off her shoulders. She welcomes the congratulatory response and beams as they make their way outside. Waiting for people to exit our pew, I scan the church until my eyes lock with another pair of eyes staring right back at me.

Did I just see?

No, your imagination is seriously on crack or something. It's the two hours of being trapped inside a church with hundreds of other people, some who could do with a bit of deodorant.

Fresh air . . . you just need some fresh air.

The eyes continue to stare at me with curiosity, then slowly, moments later, a gentle smile spreads across his face. The same face that has tormented me since the day I met him.

It's Jess.

With every breakup there is this curiosity—or perhaps more like fear—of the first time you see your ex. There's a checklist for the best scenario that you hope to achieve. You know, look your best and act like the mature one that has moved on with someone better. Be able to smile and put the past behind you.

So I looked fabulous, well at least my dress did. I had gained extra pounds thanks to the jerk.

It was a wedding. No other occasion would have me looking like a show pony, so that is a positive point.

In my head, our song, "The Flame" by Cheap Trick, is playing like a broken record. My heart is beating erratically and I'm on the verge of a panic attack. How is this even happening and why didn't Mia say anything to me? And worst yet—why do I suddenly miss him?

I try to push my way faster through the crowd, rudely motioning for everyone to hurry along.

"Zoey," Drew snaps, turning around as I push him. "What the hell is wrong with you? There's an old lady in front of

me."

I hold onto Drew's back, forcing him to move quicker. "Hurry up!"

The old lady has a walking stick, and latches onto an older man. Sure, I felt pathetic, but the thought of having to talk to Jess again made it all the worse. There is nothing worse that running into your ex, especially at a wedding, when the primary focus is love.

I had given up on the lady and dragged Drew in the opposite direction, escaping down the side of the church.

"What is going on?" he questions me, attempting to hold me back.

"I need to pee. *Really bad.*"

Outside, the crowds are congratulating the newly wedded couple. There is time to do that later. I convince Drew to take me home, which luckily, is only a couple of blocks away.

The whole way home, I make up a lie about busting to use the restroom because I drank too much water before the mass. Drew doesn't ask any questions, and retreats to his room once we arrive back home. The reception itself wasn't for another three hours, so I head over to Gigi's apartment for some much needed advice, abandoning Drew because I knew how he felt about Jess. He made that very clear when we broke up.

"Right, you said it was an emergency?"

Gigi pulls herself out of her tangled pose. With her yoga mat positioned in the center of the room, Patti and Gloria are sprawled out on the couch, watching her intently. Diana is hiding underneath the TV unit, eyes glaring at me. Stupid cat; such a fucking diva.

In the background, the music is playing the Pointer Sisters, and Gigi is dressed in her hot pink spandex one-piece.

Oh, now that's camel toe if ever I saw it.

"It *is* an emergency. It was Jess! The guy that screwed me over even though I was madly in love with him. The same guy that said we would have a family and live in a big fancy house by the beach. Promised me the world," I exaggerate.

"But he lived in a shack right?"

"What?" I ask, sidetracked. "Point is, he was my prince. Yeah, he rode in on a motorcycle instead of a horse and didn't have a dollar to his name, plus he smoked weed and spent all his wages on booze, but I loved him."

"I understand, doll. Although, all my exes are resting with the Lord Himself. I can't say I've been in your position. However, creating a relaxed and calm environment with no animosity within each other's space will alleviate the stress you are experiencing right now."

What the hell does that even mean? I stare back at Gigi, confused by her advice. "What about that guy you dated . . . the one who looked like he could be your son?"

"Oh, doll. That's not an ex. That was a fling. What your generation calls 'friends with benefits.'"

"Gigi, friends with benefits is a friend you have sex with but with the understanding that there is no romantic attachment and you're free to see other people."

"Oh." She sighs. "Well, he made me feel young and showed me a thing or two. That's it."

I shake my head, completely lost. "Uh huh. Okay, so what do I do?"

"You act like the mature one. You've moved on, and don't let him think that he has any effect on you. Don't look back, only forward, doll. Bad seeds like Jess have a tormented aura surrounding them. It's difficult for them to be at peace with themselves without harming others."

"Or," I say with eagerness, "I get Drew to pretend we are dating. That'll really stir Jess up. He hated Drew."

Gigi immediately frowns at my idea. "Do you think that's a wise idea? And what if Drew won't do that?"

It was the best idea I had in a very long time. I may have gained a few pounds since we broke up, but the black satin dress I planned to wear to the reception would be the weapon I needed. Hot, sexy and will show him exactly what he's been missing all this time.

"Trust me . . . I'll get him to do that."

"What? No way, Zoey have you lost your mind?"

"C'mon, it's just one night," I beg.

"I can't stand the guy. And why didn't you tell me he was at the church?" Drew grits, taking a long sip from his bottled water.

"Because you said you can't stand the guy. Look, he's a douche. I just wanna get him back, and he hated you," I half admit.

Drew puts his jacket back on and searches the room for his keys. "What do I get out of this?"

"Seeing him suffer."

"Or perhaps a beating?"

"Don't be such a pussy."

"I'm not being a pussy. You've gotten your revenge. You've moved on. I just don't understand why you need to do this."

It was time to call the big guns in. Issue the ultimate bribe to get him on my side. This is the only perk about Drew being a man whore. The man-whore status may attract beautiful sexy women, but it also attracts crazed stalkers.

"Remember Angela?"

He stops mid-step and cringes, placing his keys back down. "Yes, I know what you're going to say . . ."

"And remind me of what lengths I had to go to for you?"

"You had to pretend that I left the country because she was romantically attached."

"Ha," I snort. "She was stalking you!"

Defeated, he sits on the couch and rubs his face, annoyed at my *brilliant* plan. His silence carries on for minutes, then finally, he opens his eyes and answers. "Fine, I'll do it. But this better not hinder my chances of hooking up tonight."

My stomach churns at the thought of Drew taking someone home. *Let it go. You've got bigger things to worry about.*

"Promise it won't. And if it does, I'll screw you," I joke.

His elbows are resting on his knees, head bowed down with a wide grin spread across his face. "That's a dangerous promise, Zo. Plus, I don't think you can handle me."

Cocky bastard!

"Uh huh, whatever lil' peewee. Let's get going or else we'll be late."

CHAPTER Ten

Drew

I DIDN'T EXPECT THIS REACTION.

It caught me off guard.

The moment she walked into our living room, wearing that gorgeous dress. I can't even remember how it looked, or even what color it was.

My vision was fixated on her, and her alone. Breathtakingly beautiful, and nothing she wore, or anything she said, could change that.

And if nothing happens between us, and our worlds are destined to remain apart, I will forever remember the way she made me feel at that very moment.

The way my stomach flipped.

The way my *heart* did this weird fucking skipping thing.

I couldn't look away, no matter how hard I tried, even when she caught me gazing at her. There was just something about her today that made me see her in a completely different light. I only saw this beautiful woman. A woman that deserved the world. She deserved to be loved and adored.

And how quickly my admiration flew out the window when she told me who was at the church.

115

He's back.

The jerk who gives us good guys a bad rap. Okay, so maybe I didn't have the best rap. But I didn't go around treating women like yesterday's trash, especially the ones I had been romantically involved with for a year.

I was gullible enough to believe that Zoey needed to use the restroom, which is why we raced home. And so, I was blindsided when she brought up Jess being at the church.

Worst yet—her nonsensical plan to pretend we were a couple, just to anger him.

It had disaster written all over it. But like always, she had that whole Angela debacle hanging over my head, and I was just her little bitch who bowed down like a pathetic dog.

Angela—*the thorn in my side.*

Every man's worst nightmare.

Angela was a psychotic maniac who staged a fake pregnancy to get me to settle down. Apart from Zoey, she had major trust issues with any woman that stepped foot near me. At first, I thought I was lucky to score a hot chick who had her head screwed on straight. Stunning body, great career, and a stable family.

Then, the alarm bells started ringing. She would turn up at my work almost every shift, certain that I was fucking another colleague. My cell would constantly disappear, and later, I found out it was because she would raid my messages, looking for anything incriminating. She would constantly stalk my social media and bully any woman who commented on my page, which in turn, she would cyberstalk.

It was the *worst* three months of my life.

And even after a restraining order was put on her, I still had to pretend that I had left the country. Zo, of course, hatched one of her foolproof plans, and luckily, it worked and Angela moved onto another man.

But this . . . *argh.*

Again, disaster.

Just the sound of his name made my skin crawl. Yet there was something in Zo's eyes that sparkled when his name graced her lips. The mere fact that he was at the wedding should have been a good reason for Zoey to not go. I didn't understand why she, or women in general, needed closure and all that bullshit. Fucking move on I say—sayonara.

The past is the past. Let it remain that way.

"So maybe we should come up with a plan?" she suggests, tampering with the radio once again. She settles on Billy Idol, switching the volume down slightly, enough that we can still converse as "White Wedding" plays through the speakers.

My hands clutch the steering wheel as I continue to drive in silence. It's an hour trip to the outskirts of town where the reception is being held. Enough time for Zo—and these suit-pants—to drive me fucking insane. My balls feel restricted, confined in my extra-tight boxers. *If only I could unzip and let it hang free. Now that would be an entertaining conversation.*

"It just has to be believable, you know, me being your girlfriend."

Raising an enquiring eyebrow, slightly offended, "You don't think it looks believable?"

"Well, no. Only because I went on and on about how you were more like a brother and how nothing could *ever* happen between us."

It doesn't surprise me. When it came to our relationship, we were forever defining it. Like brother and sister, best friends, roomies . . . you name it. But something about her comment irked me. I could *so* be her boyfriend. Or at least make everyone in the room believe we were a couple.

"Why did he hate me so much? I did nothing for him to think there was something going on between us," I point out. "And I brought women home all the time."

"He just had a complex about you. And he thought that when we were alone, you and I . . . you know . . ." she trails off awkwardly.

"What?" I probe.

"Bumped uglies."

I laugh at her terminology, and her innocence. "Firstly, you're beautiful so it's impossible for Zoey Richards to 'bump uglies.' As for me, I would like to think I don't fall into the ugly category."

"Yeah, yeah, whatever. You know you're all hot and yummy," she rumbles under her breath. Taking her Lipsmacker out, she applies it over her lipstick. *What an odd thing to do.*

The small tube has the Fanta logo. I love Fanta, not that I drank much soda. I bet she would taste so good . . .

Rambling on, she continues, "So all I'm saying is that we need to make this couple thing look believable . . . No awkwardness, okay? Like when I kiss you or something."

Or something. That could be open to much interpretation.

If Zoey wants a boyfriend, then a boyfriend is what she will get.

My competitive streak is coming out, and admittedly, there is nothing I want more than to see that fucker suffer.

If it meant I had to touch her, I'd touch her.

If it meant I had to kiss her, I'd kiss her.

"So . . ." she begins, then stalls. "Maybe we should discuss the boundaries."

"Boundaries?"

"You know, like we should probably kiss every now and then."

"How often?" I question her.

"Does there need to be a timeline here?"

I'm thinking about her question; narcissistic Drew is

ready to play this wicked game. *How do I make this more fun . . . for me? Okay Satan, please calm down on your side of the shoulder.*

Kissing. I can handle that. I am about to open my mouth when she interrupts me.

"No tongue."

I let out a ridiculous laugh. "How do you even kiss with *no* tongue?"

"I don't know, Drew. They do it in the movies."

"The last time I checked, Zo, we weren't in Hollywood."

"Fine. Just a little tongue, but nothing porno-like."

Nothing porno-like. An interesting concept that stirs my cock slightly.

"Okay. What else?" I humor her.

"Grab my butt a couple of times," she adds.

"Right. So romantic," I note in dark amusement. "But not a porno grab?"

She shifts her body to the right, curling her legs up on the seat. Her legs are exposed until she becomes aware, positioning her dress more appropriately. "Just look like you're in love with me. Make-out like we have the best sex in the world. *Capiche?*"

I don't answer her. If she were with me, we *would* have the best sex in the world. Better than what she had with that deadbeat she calls an ex-boyfriend.

I turn the bend and the large wrought-iron gates appear with a huge sign that welcomes us to the property. Holy shit, it was a castle. An old castle that appears to have been remodeled, yet still maintains its historic charm. The gates are already open, so I turn into the long pebbled driveway.

The lawns are luscious and green, surrounded by bushes sculpted into cupids with harps. Every inch of the garden is manicured, and the flowers are bright, trimmed to perfection. The further we drive in, the larger the fountain appears, sitting in front of the property, showcasing the entrance.

Two young valets stand on the steps, and the second they see my car, their faces drop with disappointment. So Betty is no Rolls-Royce, but she was a classic in her own right.

"Huh, the valet boys seem disappointed with your ride," Zoey mentions, pointing out the obvious.

"No shit. The car in front of us costs more than a house. They better not ride her clutch hard," I worry out loud.

"I'm sure if they can drive a car the price of a house, they can drive Betty." She rolls her eyes childishly, turning to face the window so I won't catch her.

Our doors are opened by the young valet, and reluctantly I hand my keys over, but not without mentioning the clutch.

"We'll take care of your car . . . *sir,*"the valet snickers.

Lil' fucker.

The concierge extends his arm to the left, showing us the entrance. With red carpet sprawled up the three sets of stairs, there is no money spared when it comes to how grand this wedding is.

Zoey is in awe, mouth wide open as she takes in the entrance and the splashes of gold that adorn the walls. Inside, marbles floors are shining, with a small orchestra positioned in the center, playing soft classical music in the background. There are several guests lingering beside the doors, all waiting to enter the ballroom. It dawns on me that I had never been to a black tie event, wondering if my charcoal suit is formal enough. *It isn't black.*

"Thank god I splurged on a decent dress for the reception," she leans over and whispers, clutching onto my arm for support. "The invitation said formal. Do you think the low plunging neckline is too much? I can't even begin to tell you how much Hollywood tape is holding up these babies."

I had been trying my best to ignore the low plunging neckline. They—her tits—were staring me in the face.

Begging me relentlessly with their torturous pleas: *"Play with me, Drew!"*

Shit, control yourself.

I stop just before the entrance to gain her attention mid-ramble. "Zoey?"

"Yeah?" she says, distracted, eyeing a lady beside us dressed in a red silk-looking ball gown.

"You look stunning."

It catches her attention, and those green eyes of hers, the ones that had this magnetic hold, stare back at me in bewilderment. She's biting the corner of her lip, and just when I think she'll embrace the compliment, she says, "As well as hot, sexy, the kind of ex you'd wish you didn't screw over?"

My fingers move on their own accord, tracing her shoulder softly. "The beautiful kind of woman you'd never want to let go of."

"What a line, Baldwin." She smiles hopelessly. "You look mighty fine yourself. The kind of man that every woman would want by her side."

The moment is interrupted as a concierge requests our names in order to seat us. The young fellow escorts us to our table, and as soon as I see it in the corner of the room, there is no doubt in my mind that we were dumped at the singles' table.

There are ten of us at the table. A woman about our age is already sitting down, fiddling nervously with her napkin. She offers an awkward smile and I nudge Zoey to swap places with me because she looks innocent, and hey, why not have a go at bringing her home. Single ladies were vulnerable at weddings. It's probably *the* best place to pick up women. By the end of the night, she will be drunk on champagne and looking to get laid.

Except you're here with Zoey.

A little harmless flirting wouldn't go astray, so I swap the place cards and sit beside her. She tries to ignore me, but I extend my hand, introducing myself. Kimberly, as she calls herself, turns beet red and shyly says hello back, barely speaking another word.

Zoey's body presses against my arm as she attempts to discreetly get me to look at an older lady across the table. Damn, that is some beard on her. I find myself in a trance, staring, until Zoey nudges me for being so rude. I shake my head, letting out a long breath. "This is going to be one long night."

With everyone taking their places, an MC announces that the bride and groom will be making their entrance shortly. The excitement palpable, guests wait in anticipation for the big moment, unlike Zoey, who is sitting beside me, pale-faced and searching the room like a meerkat on crack.

"What's wrong with you?"

"What? Me? He must be here," she says, scattered. "Just act normal."

"I am acting normal," I remind her. "You, on the other hand, could use some Valium."

"I'm fine. See?" She extends her hand, and I stare at it, confused. "Steady hand. Just remember the plan."

Right. Remember the reason why you're here. To be her plus one. Her date. Her boyfriend.

My mood suddenly shifts, and Mr. Competitive is on guard. She wants a boyfriend? She's going to get one that cannot keep his hands off her. *Except then you'll need to touch her . . . kiss her . . . fuck—*

"Oh look, they're here!" Zoey motions excitedly.

Somewhere in this room, his eyes are on her. When the hunter sees his prey, the thirst, the desire, drives him to commence his hunt.

He isn't going to touch her.

Not if I have any say in it.

I place my arm on the back of her neck, bending down slightly as my lips touch her collarbone. Her excited claps slow down, and perhaps my imagination is running wild, but I think her eyes close for a brief moment.

And there, when I raise my head, the hunter is watching me from across the room.

I have something that *was* his.

Just not anymore.

For tonight, she is mine.

All mine.

CHAPTER Eleven

IN WEDDING FORMALITY, EVERYONE IS asked to take their places while the bridal party makes an entrance, dancing to Kool and the Gang's "Celebration." With three bridesmaids and three groomsmen, it's like one big parade as they dance and strut. One pair awkwardly tumbles down the makeshift aisle onto the dancefloor. A few minutes is spent dancing some routine, which is quite comical, until the music quiets and they eagerly take their places at the head table.

The lights dim, the announcement asking us to raise our glasses and welcome Mr. and Mrs. Bono. The music restarts, and the wide doors open in unison as Troy and Mia walk into the room amongst the cheers.

The noise dies down slightly, until some moron taps their knife against the champagne glass with the room following. With a beaming smile, Troy leans over and kisses Mia lovingly.

Drew was right. This is going to be one long night.

And I hadn't even seen Jess yet.

The guests are asked to take a seat, and as much as I wasn't fond of weddings, there is plenty of excitement in the air. Straightening the back of my dress so I'm not bare-assed against the chair, I take a seat beside Drew. The champagne sits ice-cold in buckets in the center of the table, teasing me relentlessly. The guests at our table weren't the most enthusiastic bunch, so I pour myself and Drew a glass to get the party started. Although he is going to drive tonight, a couple of glasses wouldn't hurt him.

During my second taste of the expensive champagne, Drew places his hand on my neck and plants another soft kiss on my shoulder. Amongst the soft classical music that gently plays in the background, my eyes close as the touch of lips lingering on my heated skin travels at a rapid rate, causing my heart to beat erratically.

Why does he do this to me? This unknown feeling that consumes me whole and takes me to a place that craves him to continue.

Except he can't continue.

The first time he did it, before the bridal party made their entrance, I chalked it up to nerves. This time, I have no explanation.

Just remember, this is all part of your elaborate plan to make Jess's blood boil. Stop confusing yourself, because Jess is somewhere in the room, and your aim is to make him suffer, if only for one night. That is—if he even still cares about me.

Of course he must care. Men were built with that jealously gene that drove them to the brink of insanity. I still remember one of our weekend trips when a bellboy made a snide comment about taking me back to a room. Jess almost cracked his head open. You would think I would be flattered, but in reality, he turned it around so it was my fault. My fault for wearing a short dress, my fault for wearing heels that apparently made me look like a hooker.

Yet, I still loved him anyway. Flaws and all.

Why am I doing this? *Because you're a sadistic fool.*

The waiters begin circling the tables with entrées, and on cue, my stomach growls in anticipation. The idle chitchat starts, and Drew is busying himself with the young chick beside him. Honestly, he can't for one second not think with his dick. It is so annoying. I stare at the plate that is placed before me with something orange on it that looks like a blob of goo and immediately swap it with Drew's chicken.

"Zo, I was going to eat that."

"Too fattening for you. Stick with the orange blob."

I don't give him time to respond, shoving the chicken in my mouth. The texture and flavors were questionable, but had to be better than the orange blob. As soon as I'm done, his mischievous smile alarms me.

"That was quail," he states, wiping his mouth with the napkin.

"A whatta?" I ask, confused.

"It was quail, you know, a small bird."

"Whatever, it was chicken."

I grab the menu, almost retching when I see that it was indeed quail. Without any hesitation, I pour myself another glass of champagne and down it in one go, then another. *I can't believe I just ate a bird! Turkey is a bird, you eat that.*

"I can't believe you let me eat that," I whine, sticking my tongue out, making a gurgling sound. *"Why can't they just serve pizza and fried chicken at weddings?"*

"That is so tacky. This is the only good thing about weddings. Enjoying some fine cuisine."

"This isn't fine cuisine. This is expensive and stuff that people should never eat. I mean, do you even know what that orange thing was?"

Drew picks up the menu, not looking phased as he reads the selection.

"Caviar. Honestly, I can't take you anywhere. As a

girlfriend, you've let me down with your poor taste in food."

"As a boyfriend, you're a douche for letting me eat that!"

"Since your last one was a jerk, thought I'd act like one," he shoots back.

Drew is being a pain in the ass, and his subtle arm around my shoulder starts to annoy me. Since I hadn't laid eyes on Jess in the room yet, it isn't necessary to start this bullshit act. I try to shake him off but his grip is tight, and so I have no choice but to endure his stubbornness.

The quail doesn't seem to sit right in my stomach, or perhaps it's the nerves. I tell him I need to use the restroom which is located out in the foyer. He flashes me one of his fake smiles before saying, "Sure, baby doll. I'll miss ya."

Jerk.

Weaving my way through the tables and narrowly avoiding a run-in with a waiter carrying champagne glasses, I hear my name being called. I don't need to turn around; that voice had haunted me in my sleep. It had caused me more heartache than I would wish on my greatest enemy.

I close my eyes for a split second, giving myself time to breathe. *This is it, this is the moment that you have thought about ever since you saw him being blown by your best friend. This speech . . . you've practiced it numerous times in your head. Word for word, the exact tone, the exact distance you would allow your body to be near him.*

Taking the deepest breath, I turn around slowly, pretending to be composed when truth be told, my body is having a nervous breakdown. Only an arm's length away, Jess stands before me dressed in his black tux. Nothing much has changed, still with his shaved head and his beard. His tatts are covered, except for the ones on his neck. My eyes are drawn to what appears to be a new one, an outline of a woman's torso.

What am I supposed to do now? Do I kiss him hello or just smile from a distance? Physical contact seems like a bad

idea, so I stand still, nerves getting the better of me. Christ, there should be some guide on what to do on your first encounter with your ex. I should write a book about it . . . or at least someone should.

He takes a step forward, closing the distance between us. "No kiss hello?"

Ignore the scent. Block your nose . . . do something! Do not allow Jess's scent to consume you or else you're a goner.

"How have you been, Jess?" I barely croak, still attempting to hold my breath.

"Been better. And you?"

My eyes won't focus on him, because I know if they do, he will grab onto that piece of me that still loves him. At least, I think I still love him. Inside, I'm judging myself for even thinking this. *He treated you like dirt. Disrespected you in the worse way possible.*

"Yeah, okay, busy as usual," I lie.

My gaze moves past him, pretending to be more interested in the people standing near us. I let out a small breath, and thankfully, I smell nothing but two awkward exes making polite conversation.

"You look good," he adds, not without his signature smirk.

What a load of shit. I may be all dressed up, but I had gained weight since I was with him. In my head, I'm fat.

There, I admitted it. The man who caused my binge eating is standing before me, trying to tell me I look good. The memory of the moment I saw Callie on all fours in his dirty workshop invades my thoughts and the anger rises at a fast and rapid pace. All of a sudden there are so many words I want to say, but this wasn't the time or place. I owed it to Mia not to ruin her million-dollar wedding. Remember Gigi's advice: Be the mature person.

"Thanks, I guess. So how do you know Mia and Troy?" I calm myself enough to carry a polite conversation.

"Troy's my second cousin. And you?"

"Mia and I work together."

"Right." He nods. "I notice you're here with Drew."

"He's my date," I blurt out. "And boyfriend."

His demeanor changes, and his hands instantly recoil, clenching a fist beside his thighs. If the room had been silent, the grinding of his teeth would have echoed through the castle.

"You're dating him? I always knew—"

I cut him off, placing my hand to block the distance between us. "So I better get back before he comes looking for me. He's very protective. See you around, Jess."

Walking back to the table, my urge to use the restroom disappears and I take a seat next to Drew, my body shaking. I whisper into his ear, "Okay, game on."

His smile falters, and with a bothered-looking face, he places his arm around me in a romantic gesture. From the corner of my eye, I see Jess sitting back at his table. *He looks livid.* His eyes are doing that wild swirl, his nostrils flaring like an angered animal. Okay, I'm exaggerating slightly. I can't make out his features from this far, but I can, however, see him drinking a beer in one go, then opening another bottle almost instantly.

Great! I turn to face Drew who is busily talking to the bearded lady about heart surgery complications. *Honestly, I can't take him anywhere.* To grab his attention, I squeeze on his thigh under the table. He jumps, then abruptly turns to face me. "What was that for?"

Placing my hands on his cheeks, I pull him in and kiss his lips. Closing my eyes, making it more believable, we kiss for a few seconds, no tongue, before I pull away. "I just missed you while I went to the restroom."

"Uh . . . um," he mumbles. "Okay. A little warning next time?"

"You don't warn someone when you kiss them."

He clears his throat. "Yes, you can. What's wrong with doing that?"

"It's called spontaneity. Look it up in the dictionary sometime."

Honestly, men were hopeless. Was romance seriously a dying form?

More champagne is needed for me to get through this night alive. Drew continues to sit there dazed like a fool. For someone who screwed more girls than I could count, he sure is acting funny. And we didn't even use tongue!

"Maybe you need to slow down the alcohol a bit." He takes the glass from my hands and places it back on the table.

I move it towards him. "Maybe you need to drink more."

"I'm driving," he reminds me. "Besides, someone needs to take care of you. Let's face it; you're not the best drinker in the world."

Exhaling, I cross my arms at his snide remark. "I can hold my alcohol just as much as you."

"Do I need to refresh your memory, Richards? Remember the night you went to that banana concert?"

"You mean Bananarama? Hello!" I exclaim. "They hadn't toured in, like, forever. If there is any night to celebrate, that was the night."

"I found you passed out in the janitor's closet of our building with a bottle of tequila and your panties missing."

"*My panties* were in my bag," I remind him. "That was the week I had that bad cough and took some painkillers. It was unfortunate, that was all."

"Then what about the time the police called me to pick you up because you were being a public nuisance and calling every guy on the street a cheater?"

"So I've had a few *incidents.*" I use the word loosely. "I can control myself tonight, okay? I think you need to pull the cork out of your ass and unwind."

Drew doesn't make any further comments, and luckily, dinner is being served. This time, I make sure the waiter places the fish in front of me. Something edible. We enjoy our meal and converse with the other guests at the table until the MC announces the married couple's first dance.

Mia and Troy gracefully dance the waltz to "Inspiration" by Chicago. *It is such a beautiful song.* The both of them looked so happy and in love, and it raises the questions I refuse to ask myself. Will I ever find this type of love? Someone who rocks me to the core and who I can see spending the rest of my life with? A person who will challenge my intellect, yet at the same time, love me unconditionally, flaws and all?

Ugh. This is why I despised weddings.

"Shall we?" Drew stands, reaching out his hand.

He waits patiently, much like a knight in shining armor. Or a knight in a charcoal Versace suit. His eyes plead with me to join him. How could I resist his handsome charm, especially when I look around and almost every woman has her eyes on him?

Several couples have gathered on the dancefloor to join the couple. I didn't know how to waltz, and still remember my ill-fated prom dance with my Dad that resulted in me tripping on my dress and face-planting the floor. It was *the* most embarrassing moment of my life.

"I don't know how to slow dance," I murmur, embarrassed.

"But you fast dance?"

"That's different. I have two left feet. Trust me, you don't want to dance with me."

Drew drags me to the dancefloor, not allowing me to hesitate any longer. I lift my hand to meet his and slowly place my other on his shoulder. I'm conscious of my steps, careful not to trip and to follow his lead. The pace of the music is slow, some song I hadn't heard of, and trying to

dance intimately with Drew seems very natural. He doesn't allow me to fall, holding on to my waist tightly enough and taking the lead. I find myself enjoying the dance, even more so when the music switches and The Bangles' "Eternal Flame" blasts through the speakers. Without thinking, I rest my head on his shoulder and sway softly to the music.

"I love this song," I say to myself.

"Yeah, it's kind of a classic," Drew follows.

I lift my head off his shoulder, surprised by his comment. "You mean you've actually heard of it? Mr. Never-Listens-To-Anything-That-Isn't-Played-In-A-Club?"

He stills, holding on to my waist tight. His face saddens, but he quickly covers it with a smile. "The woman who raised me for a few years used to play it a lot. I remember that."

"You mean your mother?"

It is callous of me to use that word, considering he had never spoken about her before. Drew's dad had mentioned her a few times, but like most men, he didn't want to dig up the past. I knew that she was around for a couple of years before she passed away.

"I guess you could call her that," he says painfully.

I'm not sure what to say. He is finally opening up to me, here on the dancefloor, amid a classic Bangles song.

"Drew," I whisper softly. "Despite your parents divorcing, she is the woman who brought you into the world, and is your mother."

"She may have brought me into this world, Zoey, but she didn't raise me."

"She didn't have the chance to. You can't blame her for that."

He doesn't say another word, pulling me in close to his chest. I think about his words, and how easily fate had intervened and stolen from a little boy something that most of us took for granted. A woman we called Mother—*Mom.* I want to ask him more questions, learn more about what he is feeling, but am quick to see Jess dancing with some floozy only a few feet away. His eyes are on me, tortured, yet taking a turn at playing this game we call 'who could make the other more jealous.'

Drew turns his head, immediately spotting Jess. In this moment, I feel guilty for making Drew play along, but am brutally interrupted as he moves his hands away from my waist and places them on the sides of my neck, planting a kiss on my lips. There's still no tongue, just a soft sensual kiss, enough to make my skin tingle and leave me breathless.

My arms move around his waist, and without thinking, I pull his body closer to mine and press my lips harder onto his. With Drew, it all seemed so easy, maybe because we were friends. I feel at ease kissing him, and when he returns my kisses, I don't stop him.

In fact, I want more.

To taste him. *To feel his soft lips.*

And maybe, just maybe, the roll of his tongue against mine.

The music turns to a faster song, changing the mood on the dancefloor. We pull away from each other, still keeping our bodies close. We dance to some song that Drew seems to enjoy and is singing along to, and for a brief moment he places his hands on my butt as if we were a couple.

"Nice move, Baldwin."

"Nice ass, Richards."

I let out a small laugh. "I like this song."

"But it's Bruno Mars. He's way too modern for you."

"Maybe I should change. You know, mix up my taste."

His eyes lighten, a smile playing on his lips. "I like you just the way you are, Zoey Richards. Don't change for anyone."

The way he stares back at me sinks deep into the pit of my stomach. My body is touching his, and if this were a club, we'd be grinding and dry humping like two desperate animals. "Well, I like you just the way you are, Andrew Baldwin. Don't you change for anyone."

He instantly scolds me for calling him that, but is quick to let it go. The song continues and both of us enjoy ourselves, laughing, finally relaxing by dancing some crazy moves. Maybe it was the champagne that I forced Drew to drink, but as time goes on, he relaxes and we start to have some real fun.

But fun is overrated. And I am gullible to think the night could end like this.

In the middle of the dancefloor, during the first verse of "If I Could Turn Back Time," Jess interrupts our dance to ask if he can cut in. Drew doesn't say a word and surprisingly backs off, unusually quiet for someone so opinionated.

Eying Jess with extreme wariness, he lingers for only a moment, then walks to the foyer, disappearing from sight.

Ignoring my body language, Jess forces himself on me, grabbing my waist and pulling me closer to him. There's no time to think about his touch or the way his hand rests so comfortably on my hips before he lashes out in a malevolent tone, "I knew you always had a thing for him."

My strength is weak compared to his, and so, despite my anger towards him, I continue to allow him to touch me. "Get over yourself, Jess. You were cheating on me. Don't forget that."

"Yeah, well I wouldn't have done that if I didn't think you were cheating first." His disturbing laugh that follows, coupled with his sinister gaze on my barely covered chest, should have warned me of his intentions. "Those days when you said you were busy? I knew you went home to fuck him. It's the only reason I did what I did. I was hurting. *I loved you* and you broke my heart."

I stop moving, standing perfectly still in front of him as the disco lights reflect off my body in the dim light. "Are you kidding me? Your excuse gets worse over time. Tell me, Jess, was it worth it?"

He pauses, and without any emotion in his aging face, he whispers, "No. I still love you, Zoey."

Ouch.

The words I had so desperately wanted to hear, yet in reality, they meant nothing. Empty words from someone that scarred my heart and left me to pick up the mess he created. There are words for people like him, words that sit on the tip of my tongue, itching to be said, but Gigi's voice replays in my head. *Be the mature one, the bigger person. Walk away with dignity and show him that you're over him.*

So what do I do next? I blurt out some nonsense about finding my boyfriend because I miss him and need to get laid.

Great! Pat on the back for the drunken slur, Zoey!

I pull his hands off me and scramble outside, desperately needing to find Drew. Beside the entrance, I find him, busy with some skank that is stroking his arm as he leans against the wall with a bottle of champagne in his hand. He takes a long drink straight from the bottle, wiping his mouth with the back of his hand. Oh, for the love of god. It's going to be one expensive cab ride home.

I put on my fake smile and call out to him, "There you are, babe!"

The skank backs off immediately. Standing next to Drew, I move closer and wrap my arms around his waist, burying my face into his neck. He smells so nice and masculine. My lips move against his skin and he doesn't stop me, not even when his arms move up the side of my waist, slowly tracing the curves of my breasts.

The skank mumbles something about leaving, and when a gust of wind almost lifts my dress up, I realize we are alone and there is no display for anyone. Yet we are clinging to

each other.

My pumps are extra tall, giving me a height advantage, my eyes almost in line with Drew's. And here, outside, beneath the stars, with no one to watch us but the ornamental cupids surrounding the fountain, our eyes are drawn to each other. Staring curiously, without reason, and the way he looks at me climbs into my soul. Searching for something. Something I wasn't sure I could reciprocate.

After all, it is Drew.

But I can't ignore, no matter how hard I try, the magnetic force pulling me towards him. Whatever it is in the moment feels right, and I tilt my head slightly until my lips are on his. He tastes sweet, and with his tongue kneading mine slowly, we stay locked into this kiss until some smokers come outside and interrupt us.

I touch my lips with my fingers, savoring the sensation that lingers. "We should probably head back inside, you know, save the show for where it counts."

I regret my words almost instantly.

His body instantly recoils. Taking another drink from the bottle, it appears empty, infuriating him further. He throws it into the bush, ignoring displeased bystanders. His aggressiveness is very unlike him, but I dare not say a word, for I am the one causing this huge headache.

"That's right. This is all for Jess," he almost spits.

"No, I'm sorry, I didn't mean for it to come out like that," I quickly apologize. "I just got—"

"Don't hide the truth, Zoey. You're shit at lying. You want to make him madder? Make him regret his actions? Give him a show?" he barks, the fury driving his normally calm demeanor. "Then that's what we'll do, Zoey. No more holding back."

Drew grabs my hand tightly and with force. Almost dragging me back inside, I struggle to keep up, begging him to slow down as my heels skid against the marble floor.

The lights are still dim, and amongst the crowd, Jess is leaning against the wall with a beer in hand again. The envy in his eyes intensifies the moment that Drew pulls me onto the dancefloor. Our bodies jerk forward, almost banging into each other, and Drew purposely places his hands on my naked lower back with a tight grip. I want to tell him to stop, but something reminds me that I created this monster myself.

Drew brushes his lips against the base of my neck until he reaches the bottom of my earlobe. Gently nibbling, once again stirring something inside of me, despite our argument outside.

"I don't play fair, Zoey," he says in a hushed tone, confidently holding on to me like I belong to him and only him. "You want a war? You've got one."

CHAPTER Twelve

Drew

WHEN I WAS TWELVE YEARS old, my dad and I entered a go-kart-building competition. You designed your own go-kart, and the fastest one to the end, won. It was the biggest thing to happen in our small town, and being that my dad was mechanical-minded, I had every bit of confidence that we would win. Weekends and countless hours were spent perfecting this kart, making sure it would be crowned a winner.

I was up against a kid named Jed. Jed was the town bully, and of course, talked his mouth off about winning the competition. His dad was some hotshot lawyer, and although his kart had all the bells and whistles, mine had the steady engineering.

The morning of the race, Jed approached me. He was an overly confident kid who used his manipulation to his advantage.

"Nice kart, Baldwin. Your mom help you build that?"

The idiot knew I didn't have a mom, but I didn't let him get to me. I was *that* confident we would win. My dad was the best mechanic in town. Well, the only mechanic in town.

"Good luck, Jed," I mumbled.

"I don't need luck. I'm going to win. You and your dad are

losers."

It was one thing to mention my mom, who was no longer with us, but my dad . . . you didn't say shit about my dad. I was determined to win. I *had* to win.

The race was ready to begin, and I remember my dad's words as clear as day: "Son, you've got every chance of winning. But life doesn't also end up with a win. Try your best and that's all you can do."

I lost the race that day. Jed's dad had paid some engineer to build his go-kart and won, but was eventually stripped of his title as State Champ. But that race taught me a big lesson; I didn't want the Jeds of the world to win.

And today is no different.

Zoey is the trophy.

There is no question that my jealously has been climbing by the minute, and attempting to curb it with some champagne had seemed like a good idea at the time. I should have known better; when does alcohol ever solve the problem? And despite my medical knowledge of how damaging drinking was to your liver, I had ignored any sense of reason and drank that entire bottle.

I go outside to call my dad and ask him to pick my car up. I can't drive like this, plus I need some alone time to make sense of everything that had happened inside. There is something about that jerk that rubs me the wrong way, and even more so, I just can't understand why Zoey is becoming obsessed with getting him back.

It's not long before Zoey finds me chatting with some random chick I could have scored with in the bushes somewhere. She would have been a five-minute fix—just not worth my time, to be frank. *I'm just not in the mood.*

Whatever her name is, she quickly disappears when Zoey places her hands all over me, pretending to be my girlfriend. It catches me by surprise. Kissing her did something to me— something I had never experienced before. The kisses

between us connected with the rest of my body. It was surreal, and unknown. I didn't know what it meant, and despite wanting to talk to her about it, it seemed like an unmanly thing to do. But much like the calm before a storm, her following words strike a nerve. This is all for show, and outside, there is no audience.

That's right, that's all I'm good for.

She doesn't look at me that way. She doesn't feel the same way I do.

My anger rises to a whole new level, dragging her back inside so I can show her 'audience' what the fuck I was all about. I was a man that did not intend to lose, despite her having no interest in me.

I lace my hand around the back of her dress, making contact with her skin. Running my fingers along the edge of her dress, I pull her closer until her tits are pushed up against my chest.

My mouth makes its way onto her neck, caressing her skin with a gentle roll of my tongue. She smells divine, like roses and vanilla, and all this other sweet shit I want to eat. Kissing her skin gives me an instant hard-on, one that I'm not afraid to let her feel. If she wants that dickhead to believe we are a couple, then I'm going to make her feel that way.

Then, I say the words that I can't hold back any longer. If she wants a war, then she'll get one. She appears shocked at my admission, yet as I continue to touch her in ways I had never imagined, her sweet moans continue to echo softly in my ear.

I need to get her out of here, maybe the restroom, the cloakroom. Somewhere outside, against the fancy bushes, where I can show her what it's like to be my girlfriend.

Except that she's your roomie.

Your best friend.

The one human being, the one person, who has seen you

at your worst. Been there to support you on more occasions than you can remember.

She's your definition of *family.*

She's the nagging conscience that sits on your shoulder, influencing you when you make your decisions about women. What is she saying right now? I pull back slightly and look into her eyes. They are glassy from all the champagne, but somewhere in that glance, that little devil in her is dancing around. She wants to get Jess back. That's her mission. Then it hits me again: She still loves him. She doesn't care for me. Not in that way.

I'm not good enough for her.

With every move, my blood is thickening, and anger consumes me in ways I had never imagined. I'm still holding on to her, only just, and the question that plays on my mind, I get off my chest, *"What hold does he have over you?"*

Her bleak expression, followed by her silence, tells me it's more than what I think. But she doesn't say anything and continues to dance, wrapping her arms around my neck. I pull them back off and stop, my body stilling. I want a fucking answer. Enough of this bullshit game we are playing.

"Nothing," she mumbles, eyes sidelining towards the band.

"It's not nothing," I dismiss her lie in frustration. "Yeah, he cheated on you, but how can you not see how great you are?"

The insecurity and need for revenge is now bugging me. This stupid game is slowly becoming some sick and twisted obsession. Zoey deserves better. Why couldn't she fucking see that?!

"Because . . . because he had a way of making me feel like I was inadequate."

"Inadequate?"

"Yes," she strains. "I was never good enough. I never wore

the right things, never performed the way I should have in the bedroom. I just want to prove him wrong. Like I was the best thing in his life and he missed out."

Did I hear right? That piece of lowlife scum had the nerve to belittle her in the bedroom? I clench my jaw, inviting the memory of one night when Jess stayed over. It was in the first couple of weeks they started dating. I remembered the night because it stuck with me. Her words. Her actions. But being the dedicated 'roomie' I was, I tried my best to erase the memory.

The moron is over again, but with the door shut, I'm hoping to get some sleep after a big study session. I walk down the hall to use the bathroom when I hear her voice. It's not loud, the walls just happen to be paper thin, or I'm wide awake from the pills I took to help me study for my exam.

"That feels so good. The way you rub my pussy . . ."

Oh. Just ignore it, Drew. So, every girl likes that. No biggie right?

"I'm going to turn around now, spread my ass nice and wide for you. I want you to stick your finger in my ass. Just one."

Holy shit! Did I just hear what I think I heard?

I scramble for the bathroom, shutting the door with panic and jamming my big toe in the process. No, this can't be happening. You didn't just overhear that your roomie likes it in the ass. It's all just a figment of your imagination . . . your dirty imagination.

The memory floods back, my hard-on intensifying. For a woman to tell you she wants anything in her ass is like winning the lottery. Occasionally, I would come across a woman that wanted to experiment with her dirty side. I'd play around with the rim and gently ease my way in with a tube full of lube. But then they would complain, tell me to back the fuck out, and that would be the end of that fantasy. *Cockteasers. Like staring at the lottery ticket thinking you've won, but you're one number short.*

Okay, so any anal activity was like winning a million bucks in my eyes.

You had some women who enjoyed it in a slow and relaxing pace, and others that ran for the hills if you went anywhere near their asshole.

Zoey was that woman.

The *ass* woman.

And my sudden need to get near her ass and show her what I want to do with it needs to be curbed on so many levels. These thoughts were so unnatural!

"So what do you need? A shot? One or two, maybe three?" I ask, dulling down my tone to ease her insecurity.

"Excuse me?"

"What do you need so I can prove to you that it's all in your head and you dated a loser who has no clue what the fuck he is doing?"

She laughs nervously, unable to make eye contact with me. "You've had too much to drink. *Are you asking me to have sex with you?*"

In hindsight, I am. What's so wrong with that? Maybe we could try that whole friends-with-benefits thing.

Taking a deep breath and allowing the alcohol to talk, not levelheaded Drew, "Zoey, I need to be honest with you. There was this one time when I overheard you and Jess. Basically, you asked him to finger your ass."

"Um . . . *what?*" she says, her normally pale skin flushing a bright pink.

"You heard me. So listen, women don't usually say that shit, and if they do, hallelujah. My point is, you can't be that bad. No woman that likes it in her ass can be that bad."

"I can't believe we are having this conversation on the

dancefloor . . . of a wedding . . ." she trails off, avoiding my eyes and staring embarrassedly at the floor. Her skin feels like it is on fire, and I yearn to run my hands along it and feel the effect that I'm having on her.

"Hey, it's nothing to be ashamed of. You should be proud."

Shaking her head with a cute smile, she manages to drag her eyes up to meet mine. "Proud? That I like things in my ass? Are we seriously having this conversation?"

"We've had worse conversations," I remind her.

"Oh no. I think this one tops them all."

I don't have enough alcohol in me to be able to maintain this conversation, and so, I drop the ass talk, attempting to carry on dancing. It's a lot harder than I think to forget our conversation, plus my cock is in pain from having *massive* blue balls. The only thing deflating my cock at a rapid rate is some drunken man with no teeth who attempts to dance with every woman on the dancefloor, and when that fails, he moves onto the men.

Men, myself included.

The music slows down again, a mellow and sexy beat that sets the perfect mood. I can see the fucker standing leisurely at the bar with drink in hand. He is watching us like an animal ready to attack, and with a satisfied smirk, I slowly move Zoey's hair away from her neck again and brush my lips against her skin, kissing her as I trail down to the base of her neck. This time, her eyes close and she presses carelessly against my groin. Fuck, is she even wearing a bra? Her nipples are erect and that doesn't help the fucking hard-on I'm trying to control, *again.* My eyes move up, purposely making contact with Jess. His stare is hostile, his face fueled with rage as his choice of liquor appears to be some hard scotch. The bartender speaks to him, and lashing out, he slams the glass on the counter, his body suggesting that he demands another.

That doesn't deter him from turning his attention back to

us.

Checkmate, fucker.

I'm going in for the kill.

I move my hands towards the back of her neck, directing her face so her lips are flush with mine. Kissing her softly, rolling my tongue, I pretend she is mine, and that the world around us doesn't exist.

The timing is impeccable.

The DJ switches the song, playing a popular Jason Derulo song. Maybe it's the champagne letting my inhibitions go, but damn does she look sexy with her body moving against mine.

I fucking want her.

And I don't care about anything else right now.

Just one night, one moment. When codes didn't exist and rules were made to be broken.

Just her and I on the dancefloor—the best type of foreplay. Bodies swaying, sweat glistening on our skin, creating this magnetic force that feels impossible to tear apart. She follows my lead, not allowing her body to break away. The smell of her skin is lingering in the air, and every part of me wants to take her back to our place and show her body what it needs. *What it's been craving.*

I start to think about us, and what this all means. Zoey is my best friend. What's so wrong about your best friend being more than that? The *aftermath.* The *what if it doesn't work out and things don't revert back to the way they were.* It affects everything we have: the trust, the honestly, and the friendship. Would it even be possible for us to be roomies after taking it that step further?

My head is spinning.

Stop thinking.

When the lights come on, her skin is flushed and she struggles to make eye contact with me. Reluctantly, we both

pull away from each other when the MC announces it's the end of the night, requesting that all guests form a line to say farewell to the bride and groom. *Who the fuck invented this stupid tradition?* I can barely walk, let alone form a line.

I turn to my left, surprised to find that Zoey is no longer beside me. Scanning the room, I spot her at the table and immediately start walking towards her, trying my best to act cool.

"You okay?" Losing my balance a little, I rest my hand on the back of the chair, trying to ignore the dizzy spell.

"Yeah, it's a shame it's over," she says, nonchalant.

"The wedding? I'm sure Mia and Troy have better things to do on their wedding night as a married couple," I chuckle, eyeing the leftover champagne on the table.

"No I meant the dan—" She clears her throat. "Never mind."

I do mind. Did she want this as much as I did? What did this all mean? Fuck, I need something to take the edge off. That glass of champagne remains untouched, and leaning forward, I pick it up and raise it to my lips. It may be a glass, but it feels like a drop.

Not enough. The bottle sits in the middle of the table with just a small amount left. I pour the remainder into my glass. It goes down a lot smoother, taking the edge off this unknown anxiety I am feeling.

The MC once again reminds us to join the line like animals in a circus act. *I want to go home.*

"Slow down, Drew," Zoey warns me, taking the glass out of my hands. "How are we going to get home?"

I don't answer her, following the crowd to the dancefloor. Riddled with guilt, I turn to apologize, stopping abruptly when Jess comes out of nowhere and latches on to her arm. She appears startled, switching to annoyed, then something in her face softens. I'm only a few steps away, unable to hear their conversation, till they turn in the opposite direction.

What the fuck? Instinctively, I follow them, but stop short of the foyer where they both stand.

Jess is pacing up and down, rubbing his hands along his bald head in frustration. *"Were you fucking him when we together?"*

She remains silent, not bowing down to his demands. Thank god, at least she knew how to stand up for herself.

"Fucking answer me, Zoey," he grunts, moving closer to her face, trying to terrorize her with his bullying tone.

"You cheated on me. I didn't touch Drew when we were together. I already told you that! Everything that happened between us is your fault. Stop blaming me!"

"The way he is touching you tonight. It's driving me fucking insane," he seethes. "He can't fucking touch you like that. You're mine. You understand?"

Zoey continues to stand still, crossing her arms and keeping her distance. With a satisfied laugh, she shakes her head and says, "Wow. Imagine what it's like to catch your best friend blowing your boyfriend."

"Zoey, I'm sorry," he apologizes, softening his tone with false pleas. "I had been drinking that day and it sorta just happened. I didn't mean to hurt you."

"Well, Jess, Drew and I sorta just happened too."

"I can't do this, Zoey. It was meant to be us all along. You're mine. I can't leave here tonight knowing you're going home with him."

I can hear the desperation in his voice. If this is what Zoey wanted, then she won. The fucker is suffering. But something tells me that brewing in the horizon is something bigger than this.

"I have to go, Jess. There's nothing else for us to say to each other."

"I love you," he blurts out. "Please. Give me another chance. I'll prove to you it's meant to be. I can't live without

you."

Zoey remains silent, but her sullen face says it all. His words, his reaction, they have affected her deeply, and I have no doubt at this moment that she still loves him.

Him. Not you.

The tension is palpable, and just when I think she might walk away, he takes his hands and places them on her face, kissing her passionately.

When I see that she doesn't pull away instantly, the fury inside me hits its boiling point, the adrenaline running through my veins.

My body charges forward, out of control, tearing them apart until I have Jess pinned against the wall.

Within my grip, his anger consumes him, squirming his body free and using his arms against mine. We both struggle, and my next move is paramount. He deserves this. For everything he's done, for the person he is.

And most importantly—because Zoey still loves him.

My fist makes contact with his jaw, slamming hard, the pain instantly ricocheting and causing my body to buckle in agony. Caught off guard, Jess pulls me up, punching my face in return. The pain is even worse than before, coming in waves, intensifying with every second that passes. The taste of blood lingers on my lips, the noise and commotion drowning out the yelling coming from two men trying to break us up, pushing the both of us apart.

"Drew!" Zoey cries, latching on to Jess. "Why did you hit him?!"

I don't say a word.

She just proved my point.

She defended *him* . . . she loves *him*.

Zoey caresses Jess's face, but he knocks her over in a bid to get back at me.

She tumbles to the ground. Her hair messily falls to

pieces, and she winces as her ankle twists. I push past the men holding me back, grabbing his suit until I have slammed him onto the ground. His eyes rage against mine, and together we both fight for the one person who has driven us to this point—Zoey.

"Stop it, Drew! Please," she begs.

I don't know what's come over me. This is not me. I am not the person that goes around violently hurting others, even if they deserved it. There is a lot of commotion in the foyer, then large security guards usher me outside like I'm the perpetrator. Warning me that they'll call the cops if I don't calm down.

"Fuck this!" I yell. "It's all his fault! Fucking loser. Leave her the fuck alone!"

Jess watches me with heavy breaths, wiping his cut lip with a blood-stained shirt. A couple of people have helped Zoey up, and she continues to wince, standing against the wall.

I manage to communicate—through slurs—to the valet that my dad will be picking up my car and request they call a taxi. It isn't long before the lit-up cab drives down the pebbled entrance and stops before me.

Walking towards where Zoey is standing, I demand that she comes home with me. Her face is covered in mascara from the tears, and the strap of her dress is torn. She carefully holds it up, staring back at me with a furious glance.

"Let's go." My voice is hoarse, commanding her to follow me.

"No."

"Zoey," I say, teeth clenching with utter rage. "Get the fuck in the cab."

This time she doesn't argue and gets into the cab, slamming the door behind her. She doesn't turn to face me, and instead, stares out the window, giving me the silent

treatment.

The driver keeps to himself, humming some familiar tune. Beyond the horizon, the city lights shine from afar, and this ride home seems so long when you're staring out into nothing but darkness. I close my eyes and try to forget tonight. Forget how I allowed myself to do the unthinkable. Forget about how much I wanted to reach out to her and touch her . . . just one more time before reality faces us.

Breaking the ice and the cold harsh reality between us, I switch my tone to something softer. "Is your ankle okay? Can you move it?"

"I can't believe you did that," she fumes, ignoring my question.

I lash out instantly, *"Why did you let him fucking kiss you?"*

"I didn't. I pulled away."

"You didn't pull away, Zoey. You acted like a little puppy, standing there and forgiving him for all his mistakes!" I accuse.

"How dare you say that? You have no clue how I feel."

"I think I do. He treats you like yesterday's trash, but somehow you think it's all going to work out again and that he has changed just because he says 'I love you.'"

"You don't know me," she seethes. "I'm your roommate. Not your girlfriend."

"That's where you're wrong," I bite back. "I know you better than you know yourself, Zoey. I'm the one who helped you pick up the pieces after he cheated on you. I'm the one who watches you waste your life away. Don't say that I don't know you."

"Fuck you."

"Excuse me?" I ask, shocked.

"I said, fuck you!"

Well. That's unexpected and rude. My anger doesn't

subside, and as soon as we hit the main roads, not far from home, I ask the driver to pull over at the liquor store. Zoey watches me in frustration while I quickly duck into the store and purchase a bottle of bourbon. Fuck, it's been a long time since I drank this much, but tonight calls for it.

Back in the cab, I open the cap and take a long swig, my throat clenching at the raw burn. Zoey continues to ignore me until the cab driver reaches our block and pulls up in front of our building. She immediately opens the door, leaving me with the huge bill. Serves me right, I guess. If I hadn't been drinking, I could have driven home.

The cab driver takes off, leaving me alone on the sidewalk. I have two choices: the easy road out which is to walk in the opposite direction and continue on with the night, pretending tonight didn't happen, or, walk upstairs and deal with the devil.

Unwillingly, I find myself walking in the opposite direction, until I realize that isn't the best decision. I can't maintain my balance and my surroundings becoming a blur as my body knocks into things, which I can only assume are people, judging by the threats.

Somehow, I manage to stumble back to the apartment. Fumbling with the knob, the door appears locked, and I try my best to find the right key before Gigi walks out into the hallway.

"Good night, huh?"

She's dressed in purple pajamas, holding one of her cats and stroking its fur softly.

"Great night," I say sarcastically. "*The best night.*"

Gigi opens her door, motioning for me to come inside. "Why don't you stay here tonight?"

"What the fuck did she tell you?"

As soon as the words leave my mouth, I immediately regret it. There is no need to drag Gigi into this, but Zoey must have ranted about my inappropriate behavior tonight.

The two of them were super close.

My face softens. "I'm sorry, Gigi, I didn't mean to . . . you know."

"The both of you need to calm down. Take it from me, no good will come out of you arguing."

"She just . . . she just gets on my nerves," I vent.

"You know her very well, Drew. Jess was a big part of her life. She just needs time to adjust to him not being a part of it anymore."

"She's had plenty of time!" I yell in frustration again, taking it out on Gigi. "And the way she was with him tonight . . . I wouldn't be surprised if he's in our kitchen making breakfast tomorrow morning like that other fucking jerk . . . what's his fucking face."

Gigi remains placid, allowing me to vent and not commenting further. I can tell by the look on her face that she's tired, and it's well past midnight. "I really think you should sleep on my couch tonight. Just to give each other some space."

"Go to sleep, Gigi. I'll be fine. We'll be fine. We always are."

She walks back into her apartment, closing the door behind her. Even in my dazed and alcohol-fueled state, I know one thing. I don't want her to run to Jess. And everything about my behavior tonight pushed her into his arms.

Maybe, just maybe, this was all my fault.

Time passes as I stand in the hallway outside our apartment, gathering the courage to face Zoey. So much of tonight changed our relationship, and I'm not sure that change was a good thing. After much hesitation, I open the door and find the lights turned off. She must be asleep. Down the hall, I see the light underneath her door. The closer to the room I get, the more the sounds become apparent. Like a crazed stalker, I place my ear against the door and attempt to listen. She's talking on the phone. The conversation carries on, and my gut feeling is to continue listening, until the moment she says his name.

She is talking to Jess.

CHAPTER *Thirteen*

Zoey

WHAT A FUCKING NIGHT.

If I could purchase some sort of bleach to erase what happened, I would gladly do so in a heartbeat. It was bad enough that I had to deal with Jess and his familiar jealous ways; I didn't expect Drew to follow in his footsteps.

Okay—so *maybe* my idea to pretend that Drew and I were dating wasn't genius. It worked to a certain extent; I got my revenge on Jess so why aren't I over the moon? Why wasn't I jumping for joy watching the man I gave my everything to be torn apart because he couldn't handle watching me with another man?

Sure, I missed him—a lot. But I didn't think I was in love with him anymore. Tonight only confirmed that. He's familiar, comfortable, yet there were so many elements in our relationship that destroyed me as a person. I knew better than that. At least I think I did.

What rubbed me the wrong way was Drew thinking that I would so carelessly throw myself back into Jess's bed. Give me some fucking credit! And to call me a puppy dog? I would have happily punched him in his beautiful face had he not been drunk. Not to mention he was already sporting a cut lip and bruised cheek from the fight with Jess.

I decided to leave Drew wandering the streets; he was a big enough boy to be responsible for his drunken actions. I wasn't his girlfriend or his keeper. He usually wasn't so careless and I could probably count the amount of times on one hand over the past years when I had seen him this intoxicated. Unlike myself, he only drank himself into this stupor when there was a reason.

The first time he had done it was after a big altercation with his dad. It happened another two times after that. The fourth time was when he almost got fired because of Angela stalking him, and his almost-fail on a medical assignment.

The fifth—well, something happened tonight.

As much as I didn't welcome drama, I know that I am partially to blame for the violent outburst. Okay, maybe *all* to blame.

With Drew gone, I decide to stop by Gigi's just to unleash my inner thoughts. I needed Gigi's wise words to give me guidance. Something she often did when I was clueless.

Gigi stares at me, expressionless, after I explain to her what happened tonight. All of it. No holding back.

"That's some night. So the question is, do you still love Jess?"

"No," I say with a slight cough.

"I sense hesitation in your voice."

"My throat was itchy. So what do I do about Drew?"

"You let him cool down. I agree it's out of character, but the two of you have a great friendship. Let him sober up, and I'm sure you'll have a long talk about it and smooth it over."

She's curled up on the sofa with Diana and a cup of herbal tea. Graciously, she offers me one, which I politely refuse. My stomach is feeling off with all that quail and champagne floating around.

"So this thing with you and Drew. How serious is it?" she questions.

"There's no thing with me and Drew," I quickly correct her. "We're just friends. Roomies."

"C'mon, doll. From what you're telling me, Drew doesn't feel the same way."

I'm rewinding the conversation in my head. *Did I tell her that?* "Everything was for show. Sure, it felt nice, but it could never be like that between us. I mean, it's Drew."

"Yes, it's Drew," she reiterates. "Sometimes the best relationships start as friendships."

"Gigi, he's a man whore. Plus, I'm not the type of woman he's into. He likes model-looking chicks," I brush it off. "He's all about the modern woman, you know, likes all that new music and hitting the gym."

It's past midnight, and Gigi's cats provide me with that much needed companionship that cats are supposed to. We talk a bit more about Jess, my feelings towards him, and the possibility of him changing his ways.

"People can change. Husband Number Three had a gambling addiction. Blew his entire wages each week on the slots," Gigi tells me. "Then, I packed my bags and threatened to leave. From that day on he never stepped foot near a machine."

"Then why did you guys divorce?"

"He got hit by a bus."

Speechless, I try to find the right words to say. "I'm so sorry. That must have been awful."

"He was drunk. He started drinking to replace the gambling addiction. Some things aren't meant to be."

"Like me and Drew," I say quietly.

I leave Gigi's and head back home, still with a guilty conscience. Why? I have no idea. Confused about everything and everyone, I decide to head to the shower, but am

157

interrupted as my cell dances across my nightstand. Not recognizing the number, I answer with hesitation.

"Hello?"

There is silence followed by a shallow breath. "It's me."

"Jess?"

"Yeah."

"Are you okay?"

"Yes . . . no . . . I don't know, Zoey. Tonight was just . . . fuck . . . I don't know."

There's a sharp noise in the background, the sound of glass shattering. I pause, and gather my thoughts like a rational human being. "I'm sorry Drew hit you. I don't know what he was thinking."

"He loves you . . . that's what he is thinking."

"Jess, it's not like that—"

"The man fucking loves you, Zoey. I should know. I fucked everything up between us and now he has you."

"No one has me, Jess," I answer, slightly annoyed at his reference to me being a possession.

"Tell me what I need to do, Zoey . . . I'll do anything to get you back."

His desperate pleas are exactly what I wanted to hear . . . a year ago. But now they stand like empty promises. And yet some part of him has a hold on me, and I hate that. Why can't I just let go of this man and everything we had? Why am I even thinking about getting back together with him?

"Jess, just give me time to process tonight. You and I . . . I just don't know."

"How much time? A day? A week? Tell me," he slurs.

"I don't know," I almost yell back. "I can't think . . . there's so much history between us and I just don't know anything tonight. Stop pressuring me."

The door swings open, slamming against the brittle wall.

In shock, I see Drew standing at the entrance with the same bottle still in hand. His eyes are bloodshot, and he can barely stand straight. With his dress shirt unbuttoned, I can see his chest rising and falling at a rapid rate.

"Jess, let me call you tomorrow," I tell him before ending the call without a goodbye.

I put the cell back down. "You can't just barge into my room whenever you feel like it."

"Why? We're roomies. You do whatever the hell you please, so why can't I?" he argues back, his tone malicious and very unlike him.

"What the hell is wrong with you?" I stand up and cross my arms, fed up with his antics.

"YOU . . ." he rages.

"Me what?"

"This is all your fault."

"Okay, so my plan wasn't the best. But you caused all the shit tonight, Drew. I'm not the one who hit Jess," I remind him.

He doesn't say another word, so I turn around with my back facing him to take off my necklace, hoping he will disappear to his room. My body jerks forward, his hands sliding around my waist until his grip is full and his body is pressed against mine. With my heart beating a million miles a minute, my body is trying to ignore the burning desire that is rising by him touching me this way. Count sheep, Zoey . . . think of an ugly bald man running naked in a field of corn . . .

"Drew, what are you doing?" I whisper, desperate to ignore how good he feels.

He's drunk, you're only slightly buzzed. Think rationally, Zoey.

He refuses to say any words, and instead, his hands move, tracing my hips with a slight rocking motion. Don't close your eyes . . . don't close your eyes.

Fuck.

I close my eyes.

Whatever happens in the next moment becomes a blur. My body is pushed onto my bed, and I'm forced to hold myself up on all fours. His groin rubs repeatedly against my ass, and it's impossible to ignore how hard his shaft feels against me. Don't let out a moan . . . don't let out a moan.

Fuck.

I let out a moan.

I've given him the green light. Handed him the card that says *Advance to Go—collect two hundred dollars.*

Minus the two hundred dollars . . . That sounds awfully cheap.

At the same time, I hear the low grumble escape his throat and his hands move in a frenzy that consumes me. *I can't think.* The touch of his skin, his hands, moves around to my chest, and waiting in high anticipation, I think he will circle my breasts with a gentle tease, but instead, he doesn't resist, cupping them with a tight squeeze in his bare hands.

My body shudders, my knees shaking uncontrollably on the mattress. My breaths, shallow, move unevenly, grunting softly, begging my brain to control the situation and pull away before it's all too late.

From behind I can't see his face, but maybe that's what makes this okay. Like we can erase it after. Gee, Zoey, did you have a plate of stupid for dinner?

"You're so fucking beautiful," he whispers into my ear, arching over me, controlling the way my body moves.

Just drunk talk.

Tell him to stop.

It's the bourbon . . . and champagne.

It's not your roomie or your best friend saying these words.

It's not Drew.

In just one motion, his hand glides down and skirts the outside of my panties. The aching throb is enough for me to buckle under his command, and with my arms shaking uncontrollably, I cannot find the strength to push him away. *Or you don't want to push him away. Shut up . . . shut up!*

My panties are soaked, uncomfortable, yet in a pleasurable way. His fingers move in rhythm, my clit becoming swollen with every stroke. My panties seem to be an issue, and before I know it, he yanks them down and forces my thighs open as much as possible. He continues the strokes, sliding into me with his finger . . . fingers . . . *fuck, I just can't even think.*

"You're so tight . . . and hot," he mumbles. *"I need my cock inside you . . ."*

Shit! My body wants him, every inch is crawling with a desire to have him enter and fill me, but I'm the conscious decision-maker here. I didn't drink a whole bottle of bourbon before entering the room. This moment could destroy everything between us. *Say something now!*

"Drew, we can't," I beg, drawing my body forward, away from his touch.

He senses my resistance, wrapping his arm around my stomach and pulling me back towards him. With his spare hand, he moves towards my hair and pulls the pins out, allowing my hair to fall down my back. As soon as it does, he wraps his hand around my hair, twisting it into a tight fist.

"Don't fucking fight me."

Fight him? Why did those words sound both domineering and hot?

Go to your happy place, Zoey. Your happy place will bring you much zen and steer you to make the right decision.

But what if this is my happy place? And it's no longer the time I went to that Madonna concert and met that cute boy who danced to "Like a Virgin" with me. In my dreams he was the one, but let's face it, he's probably in Ibiza now wearing a pink netted singlet and handing out Barbara Streisand CDs.

"I know you've wanted this for a long time. I bet you lie here at night and rub your pussy, begging me to find you so I can make you come."

My skin is on fire, embarrassed by his honestly, if in fact he thinks that, and by the thought of that exact image. Yes, I have done that, but never had I thought about Drew doing those things to me.

Now it's the only thing I can think about.

My thoughts are brutally interrupted as he takes his fingers out and drags them towards my ass. Shit, my weak spot.

Oh my god . . . What do I do?! *Tell him to back off . . . explain to him that if he goes anywhere near your ass . . . things will never EVER be the same.*

My chest rises and falls unevenly, panicking at the thought.

"This fucking ass. Just like you want it, Zoey."

I don't even have time to process what he says, distracted by the warm saliva touching my skin the moment he spreads my cheeks. My head falls into the bed, the pillow muffling my moans and enabling my body to focus on every single touch and sensation, and although I should protest this forbidden act, I fall into his spell, allowing him to have me.

His fingers circle the entrance, and then, it happens . . .

My roomie sticks his index finger in my *asshole.*

This can't be happening.

It's so dirty . . . so *forbidden.*

And why does that turn me on even more?

Slowly gliding in and out, in a comfortable pace, his moans accompanied by his desire to do this to me intensify the pleasure spreading to every part of my body. The familiar

build up is quicker than expected, and I struggle to curb the urge to let my body completely go. But resistance can only go so far, my inner beast pushing back against him, signaling for him to thrust deeper.

"Fuck," he grunts, sliding his middle finger inside.

I'm done.

It rocks me like an unexpected earthquake, every inch of me screaming in utter delight, until my limbs become numb and I collapse on the bed.

In midst of this euphoria, I am out of breath, swallowing dry gulps of air. The tiredness become apparent, yet I know I need to address the fact that his fingers were in my ass at some point.

In a minute . . .

He has pulled away somehow without me knowing. I can't turn around, paralyzed from the head down, the tiredness overcoming my weak body.

And like a thief in the night, his footsteps are heard, and the lights turn off.

Perhaps this is all a dream.

Either way, my eyelids become heavy, and sleep is imminent.

My dreams await me, and this time, I dream of him.

Drew.

My roomie.

CHAPTER *Fourteen*

Drew

THERE'S POUNDING, A DRILLING SOUND that is striking every nerve in my head. I want to scream, climb into a dark place of silence. Then, I realize it's morning and the stupid sun is directly on my face, my eyelids red, the severe throbbing intensifying with every twitch. Barely able to open my eyes, the blinds appear to be wide open. *Who the fuck left them open?* Attempting to stand up is fruitless, the weight of my body overcoming my strength. With the little energy I have, I manage to throw my wallet at the window, watching it tumble across the room as hits the floor just shy of the curtains.

Because that was a brilliant plan.

Brilliant plans, like Zoey's one to make her ex regret his actions.

This is how it all began: her desire to make his life hell, which in turn, has made my life hell. I remember the wedding. Remember how jealous I got and how I refused to allow him to win. It was a war, and I was standing front-row center, guns blazing. I remember smashing his face, which explains why my jaw feels like a cement block was thrown at it, and my hand is bruised.

Then Zoey told me to fuck off in the cab.

Then blank.

Blank—and no idea why I'm lying here half-dressed on my bed. My dress pants are uncomfortable and scratching my skin. The white collared shirt appears to have stains, which I cannot, for the life of me, explain. I lift the shirt to smell it, and the strong stench of bourbon engulfs my nasal passages.

Oh . . . bourbon.

Friend and foe.

I continue to lie here for another hour, attempting to ignore the persistent throb in my head. I need painkillers, and yell for Zoey to bring me some. There is no answer. *Argh.* Unsteady on my feet, I stumble to the bathroom and locate them inside the cupboard, swallowing two, praying for an instant cure.

This is why I rarely drink.

A cold shower seems like a good idea, at least to wash away the nasty hangover.

The water relaxes my aching muscles, except for the one below. Even in my exhausted state, I manage to give myself a few strokes, hoping for a quick release. My hand moves accordingly, growing my cock to its peak. Without any visuals, and following the escalating throb, it takes only seconds for my body to jerk forward and my cum to shoot out onto the shower floor. *Fuck. What was that?* My heart is beating a million miles per second, my limbs barely able to hold themselves up.

I rest my body against the cold shower tiles, slumping to the floor, catching my breath. Something inside me ignited just then. This primal need or desire to release. Usually I would have to go at it for a while, conjuring up porn in my head. *It's like I had blue balls or something.*

As I continue to sit here questioning my body, my shaft stiffens once again. *Are you kidding me?* It's like someone slipped me Viagra. Fuck, maybe that's what happened. I turn off the water, hopping out, thinking of something else

to distract me.

Back in my room, I make my bed and tidy my nightstand, opting to hit the gym instead of climbing back into bed. The apartment is dead quiet, and it's odd that Zoey isn't lounging around the apartment. But then again, her behavior has been unpredictable lately, and after last night's failed attempt at being a couple, I'm assuming she's gone into hiding.

I close the door behind me to be met by Gigi climbing the stairs with bags of groceries. With her arms full, I quickly run to her, helping her by carrying two bags. She graciously says thank you and unlocks her apartment door. Her stray cats come purring to her rescue, almost blocking my way when the fat one's tail nearly gets caught under my shoe.

"You can put them down on the kitchen counter," she directs.

I follow her instructions, carefully placing them down. As I'm about to head out, she begins to speak.

"You've got a lot of energy for someone who drank a whole bottle of bourbon. It's because you're an Aries."

Here we go. I attempt to shrug it off.

"Zoey was over here this morning."

"She was?" I ask curiously. "That would have been early."

I glance at my watch; it's only quarter past eleven.

"Hmm," she murmurs.

"Do you know where she is? I mean, in all honesty, Gigi, she's been acting weird lately."

"I'm not sure where she went," she casually speaks. "Libra women can be a little indecisive at times."

"How is that related to her acting weird?"

"She's at a point in her life where transition is natural, yet for a Libra woman, that can be quite a monumental moment."

"What transition are you talking about? It's not like she's

167

thirteen and hitting puberty," I joke.

"Just give her time to make decisions and process her thoughts."

This conversation is confusing me. Horoscopes confuse me. I studied medicine, not astrology. "I've got no clue what went down last night. I'll never drink again," I moan, seeking sympathy for my awful behavior.

"That's what you young folk always say," she laughs, handing me some herbal tablets that are supposed to rid you of a hangover. *No harm in trying.* I take them from her and swallow them whole, thanking her when I'm done.

"I didn't do anything stupid . . . did I?"

"I think it's best you talk to Zoey. Maybe you both just need to clear the air."

"There's unclear air between us?" I worry out loud.

Gigi pats my shoulder, then picks up a crystal from the table and squeezes it tight, closing her eyes. She had a habit of doing this, and awkwardly, I just stand there, waiting like some pathetic fool.

"Drew, I sense this aura around you. The uncertainty. Just wait till she comes home."

I leave the conversation at that. It made no sense to me whatsoever, and I wasn't going to waste my time solving the riddle. I loved Gigi, but boy oh boy, she had a few screws loose.

My gym workout is exactly what I need, taking the edge off my hangover. Isaac and Rob are there, and so I chat for a bit, Rob worried about Zoey. I tell him she's fine but a little shaken up, so best not to call her.

Deceitful—the only way to describe yourself right now. It's not like I could stop men from coming into her life . . . or could I? My head hurts thinking about it, and if only for today I've pushed away another one of her interests, then my

job is done.

I'm due for a late shift tonight, and when I arrive back at the apartment, still no Zoey. It starts to worry me a little, so I decide to send her a quick text.

I hope you're not avoiding me. Where are you?

She never responds, and a couple of hours later, she casually strolls through the front door, carrying some shopping bags. As I look at the logos printed on the front, I see a popular shoe store. *Women.* Then, behind the white paper bag, I see the familiar pink *Victoria's Secret* bag. *Oh. Don't think about sexy lingerie now!* I've had enough trouble trying to curb that boner all day long.

"There you are! Jesus, Zoey, you had me worried." Even I can hear how distressed my voice is, yet Zoey seems unaffected.

She places the keys down, avoiding my gaze. "Why would you be worried? It's still light out. Aren't I allowed to go and do whatever I want on a Sunday?"

Her tone is off, and her refusal to look me in the eye warns me that maybe I did or said something wrong yesterday. How am I going to get this out of her without looking like a dickhead? *Well, you are a dickhead. You punched Jess in the face . . . though, he deserved it.*

"It's just . . . never mind. I just wanted to make sure you're okay."

"I'm fine."

There's that phrase again. The *'I'm fine.'* When a woman says she's fine, she's never fine. It doesn't take a rocket scientist to figure that out. I scurry behind her, following her to the bedroom, and hold the door open before she shuts it.

"Quit the weird act, Zo. Did I do something? I want to apologize for last night. I drank a lot and I don't remember much after—"

"After what?" she brutally interrupts me, stopping at her

heels as she turns to face me. She's wearing her silver ballet flats, and falls just under my chin. But even then, her glare is enough to intimidate me. Shit, I must have done something really bad.

"After you told me to fuck off in the cab."

With an odd stare, she withdraws, turning her attention to the shopping bags and unpacking her lingerie as if I'm not even in the room.

"So you remember nothing after that cab ride?"

I shake my head.

"Nothing at all?"

"Nothing, Zo. C'mon, you're freaking me out. Did I do something? Or say something? I'm sorry."

"Nothing. You did nothing. Except for smash Jess's face at the reception," she adds.

He deserved it. That much I know.

"Yeah, I know you'll pull out some macho comment, so I don't want to hear it. I've got some stuff I need to get done if you'll excuse me."

I back off until she turns around. "And just so you know, I was with Mia having lunch today before she left for the airport. She was distraught over your altercation."

Okay, so now I officially feel like shit. Even though the guy deserved it, Mia and Troy didn't. I remind myself to make the effort to apologize in person upon their return.

Zoey stays locked in her room all afternoon, and I make the conscious decision not to bother her.

With boredom comes hunger. It's not until I raid the kitchen cupboard that I realize we are low on food. I have a crazy idea: the both of us could go grocery shopping together. We haven't done it in years, and maybe she would tell me what I did that has made her so moody. A bonding session . . . over food.

"Zo," I yell out. "Let's go out. We need groceries."

No response. I walk to her room and hear some music playing. Upon closer inspection, I can hear the sounds of Pink playing. How odd and very unusual for her to play something modern. Something in the universe is not right. I bet it's a full moon tonight. I bang on the door again, repeating my words.

"What?" she says, opening the door.

"Let go grocery shopping. We've got nothing."

"We haven't done that since you first moved in," she points out, eyeing me dubiously. "Besides, I'm busy."

My glance moves past her. The iPad sits on the bed; the screen is on with a game of solitaire playing.

"No, you're not. C'mon. The fresh air might do us both some good."

I remember why we never shop together anymore. Zoey throws junk into the cart while I sneak it out. Behind the organic carrots and fresh parsley sits a box of Oreos and a jumbo pack of Cheetos. She knew how to rile me up, but I allow the items to sit in the cart, hoping that she will finally open up to me about last night.

The six-pack of Coke, bag of Reese's, and some bacon-flavored candy push me over the edge. The second she turns around, the candy and Coke go back onto the shelf.

"If you're going to keep doing that, I don't know why you bothered to ask me to come," she says blankly, pretending to read the back of the Lucky Charms box.

Is she seriously reading the ingredients? Sugar, sugar, plus more sugar?

I grip the bar on the shopping cart, fed up and frustrated with her attitude. "For the love of god, just tell me what the fuck I did wrong so we can move forward like we always do."

She pretends to be interested in a magazine she had dumped into the cart earlier, but I know she's procrastinating. I grab it out of her hands, placing it back on the shelf, certain the store workers would be angry at me for discarding it in the cereal aisle.

"You didn't do anything wrong, the whole night was just not what I had in mind," she finally admits.

I watch her, confused. "You were the one who wanted to make him jealous. I just did what you wanted."

"I know. Maybe we just took it too far."

"Well, I'm willing to move past it if you can. It's not like we had sex, Zo. So we kissed and I grabbed your ass. No biggie, right?"

"No biggie," she copies with a softer tone, pursing her lips.

"Okay, so let's just forget it. I can't handle you being like this with me. And look, I'm sorry about hitting Jess. He just . . ." I trail off unable to find the words to describe how much of a scumbag he is.

"It's not your fault. I shouldn't have acted so childish. What's the point of making someone jealous?"

"Exactly."

I breathe a sigh of relief that maybe we can move past this. Also, that she will see Jess for who he is truly is and learn from her mistakes. I know not to push her any further, and hopefully, this will blow over and things will go back to normal.

She doesn't say another word, taking the cart from me and moving towards the deli section where she peruses the cheeses. I wasn't about to point out all the fat in the cheese she's staring at, and instead bring up her birthday since it's only two weeks away.

"So . . . what are your plans for your big three-oh?" I ask, switching the subject.

"I was thinking of having it at that new amusement park that opened up. It's supposed to be really good."

"As in rides and cotton candy?"

"No, as in unicorns and cocaine."

"Ha, ha," I mock her. "I haven't been on a rollercoaster since I was like ten."

"It's like riding a bike; you never forget. It'll be an intimate party, maybe just a few of us." Her mood picks up a little, a smile gracing her lips.

"The last time you used the words 'intimate affair,' fifty people showed up and you almost got evicted from that Italian restaurant."

"Geez, Dad. Lighten up. I'm turning thirty, not twenty-one."

"Dirty thirties, isn't that what they say?" I tease.

"Who says that?" she questions like I just told her I committed a murder and buried the body somewhere in the bush.

"Uh . . . people? Don't get oversensitive about it. It's just a number."

"Off course you would say that. You're only twenty-eight."

She drops a massive block of cheddar cheese into the cart. I wait seconds, maybe a minute tops, before I open my mouth.

"Do you even know how bad that is for you?"

"What? The cheese?"

"Yes, the cheese." I roll my eyes at her, removing the block and placing it back on the shelf.

"You know," she says, hesitating. "Friends don't make their friends eat low-fat cheese. And you are my *friend* aren't you?"

Standing beside the cart with her arms folded, she waits for me to answer. What kind of question is this? And why did she drag out the word 'friend'? I can't shake the feeling that there is more to this again, another secret or emotion she is holding back.

So what do I do?

What most guys would do in this situation.

I grab the cheese and throw it back into the cart, not wanting to fuel the beast any further.

Avoidance. The key to making a woman think they won the battle, when in reality, I just couldn't be bothered dealing with it.

"There, you happy?" I bark, waiting for her to gloat.

She doesn't, and instead, avoids my gaze again. Her face, as easy as it is to read, looks melancholy, even pained. The sadness in her eyes shadows her normally vibrant self. Something is troubling her. And if I'm thinking clearly, it must have something to do with Jess. *She still loves him.*

Bits of yesterday come flooding back. He told her he still loved her. And if memory serves me correctly, she didn't push him away. She allowed that kiss.

You were there, through it all. You know how much she loved him, even after he hurt her. You were there throughout their entire relationship. You saw the ups, but mainly the downs.

And, you know Zoey very well.

She's hurting because she still wants him.

I don't ask; I have no interest in finding out the truth. Instead, I pick up my sore ego and carry on, reminding myself that I'm not who she wants.

I'm not who she loves.

And why, out of everything that happened, is that the only thing I can think about?

CHAPTER Fifteen

*H*E HAD NO CLUE WHATSOEVER.

    I didn't know what was worse: the fact that he had no clue, oblivious to his actions that have changed the whole dynamic of our relationship, or, if he did remember, how would we move forward from what's happened?

Confused and way out of my depth, I finally confided in Gigi that Sunday morning. I woke up early, not wanting to confront Drew. His heavy snores echoed in his room, so I slipped out, avoiding him completely.

Gigi's reaction didn't surprise me one bit. She told me to watch out, questioning me relentlessly on whether or not it was worth damaging our friendship because of one night.

I struggled to admit to her, and myself, that last night not only changed things between us, it changed the way I felt about him. And finally, I admitted that I saw Drew in a different light.

A light that's painted with roses, romance, and all that mushy stuff I never expected to feel for my roomie. And the worst part was . . . he had no idea.

No idea how his touch ignited me.

No idea how I tried to pull away but just couldn't.

No idea that I couldn't look at him without wanting him.

I was able to catch up with Mia for a quick cup of coffee before they were due to fly out. Troy, had organized their honeymoon on a remote island near the coast of Mauritius.

Mia was upset that her perfect wedding had drama not even related to her. I apologized a million times, because in the end, I hatched that stupid plan and it backfired in my face, big time.

I prayed that I didn't ruin our friendship, but Mia was forgiving, and with a honeymoon destination of a secluded resort on a tropical island, you could only move forward with a positive attitude.

With minimal sleep and a brain that wouldn't stop ticking, I ran through the night over and over in my head. Stupid and idiotic don't even cover how I felt about myself. I was so focused on getting Jess back that I didn't see what I was doing to myself, and to Drew.

I was almost thirty years old, acting like a teenager. I had nothing to show for my life. No, I wasn't suicidal, I wouldn't be that dramatic. But fuck, I had no idea how to untangle myself from the web of mess I somehow continue to create for myself.

Avoiding Drew allowed me time to clear my head, but that, only lasted so long. When he sent me that text asking me where I was, I knew I couldn't avoid him any longer, and so, I reluctantly made my way back to the apartment, armed with shopping bags and a massive credit card bill.

I hadn't shopped in forever, yet all of sudden, I had the desire to update my wardrobe, especially my lingerie. And several times throughout my Victoria's Secret binge, I shoved aside the nagging feeling that I was doing this for someone else, and not me.

Yellow thongs weren't exactly my thing.

Drew's favorite color is yellow.

I had put it back on the shelf, remaining strong willed. Did I expect him to see me wearing it? Did I expect to be intimate with him again?

Questions, too many of them, swirling in my head, ready to cause an explosion.

And when I reached the checkout, I slipped it back into my basket.

I guess I just answered that question.

Seeing him was hard. Even with a massive hangover, he looked so beautiful. He had come back from the gym, covered in sweat and wearing those shorts that made his legs look muscular and sexy. His tank was drenched, only showing off his bulky arms.

After we discussed last night and his failure to remember a single thing, I wanted to scream at the top of my lungs and remind him of what he did to me. *What I allowed him to do.* I wanted nothing more than to refresh his memory, even if it meant getting down on all fours and re-enacting the moment.

But that would have been greedy. Just because I experienced the best orgasm of my life, didn't mean a single thing.

There—I admitted it.

Playing the avoidance game worked well for me, until he dragged me out to go grocery shopping.

I bit my tongue as hard as I could, channeling out all these unwarranted thoughts.

Throughout our grocery trip, Drew kept rambling on about everything and anything not related to the wedding. I pretended to listen, but every time he bent over or pulled up close to me, my body betrayed me and refused to ignore how much I wanted him.

And in the end, I gave up.

He wanted everything to go back to normal between us. We were friends. He couldn't have made that any clearer.

Thank god it was over. He had a late shift at the hospital, leaving shortly after we arrived back at the hospital.

Being alone, as much as I wanted it, gave me too much time to think. Jess had been texting me, asking me if I had made a decision. Drew had sent me a couple more texts, just checking in to make sure we were still okay.

Gigi came over with some ice cream, the answer to all my problems. I welcomed that, until I found out it wasn't really ice cream, rather some soy substitute.

From every direction, every angle, I felt pressured. To make decisions, life-altering ones, in the space of a short time. *Ignorance is bliss.*

The only thing that comforted me was my music, and so, I scrolled through my iPod and listened to Pink's album again. I normally didn't listen to pop music that was released after nineteen eighty-nine, but tonight, I wanted to try something different.

I wanted to *be* someone different.

I kept to myself for most of the week. Jess didn't relent, his texts bordering on obsessive. I should have just said no to getting back together, but instead, I kept telling him I needed more time to process.

Apparently time was of the essence with him, giving me yet another ultimatum. I chose to ignore his childish bribes, deleting his text until I could think about the whole situation properly.

Work was extremely busy, starting the week off with a mountain of tasks to get through with a ridiculous deadline. By Wednesday, shit hit the fan.

Mr. Becker had major attitude, slamming doors and raising his voice at anyone that came near him. With Mia gone, our department was under the pump, and everyone was feeling the pressure. I was due to have a meeting with

some key stakeholders when Mr. Becker told me to stay in reception and answer calls. It was a big slap in the face, but with everything else going on, I didn't know how to fight for what I wanted.

It felt like everything in my life was falling apart.

With my birthday looming, I'm looking forward to spending it at the amusement park. According to all the media press, it had one of the fastest rollercoasters in the Northern Hemisphere and a haunted house guaranteed to make you shit your pants. *Exactly what I need.* A day to let my inhibitions go, and forget that turning thirty means I'll need to be responsible with my life. The joys of turning back the clock and being a kid again, if only for one day. But with alcohol. Booze and a haunted house. *Now that sounds like fun.*

Given that the tickets are almost sold out, I decide to head over there this afternoon, making sure I secure some for next Friday night. I ask Mr. Becker if I can leave half an hour early, given that I have finished all my work and stayed late each night this week. He mumbles something, which I take as a yes.

With my bag packed and computer shut down, he calls my name, asking me to come to his office. Given his foul mood and threat to fire everyone in this building, I figure this is it. My severance pay. The final hurrah.

"Close the door behind you, Zoey."

Nervously, I shut the door and take a seat, fiddling with the hem of my skirt as I wait for the inevitable.

"I've been watching you, Zoey. For a long time. And I'll be honest, you don't belong here."

I knew it. My hands begin to shake, and I don't want to be one of those people who cry at work, but the tears are gathering on the surface. The struggle to compose myself is becoming too hard, my lips quivering in anticipation.

"You've got talent, Richards. And you staying here would be wasting that," he says, offering a smile. "We have an opening in London. It's a two-year contract with my brother's company."

"Excuse me?"

"I know it's a big move, but my brother is willing to pay for a fully furnished apartment and any transfer costs."

"You want me to work in London?" I ask, unable to get a grip on the enormity of his proposal.

"Yes," he confirms. "Unless, of course, there's a reason to stay here. Like a boyfriend or something."

"No boyfriend," I answer quickly, shutting down the notion. "It's just a lot to take in."

"Let me give you this advice. It's a great opportunity, one that only comes once in a lifetime. Grab it with both hands, Zoey. Like I said, you're talented and they could really use you for this project."

"When do you need to know by?"

"By the end of the month," he states firmly.

"But that's next Friday?"

"Yes." He stands up, placing his briefcase on his desk and inserting some paperwork.

"I have to get to that meeting. How about we meet on Monday morning? We can talk more about what's involved."

"Okay," I stammer, nervous and barely able to think.

"Have a good weekend, Zoey."

He smiles kindly, something rare, and leaves his office. I continue to sit in shock, not understanding how only moments ago I was terrified that I would lose my job, let alone be offered an opportunity that seems too good to pass up.

But London was so far away, and cold. Everything I knew was here in the States.

This is home.

I rush out of the office, not saying goodbye to anyone, jumping in a cab to pick up the tickets. The entire cab ride is spent staring out the window, dazed and unable to grasp how big moving to London really is. I'm desperate to call Drew, run the thought past him, given that he is usually good at the whole advice thing. But things aren't exactly back to normal, despite what he may think.

The only person who would understand is Gigi. Honestly, she should charge by the hour for the amount of times I've knocked on her door with what I deemed the biggest problem ever.

Although this time, it is pretty big.

"London." Gigi follows with a whistle. "Wow, doll, that's a great opportunity."

"But all I know is here. My family and friends live here."

I have to admit, being away from my parents wouldn't be such a bad thing. I love them, but my mom had a way of smothering me. Probably because I am her only daughter. Dad is even worse. The boys got away with everything. They always did. Not Zoey. She's too fragile, like a baby bird. If they could wrap me up in bubble wrap, I'm sure they would.

Gigi offers me some tea, another herbal concoction. It is supposed to alleviate stress. A splash of vodka could also do that.

She dips the teabag in and out of the boiling water. "There are so many pros to living in London. I spent three years there back in the eighties."

"Apart from the actual job? Like what?"

"Pro: the British men and their sexy accents." She smiles.

"Con: the British men and their bad teeth."

She finally removes the teabag, taking a sip from the small cup. "Pro: all the architecture and things to see."

"Con: it's always cold and rainy. How could you deal with that?"

181

"Pro: the queen."

"That's a con," I complain.

"Pro: You would be away from everything in your life that is toxic. A fresh start, new friends, new life. A chance to reinvent yourself. This could be the beginning of a new life, Zoey. The life you keep telling me you envision yourself living."

There is no other con left on my list. Except one. Drew.

I would be leaving him. Yet my heart and head weren't sure if that was a con. Drew and I . . . whatever happened or is happening, there is no right answer to that riddle.

He is my best friend. One that I would leave behind. I really need to talk to him, and contemplate calling him at work. But the rational side of me knows that this conversation has to be had in person.

I spend the next hour talking to Gigi and looking at her photos from her time in London. It's late, and I decide to call it a night, saying goodbye and thanking her for listening to me.

Exiting Gigi's place, I close the door behind me and stop just shy of my apartment. My body freezes on the spot, and sick to my stomach, I begin to shake, fueled with anger.

Standing in front of me is Callie.

My former best friend.

She gives me a warm smile but all I can see is the image of her on all fours, sucking on my boyfriend's cock. Her jet-black hair scattered all over her back, as Jess pushes her deeper, causing her to gag as he demands she take him all in.

"Zoey," she calls, breaking me from the unpleasant memory.

I'm quick to ignore her presence and anxiously fumble for my keys.

"Please, Zoey. We really need to talk. It's important."

I almost pull a muscle in my neck with how swiftly my body turns to face her. "Talk? What on earth would you have to say to me?"

"Please, Zoey. Can I come inside?" Her big brown eyes beg and plead, targeting the compassionate side of me that I strongly believed lay dormant when it came to her.

She *was* my best friend. The one person I confided in. Yet, the betrayal, it was difficult to ignore. I didn't only lose a boyfriend that day, I lost someone I considered family.

I don't say a word, opening the door as she follows behind me. I throw my keys onto the nightstand, missing it narrowly. Walking towards the living room, I sit on the couch, pretending to sort through my mail, disinterested in her presence.

She sits down on the armchair, but at the edge of the seat, looking extremely uncomfortable. With the corner of my eye, I can barely catch a glimpse of Callie.

Two years had gone by since I last saw her, and boy had she changed. She was never a skinny girl, voluptuous but with curves in the right places. With her South American heritage, she had olive skin that often looked fresh and vibrant. But something is different, her skin pale with traces of yellow. Her weight had dropped dramatically, her collarbone exposed and gaunt. Even the dark circles around her eyes can't hide whatever she is feeling.

But that shouldn't be your concern.

You're no longer her best friend.

I'm not completely devoid of emotion, and as much as I want to reach out to her, a part of me, the burnt and betrayed friend, decides it's best to listen to what she has to say.

"This is hard for me to say . . . to tell you," she says in a somber voice.

I open my big fat mouth with a sarcastic laugh. "That you're sorry?"

Her eyes leave the floor and look directly into mine. "Yes,

of course I'm sorry. It was the dumbest thing I could have done. I don't know what I was thinking," she apologizes, her posture slouched as she nervously bites her fingernails. "I wasn't thinking. Jess had a way of . . ."

I'm waiting, suddenly intrigued as to what possible excuse she could come up with.

"A way of making it seemed like no big deal. That he wasn't going to stay with you, that he wasn't happy and that he was in love with me," she finishes.

Ouch. I didn't expect that. Even though the words came from her, it stung. All the texts he had sent over the past week seemed insignificant and all one big fat lie. I make a mental note to respond to him as soon as she leaves.

"I was young. I didn't know better," she adds.

"It was two years ago, Callie. That's a pretty poor excuse, don't you think?"

She doesn't comment, the both of us sitting in silence. When time passes and neither one of us talk, I'm about to ask her again why she's here.

"I've met someone. In fact, we got married a few months back." She extends her hand, flashing a simple gold band. "His name is Rodrigo. We met on a cruise."

"Congratulations," I say, monotone.

"Thank you." She smiles. "He comes from a big family. Has five sisters and one brother." She twists her hands nervously, the sweat beads forming on her forehead. "He wants to have kids straight away. He wants a big family."

I let out a long sigh, something telling me that I need to move on and forgive. There's more to this story. We may no longer be friends, but I know Callie like the back of my hand. Something is way off. The anxiety is written all over her face.

"He sounds great, Callie. I'm really happy for you."

She nods her head with a small smile that shortly disappears as the darkness overshadows her once-beaming

eyes. "We've been trying for a while and I finally decided to see a specialist. Zoey, I have chlamydia."

An STD? I had heard of it before but wasn't sure what it was. *Fuck! Is she dying?*

"Apparently, I had it for years, but because it went undetected and I had never been tested . . . I'm not fertile anymore."

In a state of shock, I can see how upset Callie is as she tells me her story. I haven't been in love and gotten married with that desire for babies straight away, so I can't imagine what she's going through. But to know you could never have children is such a huge slap in the face.

"I'm so sorry, Callie. That must be hard for you and Rodrigo, considering you both want a big family."

"He left me. Well, he's leaving me. It was his deal-breaker. And I'm not a woman if I can't produce babies," she says faintly.

"You're still a woman and there's other ways to have children. Adoption, for example."

"If it isn't both our blood, then he doesn't consider it family."

He sounded like a selfish prick. So much for better or worse, till death do us part. *I'm not going to say that out loud.* I may be cold sometimes, but kicking someone when they're already down is just mean.

"Zoey, I need to tell you something."

Her voice is low, and barely above a whisper. The sweat bead has trickled down her face, and instantly, she wipes it with her sleeve, embarrassed.

"It's Jess," she begins, then stalls. "Jess infected me. He gave me the STD."

My stomach drops, the bile rising in my throat. I cover my mouth instantly, running to the kitchen and barely making it to the sink as I vomit profusely.

I do all the mental calculations in my head, rewinding back to the time we were together. I wasn't stupid, we always used a condom.

Except that one time . . .

The one time Drew and I stood in the bathroom, fighting for the last one. He had brought a girl home, and Jess was going away for the weekend.

It was rock, paper, scissors that decided our fate, and I lost.

Drew happily walked away with the gold packet while I walked back to my room to a livid Jess.

He begged me to fuck him, bareback, saying that if I loved him, I would do it.

And I did.

CHAPTER *Sixteen*

Drew

IT WAS THE KIND OF night that dragged on. I got stuck with admin work. Boring and mundane, filing out form after form until my hand cramped up. The hospital was quiet, the emergency ward practically empty.

The problem was, it gave me way too much time to think. I didn't mean to get all obsessive, but I had texted Zoey several times to make sure all was good between us.

Despite our shopping trip, something didn't add up. I knew her too well. And on top of this, I tried my very best to be her friend and ignore the sexual feelings towards her.

Take, for example, when we got home from grocery shopping. She escaped to her room and emerged in her ratted tee and these skimpy boxer shorts. I could barely peel my eyes away from her legs. The same legs that had been draped over me a million times on the couch, usually covered in hair during what she called her 'winter season.'

And now, they were calling my name. Begging to be touched, to run my fingertips along them until I reached her . . .

Never mind.

"Hey Drew," Kristy calls, bumping into my arm on purpose.

"Hey." I glance at the chart she is holding. Lucky Kristy got all the good cases tonight.

"Admin work?" she asks, followed by a laugh. "Enough to bore you to death. You look a million miles away."

"Yeah, just . . . argh it's stupid."

"I've got five. Wanna grab a coffee?"

I nod my head and tell the nurse I'll be back in five minutes. We walk along the quiet corridor, taking the elevator down a level. We order our coffees, waiting aside until they're ready.

"So, what's causing Dr. Drew to be all down in the dumps?"

"I wouldn't call it down in the dumps. There's this . . ." I hesitate, extremely uncomfortable talking about my feelings.

"Girl," she finishes. "Has to be a girl making you go cray-cray."

"Yes," I admit. "It's complicated."

"When isn't it complicated?" She smiles. "So what's the deal?"

"She's a friend. Been a really good friend for years. In fact, my best friend."

"Zoey?" she asks, smiling as she says her name.

"How did you know?"

"Because you'd be a fool not to see it. Every time the two of you are in a room there is this spark. It's cute."

"Cute is not what I'm looking for."

"You know what I mean. So what's the problem? You guys already live together. You know each other better than anyone else."

"Let's see. Number one—her ex, Jess. She's still in love with him," I point out, trying to control my anger as I say his name.

"Are you sure about that?"

If yesterday taught me anything, revenge was also code for 'I still love him and want him back.' She still hasn't denied any of my accusations, and her odd behavior only confirmed that. "I think so."

"Okay, that didn't sound very convincing. What else?"

"She doesn't think of me that way. She always refers to me as just her friend, brother, roomie," I complain.

"She could be in denial. Have you spoken to her about it?"

"Yes. No. It's awkward. Why can't I get her out of my head?"

Fuck! Did I just admit that out loud? That I have feelings for my roommate? Feelings . . . like a crush or something. It's not like I'm in love with her.

Am I?

The barista hands us our coffees, and we both stand at the counter with our sachets of sugar. I tap the packet gently, rip it open, then pour it in, simultaneously stirring it.

"Drew. The question is, do you have anything to lose by expressing your feelings?"

"Kristy, I have everything to lose if she doesn't feel the same way."

"And you have everything to gain if she does."

I think long and hard about Kristy's words all night. Yes, I did have everything to gain if she felt the same way. Being in a relationship with her didn't scare me, but if it didn't work out, then what? Could we go back to being friends?

I decide to go home and try to talk to her about it. Maybe I was being stupid. Maybe I was conjuring up all these ridiculous feelings in my head because I knew it was difficult to express. She hadn't directly said she loved Jess and wanted to get back together with him.

Again, this is why I didn't drink. The hangover clouded any rational thoughts.

With my keys in one hand and a bag of bananas in the other, I open the door to a dimly lit apartment. Placing my keys quietly on the nightstand, I walk softly towards the living room, almost tiptoeing, startled to see Zoey sitting on the corner of the couch, hugging her knees. She stares blankly at the TV, which is switched off. She doesn't turn to face me, and her stare is oddly terrifying.

"Zo, what's wrong?"

Silence falls over the room. And not even a twitch, a blink of the eye leaves her gloomy face. I sit down beside her, worried and anxious. "Zoey, talk to me."

Her face turns towards me, slowly, like one of the clowns at an amusement park. She has been crying. Her eyes are bloodshot and puffy, mixed with fear and terror. Using the back of her hand, she wipes her nose. I lean towards the coffee table, pulling out a tissue and handing it to her.

"I fucked up, Drew."

My pulse is racing, paranoid that she is in trouble, that she's been *hurt.* "What did you do?"

"Callie . . ." she whispers.

Her short statements, stretched out in a sedated tone, only cause me to panic further. "Callie what?"

"Callie came over. She can't have kids, Drew. She's lost everything."

Nothing she is saying makes sense. Why would her ex-best friend come over to tell her that she can't have kids, and why would that affect Zoey so much?

"You're not making sense, Zo. Start from the beginning."

I take her hand and place mine over it, gently rubbing her skin to calm her down.

"Callie's husband left her. They couldn't have a family. When they tested to see why, she found out she can't have kids. She has chlamydia," Zoey says in one breath, gulping for air as soon as she's finished.

How awful for Callie. Chlamydia is a nasty disease. If left untreated, it could lead to infertility, which in this case, it has.

"I'm sorry, Zoey. But I don't understand." I shake my head, confused. "You haven't seen or spoken to her since she betrayed you. Why the sudden need to knock on your door and tell you this?"

She continues to weep, discreetly. Wiping her fallen tears with the back of her hand, she wraps her arms around her knees, rocking herself back and forth. "She caught it from Jess."

And the penny drops.

Fuck! He gave her an STD!? The fucking lowlife degenerate. All along I knew this guy was trouble. Screw the drinking problem, this was dead serious. To think of how many women he cheated on Zoey with.

"I'm scared, Drew." Her body begins to shake, and within seconds, the loud sobs leave her heaving chest.

"Why would you be scared, Zo?"

As soon as the question leaves my lips, my heart tumbles to the ground. Trying to rid my head of the emotions, just for one fucking moment, I attempt to put on my medical thinking cap.

If Callie caught the STD from Jess and they were fucking behind Zoey's back, chances were, Zoey could have been infected.

FUCK! Calm. The. Hell. Down. Don't show her you're scared.

"I'm sorry. I don't know why I didn't think of the medical side of things. I'll take you down to the clinic tomorrow. We'll have you tested. It'll be fine, Zo."

"How do you know?" she sputters, momentarily beyond words. "If Callie caught it, why wouldn't I? And what about Noah?"

I grit my teeth, shaking at the core. The blood in my veins is pumping hard, on the verge of combusting. I'm seeing shades of red, crimson, and then I see Jess's smug face staring back at me. My fists curl into a ball, the tightness in my chest constricting my breathing. Do I dare ask the question that is eating me alive? The rage is consuming me, and madly, I unleash. "You used protection, right?"

She's quick to respond in her defense, "Always. But with Jess . . . I loved him."

Savagely, I attack, "Fucking hell, Zoey! Love isn't a reason for going bareback!"

"Oh, don't pull that crap with me, Drew. You of all people have probably slipped up once or twice."

"No, Zoey. That's where you're wrong. I'm always safe. The amount of cases that walk through that hospital door every day is enough for me to protect myself."

"So I'm stupid? I get it."

I soften, and have no clue why. This was no joke or laughing matter. I shouldn't be comforting her. What she needed was tough love.

"Yes, you were stupid," I tell her in a hushed tone. "Look, I'll be right there with you. I know you're scared, but not matter what happens, we'll get through it together."

Shuffling closer to her, my arms cradle her body. She rests her head on my shoulder, sniffling quietly as we sit in silence. The shadows in the dimly lit room taunt us, the wind outside picking up. The weather bureau had predicted a storm earlier. *Perhaps this is it.* The moon is hiding behind the dark clouds, refusing to grace us with its presence.

"Drew," she whispers softly. "I need to confess something."

Here it is. She's about to tell me that she's back with Jess, and that's why she's so upset. Instantly, my body recoils, waiting with barely a breath. I'm mentally preparing my speech; its hateful, ugly, and is full of colorful words that would even offend a sailor.

"This is hard for me to say." Her words linger with renewed wariness. "Extremely hard. And I'm scared it'll change everything between us."

"You're back with Jess," I blurt out violently, removing my arms from the touch of her skin.

"What? NO!" she shuffles away from me, offended and surprised. "The night of the wedding. You were drunk and you made a move on me."

Huh? I made a move on her. I'm notorious for making moves, and usually, they resulted in a nice session of . . .

Did I?

I fucked her.

No way! This is why she's been acting all weird.

I rush to get my words out. "What kind of move?"

"I don't know how to say it."

Even in the dark, her cheeks appear flushed as she fiddles with the loose thread hanging from one of the cushions. The tension in the room is palpable. What I would give to have a bottle of *anything* in my hand right now.

"You . . . you touched me. In places that you hadn't touched me before."

She says the word 'touched' so innocently. Despite what she's about to tell me, I want to hold her in my arms and kiss her. Promise her that everything will be fine, and that no matter what, nothing will change between us.

But like always, my ego intervenes. "Did we . . . did we, you know?"

"No," she's quick to answer. "You wanted to but I um . . . kinda, you know . . . finished. Then, you kissed me on the shoulder and walked away."

She finished? What did that mean . . .

Oh.

Once again, the penny drops. Damn, there's been an awful lot of penny-dropping, and metaphorically, it's sending me broke.

I'm aware that my palms are sweaty, and the room is stifling hot. This explains why she had been acting weird, why I had no clue what happened, and why I found myself shirtless on my bed.

The question remains: What exactly did I do to her?

She finished. So she came. *I made her orgasm?* It had to be more than kissing, more than a grope of a tit. I would have touched her . . . *there.* Fuck! My cock stirs beneath my scrubs. Such an inappropriate time to feel anything but concern over her wellbeing . . . and mine.

Another penny drops. *A big fucking one.* The loud bang as it hits the ground reminds me of why we are here. The purpose to this discussion.

"Okay, shit. You need to tell me everything, Zoey. We're talking about an STD here. It's not only about you and me, my job . . . fuck."

My words choke out, my head spinning out of control. What about my patients? No, it's okay. I've always tested myself regularly and have been clean. Zoey just needs to be honest and tell me exactly what happened between us.

"I . . . I didn't even think about that . . . I don't know how to say this . . ."

"Well fucking say it!" I yell, frustrated and irate. "Do you not understand the severity of the situation?"

"*Don't yell at me,*" she cries in a panic. "I didn't know. And I tried to stop you but you forced yourself on me."

"I forced myself on you?" I struggle with the notion. I had never forced myself on someone. What did that mean? Did I hurt her? God, could this get any worse?

I switch my tone, apologetic for my actions. I wish I could remember what happened. I want to tell her I'm sorry, that I didn't mean to hurt her.

"Zoey, I'm sorry I hurt you. I would never do such a thing

if I was sober. But you need to tell me exactly what happened?"

"You didn't hurt me," she barks, unleashing her frustration. "You want to know what happened? You came at me from behind and rubbed yourself against me, with clothes on. You then grabbed my boobs and slid your way down, playing with my you-know-what, then stuck your finger in my . . ." I can hear the struggle in her voice. *"Behind."*

Her words only added to my confusion. Boobs, you-know-what, behind. My brain is scrambling, trying to solve the mystery puzzle. I'm stunned, shocked beyond belief, that this happened. That my brain has some mechanism in erasing something I desperately want to remember.

"Wow . . . that's um, a lot to take in," I openly admit.

Throwing fuel onto the fire, she adds, "And you said you wanted to stick your cock in my pussy."

The second she says it, my head spins with the image of her bent on all fours. Imagining how good her moans would sound, like music to my ears. The look on her face, mid-orgasm, the delight and sheer pleasure sketched all over her beautiful body.

Thank god I'm sitting down, barely able to contain the desire that riddles me with guilt at this moment. I rest my elbows on my knees with my head buried between.

"Fuck, Zoey. I'm sorry. What does this mean?"

"You tell me, Dr. Drew."

I let out a long breath. "Look, if I touched you, it's safe. Did I . . . you know . . . do anything orally?"

She is quick to shut me down. "No."

"But you said you came?"

"Jesus fucking Christ. I can't believe we are having this conversation," she moans, standing up and walking to the other side of the room, creating some sort of distance between us. "Yes, you touched me and I came. There. I said it. Bottom line was that I should have fought harder to stop it. I forgot it was you and got lost in the moment."

Glancing aside, and unwillingly, small chuckles escape my mouth. This situation is unbelievable, comical to say the least.

"Why are you laughing?" She watches me, grimacing at my relaxed demeanor.

"Because this is the most bizarre thing ever. You're telling me I fingered your *ass* and I have no recollection. Don't you think that's funny?"

"No. I think it's mortifying. And I'm finding it hard to see the funny side of this, considering that I may be in danger of having a sexually transmitted disease," she argues.

I immediately stop laughing. She's right. This wasn't a laughing matter.

Only one thing stayed true; I have to be her friend. Support her no matter what the outcome. Ignore any romantic feelings, any sexual desire towards my best friend, my roomie, who is hurting right now.

"First thing tomorrow morning, we'll go to the clinic. I promise, Zoey, everything will be alright."

"How many sexual partners have you had?"

Dr. Taylor sits on the stool, chart in hand, waiting patiently for Zoey to respond.

She turns my way, flushed with embarrassment, her lips moving as she quietly does the calculation. I want to reach out to her, tell her to breathe and just answer his question truthfully. Instead, I sit uncomfortably on the plastic chair, wishing for this to be over.

Maybe me being here is not such a good idea.

"Um . . ." she pauses. *"Six."*

"And with these six men, how many have you had

unprotected sex with?" Dr. Taylor questions, scribbling down notes as Zoey procrastinates.

She bows her head, refusing to look my way, clutching to her gold pineapple which she brought to the clinic. *Like that is going to protect her.* My gaze purposely focuses on the poster pinned to the wall. It's a picture of the human anatomy, and although I'm extremely familiar with it, I study it again, welcoming any distraction.

"Just the one . . . wait, what about oral sex?"

Oh fuck. Did she have to ask that? My hand is gripping the chair, the sweat in my palms sliding against the plastic. The anxiety begins to eat away at me, my stomach churning, anticipating her response.

"Oral sex as well," Dr. Taylor confirms.

"Like three . . . no, wait, maybe four."

I want to block my ears. Rock myself in the corner wishing I could erase everything I'm hearing. A childish act, but I had not expected to feel this way. Overcome with jealousy, *again.*

Women never made me jealous. A few tried, but failed miserably. I really wasn't *that* guy. I never emotionally attached myself to someone in order to experience that emotion. Does my being jealous mean that I love her? I do, but just as friends.

I don't even know what love is. Sure, I care for her, deeply. I want to protect her, from everything and everyone. And most importantly, I only want her to be happy. For the world to be blessed with her beautiful smile every day.

I only want good things for her.

And whether or not I'm a good thing is yet to be determined.

"Okay, Miss Richards. I need to take a swab. Do you want Mr. Baldwin present?"

I answer yes, the same time she says no.

"No," she warns me sternly. "This is already so embarrassing. It would be nice to leave with some sort of dignity."

I walk out, shutting the door behind me. Outside the room, I sit in the waiting area along with the other patients. It feels like eternity, the clock taunting me with its slow movements. The magazines that casually sit on the table beside me are dated, and seem uninteresting. There is nothing else to do but close my eyes and wait.

Sometime later, she emerges, eyes swollen and bloodshot. Her lips are quivering, and with shaky legs, she walks towards me, almost collapsing in my arms. I jump to my feet, just in time, catching her as she falls.

"It'll be okay, Zo. I swear my life on it," I whisper, kissing the top of her head while she weeps into my chest.

It's a big promise to make.

I have everything to lose, my whole life riding on it.

And that only confirms my feelings for Zoey.

She *is* my whole life.

And without her, I have *nothing.*

CHAPTER *Seventeen*

I *HAVE NEVER BEEN SO terrified in my life.*

Dr. Taylor explained more about the STD, how it's contracted, and if found positive, ways it could be treated. I told him about Callie and how she couldn't have kids. He went on and explained further about the symptoms she would have experienced that led to her being infertile. The thought of not having kids weighs heavily on my mind. Much like Callie's predicament, what man would want me if I couldn't have children? It's the only thing I can think about, now that there's this possibility of it being taken away from me.

I want nothing more than to pee on that stick, see the two blue lines, and feel the pure joy that many women have told me they experienced. I want to attend an ultrasound, see and hear my baby's first heartbeat. *I want that first kick.* To have weird cravings and eat pickles with ice cream at three-o'clock in the morning.

I want to go into labor, scream my lungs out, all the while blaming my husband that it was all his fault, and march on over to the operating room for a quick snip.

I want to be a mother.

And that feeling alone is what hurts the most. That it may never be. Granted, I know there are other options, but this . . . this can't be happening to me. I'm only twenty-nine. I studied in college and finished my degree in architecture. I wasn't a complete airhead. I should have known better.

My head is on the verge of exploding. The clock ticking, counting down to the grand finale. The explosion that sends me cuckoo and shaving my head like Britney Spears.

Jess and his need to fix things between us is an afterthought. Drew and our almost, but not quite, sexual encounter is placed on the 'I'll deal with that later' list.

I just want to grieve the loss of something I never knew how much I wanted till this very moment. When the world feels like it's spinning and I'm completely standing still.

I had stepped out of Dr. Taylor's office feeling lightheaded and woozy, collapsing into Drew's arms. Confiding in Drew about what happened between us was extremely difficult, but absolutely necessary. And the hardest part about this all was that I knew I was hurting him. Communication wasn't our strongest trait at this point, and much like an ostrich, Drew buried his head in the sand, ignoring the obvious problem at hand.

Since my admission of our encounter, things have been awkward between us. You'd be a fool not to see it. Drew tries his best to be supportive, but also uses every opportunity to pick up extra shifts at the hospital with the excuse that they are down in numbers.

He struggles to make eye contact with me at the best of times, and maybe I was reading way too much into this, but even his mannerisms and body language just aren't the same. If I got too close, he would flinch.

It's almost like I make his skin crawl.

And that *cut me like a knife.*

Despite everything going on, my feelings grow stronger

every day. It should have worked in reverse. He isn't Drew, my roomie. He is *Drew,* the guy I have a crush on. Yes, call me juvenile, but love is such a powerful word, and one that I'm not ready to use.

At least, I don't think so.

It's what happens when you've used the term so loosely in the past. In our teens, we threw around the word 'love' like it was a bag of potato chips. It didn't matter who it was, you called out 'love you' to every Tom, Dick, and Harry.

In our twenties, our maturity weighed in. You only used the word 'love' after a mind-blowing orgasm. Sex and love came in some sort of package. The better the sex, the more you *apparently* loved the guy.

And since I'm a week away from being thirty, the theory behind the word 'love' has become clearer. It means so much more than sex.

With life being one giant mess, the optimal thing to do would be to call in sick to work and stay in bed with a block of chocolate and The Cure on repeat.

Instead, I wake up at six am every morning and hit the gym. I go grocery shopping and rid the fridge and pantry of any junk. I even find myself dressing more nicely each day, and I hate to admit that part of me is doing this so Drew will notice. His type of woman is the gym-hitting, healthy-eating, nice-looking type of gal.

I am appalled at myself for even factoring him into my wardrobe decision. It's high school all over again, minus the braces and pom-poms.

Work is my haven. Mia is still on her honeymoon, due to return in a couple of days. We have so many new contracts with a ton of work to complete, which would have been easy to get through if Mr. Becker was around to answer our questions.

On Tuesday afternoon, he turns up out of the blue, and is quick to corner me at my desk.

"So, Zoey, any thoughts on the offer?"

"I've had a busy week. Been unwell. Sorry, I just haven't had a moment . . ." I trail off.

"I understand, Zoey, but this is a once in a lifetime opportunity," he laughs, shaking his head in amusement. "What is there to think about? You're not tied down here."

I could tell him about a number of things. How this is my comfort zone. How my family lives only an hour away, and as much as they drive me crazy, I can't imagine being across the world from them.

I'm worried that the food tastes different. That I won't fit in. That the Brits will judge me by my accent, call me an arrogant yank, maybe even a wanker if I rub them the wrong way.

And how the thought of leaving Drew seems incomprehensible.

But they are all excuses.

And the more I think about it, the more it makes me seem stupid and unappreciative of his offer. I'm a grown woman for Pete's sake. An independent, grown woman who should be able to get on a plane—by herself—and live in a foreign city for the sake of my career. I don't need my mommy to hold my hand, and I shouldn't be staying in a place for a man who can't stand to be near me right now.

"I'll have an answer by the end of the week, Mr. Becker."

He leaves me alone for rest of the day, emailing me links to a few apartments in London that his brother had sent him. Curious, I open the links and browse through the pictures attached. It is completely different, yet exciting. Small, I have to admit, but quaint. The thought of London is growing on me, but could it grow enough that I could leave everything behind?

I welcome the short distraction, until Wednesday morning, when the results come in.

I ask Mr. Becker for the morning off, telling him that I

need to meet with my realtor about renting my place out should I accept the offer to move to London. He is quick to say yes, even suggesting I take the whole day off. I hate lying, but telling your boss you're going to find out if you have an STD or not seems extremely disturbing.

Finding the courage to ask Drew to come with me to Dr. Taylor's office had been difficult to say the least. The tension between us only grew, given that we were both on edge, waiting for the results. I needed him in case things went wrong. The thought alone made my stomach churn, and several times over the past couple of days, I found myself hyperventilating, driven by panic attacks. I didn't have the guts to tell him, worried that he would send me to the hospital for a check-up. The last thing I needed was to be in the hospital again.

Dr. Taylor is quick to read out my results; I tested negative for any STDs. Accompanied with the results is a lecture on safe sex. Not only does Dr. Taylor give me multiple pamphlets on how to practice safe sex, he also gives me a handful of condoms. With Drew in the room, my embarrassment is taken to a whole new level. Vaginal, oral, anal, you name it—Dr. Taylor went on and on. I don't expect to be sexually active with a man anytime soon, but then again, my mind is only thinking about one person.

The person squirming uncomfortably beside me.

Then, it finally hits me. *This nightmare is over.*

My body had instantly breathed a sigh of relief when he gave me the all clear, but soon followed with heavy, drawn-out sobs. Dr. Taylor leaves the room, allowing us a moment of privacy.

"How could I be so stupid?" I whimper, grabbing a tissue from the box sitting beside me, rambling utter nonsense. "I had the safe-sex talk in school. They even did the whole banana and condom thing. Sure, I thought it was hilarious, and maybe my witty jokes which were a hoot in class distracted me from actually paying attention. I mean, that bubble thing you have to do . . . is that necessary? And what happens if you don't? Do the sperm free themselves or what?"

Drew rubs my thigh, letting out a breath. "We've all had our moments, Zo. This was just a stupid mistake." He pauses, then continues. "Just . . . just next time listen to the doctor and be safe."

"There's no next time," I blurt out.

He shakes his head, trying to rid the involuntary smile gracing his lips. "C'mon, you're not joining the nunnery."

"Why not? Sex only leads to trouble. What a mess this has been. Plus, I read an article that nunnery enrolments are low. They predicted by the time two thousand and forty rolls around, we could be nunless."

"That's absurd. I don't know why or how you end up reading articles like that. And besides, if you do become a nun, some guy out there will be missing out on something good," he says with a low voice, removing his hand from my thigh.

I purse my lips, unsure of where to go from here. I swiftly change the subject, wanting to leave this sterile environment that makes my skin crawl. "Can we get out of here? Could we maybe grab a bite to eat for lunch? I think we need to talk, Drew."

"I've . . . um . . . actually promised my dad I would visit for a couple of days since the hospital allowed me to use some leave."

"Oh," I say, a little hurt. "Okay, so you'll be back when?"

"Hmm . . . Friday, I guess."

"Are you still coming out for my birthday?"

"Sure." He smiles unconvincingly before walking out the room and saying goodbye.

The apartment is lonely without Drew. True to his word,

he left that day with his bag packed for his dad's. I wanted to tell him to stay, to be with me. I wanted to open up about my feelings towards him. Be honest about how I felt that night when he touched me, and tell him how I'm sick of walking on eggshells when we are in the same room.

But that had seemed so selfish, and my heart didn't want to hurt him anymore.

The one thing I had learned throughout this was my ability to hurt the ones I love. I don't want to be that person. I am hell bent on changing my life and finally making grown-up decisions.

Drew's absence has created more time for me to think, and when Zoey Richards thinks, no good can come from it. I busy myself with cleaning the apartment, every single inch of it. Even getting down on my hands and knees to scrub the orange stain I left on the hallway rug when I was on a bender one night and accidentally spilled a jar of Tang on it. The powder was dry and could have easily been vacuumed had my tears not fallen on the same spot. The rare jar of Tang was a gift from Drew. I had gone on and on about how much I loved the stuff when I was growing up. One day, he surprised me with it. I was shocked, ecstatic, and extremely thankful for the thoughtful gesture.

And let's rewind back to why I was on a bender on a Wednesday night. *Jess.* He drank every night, afternoon, and morning, and somehow I was dubbed the party pooper for not joining him. The more I thought about him, the easier it became to let go.

He didn't care about my feelings. He wasn't the one constantly nagging me to continue studying to further my career, nor was he the one circling job opportunities in the paper and leaving sticky notes with motivational quotes on them next to the pot of coffee some mornings.

Draining my bank account was his priority, making me pay anytime we went anywhere. He didn't secretly pay our electricity bill and not tell me about it, saying that it got lost in the mail.

And he didn't buy me a jar of Tang to cheer me up.

Drew. All Drew. It became more and more clear that all along, Drew looked out for me. He had my back.

I'm desperate to call him, yet my insecurity is getting the better of me. He did all those things for me as a good friend. Not as someone interested in being my boyfriend.

On Wednesday night, he sends me a text. I almost fall off the couch when I see his name on the screen, beyond excited and nervous.

Don't forget to water the plants.

The text alone is boring and uneventful. Usually he would add something fun, just to rile me up. I couldn't blame him. I had ruined things between us. Lost that spark or whatever it was that made our relationship special.

We have plants?

Relax, control freak. Your precious plants are still GREEN.

He never responds. On Thursday night, he sends me another uneventful text.

It's bin night. Don't forget to take out the trash.

Again, I respond to him, trying to goad some sort of reaction.

Does that include the hussy that's been banging on our door every night asking for you?

I manage to laugh at my own joke, lying in bed, thinking that if a hussy was banging on our door, I would get all kung-fu on her ass. *Cue the jealousy, Zoey.* I wait for his response, picking up my Kindle and trying to lose myself in a stepbrother romance that was the latest craze in the book world. I find it hard to get into, given that every few seconds, my eyes glance towards the screen of my cell. Then, I hear a bubble sound and drop the Kindle, picking up my cell, waiting in anticipation.

Funny.

That's it? Funny? I'm starting to get annoyed and I type fast, knowing his phone would be in close proximity to him.

> What are you up to? I'm reading a stepbrother romance. Do you think it's weird that the stepbrother and stepsister do it in the house and the parents have no clue? Sure, you can block the noise, but what about the smell?

The bubble teases me again, and unwillingly, I find my legs twitching, waiting impatiently for him to respond.

> Sex doesn't have a smell, Zoey.

And he calls himself a doctor. . . .

I type quickly.

> Yes, it does. It's a combination of sweat, heat, and something I can't put my finger on.

He quickly responds.

> Cum?

I immediately blush with him using that word. Why, I have no idea. My palms begin to sweat, and suddenly the room is stifling hot.

Removing my shirt, I lie in bed wearing only my tank and shorts.

> Uh . . . sure?

> I don't know but your room reeks of it.

A witty response that is sure to fire him up.

> Stay out of my room, Zoey.

I can tell he's trying his best not to encourage my immature behavior, but I have to admit, this is fun. Just like in high school when you would pass notes in class, hoping it would make it to the back of the room and into the hands of your crush.

Mine made it halfway, into the hands of Cindy Matthews.

Word on the street is that she is now a lesbian. I often wonder if it had anything to do with my note.

I type quickly, then hit send.

> Sorry, I went in earlier when I was short on cash for the pizza guy.

I put the cell down for a moment, rushing to the bathroom. Since I adopted healthy eating habits two days ago, I've started drinking two liters of water a day. According to online articles, that's how much water your body needs to stay hydrated. In turn, I need to pee every god damn minute. *A glimpse into life as an old lady with a bladder problem.*

Feeling relieved, I wander back to my room and see his response.

> Stay out of my room, Zoey!

I quickly type, noticing my battery is down to one percent. I can make it . . . live on the edge! Drew hated it when he would see my battery so low. He started panicking at twenty percent, searching for a charger like he only had seconds to live.

> Kidding! I haven't had pizza since last week. You'd be proud of me, I bought a pineapple instead. Bringing fortune and healthy eating into the house.

A smiley face appears on my screen, accompanied by his message.

> Good girl. I'll be back tomorrow for your birthday.

> Stay out of my room!

Only one more day till he's back. I'd be glad to have him back home, despite the awkwardness between us.

> I will, drama queen. See you tomorrow, roomie.

I assume it's the end of our conversation and am surprised to hear my cell chime again.

> And Zoey . . .

The bubble appears . . . *And Zoey what?* I'm sitting on the edge of my bed, tapping my feet nervously on the ground. Staring at the screen, watching the bubble do its thing as if he is writing some *long* message. Dear god, hurry up! Then, because the iPhone gods want to punish me, my screen goes completely black.

Battery dead.

Noooooooo!

Serves me right for being an adrenaline junkie. I race over to my desk, plugging it in. The few minutes it takes to charge and power up feels like a lifetime. Worse yet, I need to pee again. I don't, and instead, cross my legs and skip on the spot, trying to ignore the urge.

When the screen turns on, I enter my passcode at record speed and open my messages. Staring at the box, there it is, the long message I assumed he would send.

> I miss you.

Oh.

He misses me. It's the perfect opportunity to tell him that I miss him, yet I just don't know how. I want to say so much more than that. Gosh, I want to pour my heart out to him and tell him how the butterflies in my stomach are all because of him.

But I don't.

I grab my iPod and walk across the hall and into his room. The second I enter, I only smell *Drew*. It feels right, and it feels like home. His room, as usual, is neat and tidy. His bed is made, the navy-blue cover tucked into the sides of the bed. The pillows are positioned perfectly, just like in a hotel room.

I lie down on his bed and turn the iPod on, playing "All Through the Night" by Cyndi Lauper, realizing that Drew and I have a past. One that could never be erased. We've gone through so much, and leaned on each other more times than I could count. Yet everything we experienced was as *friends.* Taking the next step would be huge—that's if he wants to do that.

There is only one thing I am sure of: Despite everything going on, I want to go to London. To finally do something for myself and be the person I know I can be.

And if Drew has any feelings for me, he will understand and encourage me to go.

Long distance—we could make it work.

The next morning, I march straight into Mr. Becker's office.

"I've decided to take you up on your offer. I'm going to London," I tell him.

With a satisfied smile, he stands up, shaking my hand.

"Smart move, Zoey. It's only up from here. I'll get tickets booked. A week from today, you'll be in London."

Wow. I did it! A week from today, I'll be saying hi to the queen.

I can't wait to tell Drew; the look on his face will be priceless. I know he will be proud of me, taking this massive leap. And if he'll take it with me, it could be even sweeter.

We could chat on the phone every day, use Skype, and maybe once a month he could fly over or I could fly back for a couple of days. We could visit Spain and attend La Tomatina, something we both dreamed about doing after we watched a documentary on it. Drink beer at Oktoberfest, then get drunk and into a fight, Chevy-Chase style. We could fly to Paris, eat croissants, and visit the Eiffel tower.

It could be so romantic.

Me and him, long-distance lovers.

I have it all planned out, and as soon as Drew comes back home, the first thing I will do is tell him the good news.

Drew

"**H**AND ME THE WRENCH, SON."

I pass the wrench to my dad, sliding it underneath the car. The engine on Betty is way worse than I had originally anticipated, my dad quick to berate me for letting her run this poor for so long.

After the drama that unfolded last week, spending the days at dad's property gives me the quiet time I need. Being outside the city, staring at nothing but green acres, is very therapeutic. My head needs clearing because so much of what happened last week frightened me. *A rollercoaster of emotions.*

At first, we went from Zoey playing coy with me after the wedding. Then, the whole Jess, Callie, can't even get *into* how angry that made me feel. A fucking nightmare.

And, of course, Zoey dropping that massive bombshell. *We had a moment.* A moment that could have changed everything between us, if I hadn't been blind drunk. I'm so desperate to remember what happened, anything at all. The slightest touch, the sounds her body made . . .

The worst moment of them all is the peak of the rollercoaster, just before you're about to go down. Playing the waiting game. Climbing slowly, your whole body filled with fear and anxiety, seeing the top and waiting for the unknown.

When my mother passed away, I was too young to understand the enormity of the situation. Studying for my medical exams, another terrifying moment. It was a make-or-break situation. Then, the first time I stepped foot in the ER. My heart was beating a million miles a minute and I was certain that I would choke on the spot and forget everything I had learned.

But waiting for Zoey's results . . .

It almost *killed* me.

When the results finally came through, I breathed a sigh of relief that she was okay, but it was accompanied with much anger. How could she be so careless? Everyone knew you didn't go bareback. Not unless you were in a long-term relationship. In hindsight, they were. The more I got to thinking, the more I realized, it wasn't really her fault. She was in love; she had been with the guy for well over a year. She was faithful and assumed he was too, given the length of their relationship. Although it seemed selfish to blame her, I could only think about myself. Self-absorbed and jealous that Zoey was intimate with a man I loathed.

Dad slides himself from underneath the car and moves onto the engine bay. I hand him a beer, something cold to quench his thirst.

"So how's my girl, Zoey, doing?" Dad asks, stopping for a moment to sip on his beer.

Dad loves Zoey. She had a way of making him laugh and he always tells her that she's the daughter he never had. It fed her ego. Occasionally she would throw jokes at me, that she would make the perfect daughter-in-law, and if neither one of us was married by the time we hit forty, we should consider it. Empty promises fueled by alcohol. No surprise that when I would remind her of that the following morning, mid-hangover, she had no recollection.

"Fine. The same, I guess."

Placing his bottle down, he grabs the dirty rag that's hanging from his waist and opens the radiator. "What's she doing these days?

"Uh, the same. She's still working at that architecture firm. She'll probably be there forever."

Dad lifts his head, glancing my way with a raised eyebrow. "Is she seeing anyone?"

"Not that I'm aware of. But who knows with her," I respond matter-of-factly.

He doesn't ask any more questions, shifting the topic to Betty, cars being his favorite topic of conversation.

"You've really let her go, son."

"I know," I admit. "I was thinking of buying a new car anyway. Something modern. Was hoping we could look at something?"

He pulls himself out of the hood. "Since when do you want something modern?"

"The chicks dig it, Dad."

I loved Betty. She was a classic and irreplaceable in my eyes. But she was old, and hard to get around in sometimes. She's very temperamental, and occasionally she would break down and be more of a headache than she's worth.

And every part of me hates saying this, because I wasn't someone who fell head over heels for a girl and followed them like a sick puppy dog, but part of the new car idea was because Zoey loved them. She forever complained about Betty, and maybe she would be happy that I finally moved forward.

"If that's what you want, son. When do you want to go?"

"How about this afternoon?" I say, eager to start looking.

We head out in the afternoon to a local dealership that sold almost-new cars. The second I see the sexy black beast in the car lot, I know she's the one. Only a year old, with low mileage and paint in mint condition. As an added bonus, it has a sunroof and decent wheels.

"Is this your new girl?" Dad asks, lifting the hood and checking the engine.

"I think she is." I grin, sliding my hands across the door panel and admiring the new metallic paint.

Dad utilizes his negotiation skills and manages to knock down the price. With the paperwork signed, the dealer tells us the car will be ready to pick up tomorrow.

"So what are you going to do with Betty now?" Dad questions on the ride home.

"If you don't mind, I'll leave her at your place. Time to make changes in my life."

The road home is bumpy; Dad's truck wasn't the most comfortable vehicle to sit in. We take a turn into the local diner, stopping for a bite to eat.

"I think you're doing alright, kid. If it ain't broke, don't fix it."

"I'm trying, Dad. It's just hard."

"Life ain't easy, son. And if it's easy, then maybe you ain't trying hard enough for what you want."

Life *was* complicated. Zoey complicated my life. We had been texting, but like always, she had reverted back to normal as if nothing between us had happened. I struggled with not responding to her and unleashing my thoughts. Instead, I was cordial and polite in my responses.

But then, I caved.

I told her I *missed* her.

Because I did. I just fucking missed her.

I just didn't know how to articulate my thoughts, tell her that I have these feelings towards her without ruining our relationship.

On Friday I wake up refreshed and with a clearer headspace. With my bags packed, we drive into town and

pick up my new car. I was never a fan of new-car smell and I'm still not. Zoey reckons they should capture new-car smell in a can and make it an air freshener.

To be honest, the smell is kind of nauseating.

I say goodbye to Dad, and with the keys to my new car in hand, I'm ready to hit the open road.

That plan is shot down, heavy roadworks delaying the drive home. Thanks to my new sound system, I've hooked up the Bluetooth, and I scroll through my phone, settling on some Ed Sheeran to ease the annoying drive back. By five pm, I am still an hour out of the city. I text Zoey saying I will be late, and that I'll meet her at the amusement park. I still think it's an odd choice for a birthday party, given that she is turning thirty, not thirteen.

The traffic moves at a snail's pace, cutting short the time I need to make a pit stop to pick up Zoey's present. I had put a lot of thought into her gift, yet the more I thought about it, the more uncertain I became. *What if she didn't like it?*

The second I lay eyes on it, I smile. It's her . . . *all her.*

Thanking the shop assistant, I grab the paper bag and rush back to the car. The traffic has eased, making the trip short.

I turn into the parking lot and make my way to the entrance. The amusement park is busy, families and kids scurrying around trying to line up on all the popular rides. The screams from the rollercoaster can be heard, combined with music coming from the merry-go-round. Everywhere I look, there are booths. Some with games, some selling food. *All junk food.*

Gigi is the first person I see, walking away from one of the booths, busily eating some cotton candy. Dressed in her usual attire, she's wearing a long purple dress and draped in different colored beads.

"Drew," she calls, walking towards where I stand.

I give her a quick hug, scowling at her choice of food.

"You're really getting into that, Gigi."

"To be a kid again," she beams. "I've also eaten a corndog and a candy apple. Very naughty, I know."

I laugh, placing my arm around her in a friendly gesture. "You only live once, right?"

"Maybe twice. Reincarnation is making a comeback," she notes with dark amusement. "How was your trip to your dad's?"

"Good," I say. Then I add, "Great. Nice to spend time with him."

She links her arm into mine, guiding me towards the bumper cars. There's a very long line, many whiny kids impatiently crying as they await their turn. Their frustrated parents are on the verge of nervous breakdowns.

"And did you think about your relationship with Zoey?"

Gigi knew me too well. She'd been there for me more times than I could count. Zoey is a great friend, but sometimes I needed wisdom. An old soul to vent my frustrations to, especially with all the emotional baggage that came along with working at the hospital.

I contemplate telling her how I feel, but we are interrupted as hands cover my eyes.

"Guess who?"

I can smell the tips of her fingers. They smell like *pineapple.*

A smile spreads across my face. I place my hands over hers, and as our skin touches, it electrifies every inch of my body. This wonderful, electrifying jolt that takes my senses to a place it's never been, yet at the same time, calms my anxious nerves.

The breath I'm holding in gently releases. Removing her hands off my eyes, I turn around slowly until her eyes meet mine.

And there she is, standing before me, her beauty killing

my soul.

There's this light shining all around her, radiant and sweeping me up as I stare, unable to turn away.

I'm seeing Zoey.

Not my roomie, not only my best friend . . . but Zoey. *This beautiful woman.*

Despite her braids and what appears to be a new Rainbow Brite shirt, this beautiful woman is staring back at me. Her cheekbones are covered with a tint of pink, and her lips appear luscious and soft. My focus on her lips shifts, the effortless grin on her face causing this unknown feeling inside my stomach. Like a million bees let loose, or what Zoey often referred to as butterflies.

So this is it, this oddly nauseating feeling mixed with excitement.

"Glad you could make it, roomie." Zoey punches my arm softly, grinning from ear to ear.

"Wouldn't miss your birthday for the world, kiddo."

"Kiddo?" she grimaces.

"Not a fan?"

"I'm thirty. It's so old."

"Age ain't nothing but a number, baby." I gently tug on her braid, teasing her. "If it makes you feel any better, you look eighteen."

"Would an eighteen-year-old have this?" She glances back and forth, then pulls a flask out of her jacket. "I got some juice."

"The last time I had some juice, I did things that um . . ." I trail off.

"You stuck your finger in my ass?"

"Zoey!" The kids beside us stare at my outburst. "So, haunted house. Terrifying, right?"

The kids continue to rudely stare. I yank Zoey's arm and pull her closer to me. "Curb the ass-talk till we're alone,

Richards."

"I may have drunk some juice already."

"Oh . . . you think?" I answer back sarcastically.

Gigi and Mia join us, handing Zoey a bunch of tickets. I pull Mia aside, wanting to apologize for what happened at the wedding.

"I'm sorry, Mia. It was really immature of me."

She folds her arms, keeping her distance, then follows through with a smile. Am I missing something here? Women confused me. I could never predict their next move.

"It was immature of you, but I get it. It's easy to get jealous when the person you love is the apple of somebody else's eye. On our honeymoon, one of the old maids kept batting her eyelashes at Troy. I didn't think I would be so jealous, but turns out I can be."

Brushing it off, not wanting to admit any truth to what she said, "It's not like that."

"Then tell me what it's like, Drew." She laughs. "It's so frustrating watching the both of you. It's like watching a trapeze; both of you are swinging but no one will let go. It's about being in sync and trusting the other person."

I turn my head to the left where a trapeze is set up with a big net beneath it. A couple are swinging, and failing miserably at letting go.

"Did you come up with that because you're staring at that couple trying to do it?"

"Yes . . . no. It all makes sense now," she says to herself.

"That's nice. Because what you're saying makes no sense to me."

She shakes her head, breaking her sudden daze, and grins. "It'll all work out. Plus, London is so romantic. Some of the greatest love stories began there."

"Mia, what does London have to do with Zoey and me?"

"Uh hello, because Zoey's moving there in the next week

for wo—" She pauses, her face pulling back in shock. "She hasn't told you."

"Told me what?" I grit.

"I thought she told you! Don't rat me out, Drew . . . I had no idea."

"She's moving to London?"

"Mr. Becker offered her a role with his brother's company. It'll be a step up from what she's doing, a promotion really, plus they're footing the bill for her apartment and moving expenses. She'd be silly not to take it . . ."

Mia's voice fades out and my head turns to where Zoey is standing with Gigi. She's clutching over, laughing along with Gigi. Her annoying yet cute braids in the way so that I cannot see her face. When she composes herself, she's all smiles, and the vibrancy in her eyes displays her happiness.

Yet on the inside, my anger is slowly bubbling. *How could she not tell me?* Pick up the phone and give me a call. Our relationship must mean more to me than it does to her. I told her I missed her and she didn't even fucking respond!

In a daze, filled with animosity, I walk back towards her.

"Oh, there you are. Let's go." She smiles.

The man takes our tickets and we walk towards the painted black door. "Enjoy," he says before the doors swing open and all we can hear is moaning.

"I can do this," Zoey breathes. "I won't crap my pants, I won't crap my pants," she chants repeatedly.

She links her arm into mine and I try my best to contain my thoughts until we got home, not wanting to cause a scene here and ruin her birthday. *I'm biting my tongue . . . barely.*

A loud sound startles us, followed by a masked man jumping in front of our path. Zoey screams, throwing herself at me as I almost topple over.

The masked man moves, and with Zoey's face buried deep into my chest, I pull her along, not wanting to delay the people behind us. We turn the corner into a small hallway with bloodied walls. A steam machine blows over, blurring our vision. The sound of a witch laughing echoes in the room, and just before the door opens, a hand lingers over our shoulders, causing Zoey to scream once again in my ear.

"I'm moving to London."

"What?" I can barely hear, the haunting screams damaging my eardrums.

"I'm moving to London. Next week. For work. Mr. Becker offered me a position and it was too good to pass up."

"You're moving to London?"

I move away from where she is standing. Even though Mia had told me, hearing it from Zoey adds a whole new meaning. Zoey had a tendency to not follow through with plans, but something tells me this time is different.

"Aren't you happy for me? You keep telling me to live my life and . . ."

"Did you even think about how I would feel in this? And you spring this on me now? Here?" I shoot back, struggling to compose myself.

"But I thought . . ."

"You don't think!" I yell back. "It's all about you!"

Taken aback, she ignores the ghoulish man walking towards her. "Who else would it be about?" she says, puzzled.

I look into her eyes and I know she can read my thoughts. Her face changes, almost a look of pity, then she reaches out her hand to touch my arm and I instantly recoil. Pulling back, not wanting her to feel sorry for me because I'm the fucking dick that has feelings for her but she doesn't feel the same way.

"Don't," I growl.

"Drew. I think we need to talk."

I turn around quickly, desperate to get out of here. "We're done talking."

Even in the darkness, I find my way, ignoring the masked men with chainsaws, zombies attacking, and even the eerie-looking clown at the end. The exit is illuminated, and easily, I am outside amongst the busy crowds of people.

Gigi and Mia are standing at the game-stand, shoving ping pong balls into the clowns' mouths. Zoey continues to call my name, but I ignore her, walking fast towards the exit of the amusement park.

Fumbling for my keys, I hit the electronic button until the alarm sounds and the lights flicker on the car. She's on my tail, out of breath.

"Whose car is this?" she strains, holding her side as she catches her breath.

"Does it matter?"

"It's yours? But you hate cars like this. This isn't you."

I ignore her comment, opening the door. "Drew. Will you *fucking* turn around and talk to me?"

I stop, turn around, glowering while she watches me with doleful eyes. "What do you want to talk about, Zoey?"

"Oh, I don't know. How about the fact that you appear to be angry at me? That you're running away from me."

"I'm running away?" I laugh. "You're the one moving to the other side of the world."

"For work," she says, exasperated. "For months, all I heard from you was how pathetic I was. How I've let myself go. I'm doing this for me. Why can't you see that?"

Not once did I call her pathetic. Yes, she's let herself go, but she doesn't need to go to London to find herself. The idea alone is preposterous.

"All you're doing is running away. Like you always fucking do. I'm done, Zoey."

"You're done?" she hisses, crossing her arms as she takes a step back. "With what?"

"Done with all the drama you seem to bring along with

you. I can't continue feeling this way about you," I throw back at her, admitting the truth.

"What way, Drew? We're roomies," she chokes, turning away and refusing to make eye contact with me.

"What's the point anymore?" I put my hand in my pocket and pull out the small yellow box. "Here you go. Happy birthday, Zoey."

I should turn away, get in the car, and drive off at record speed. Instead, I wait, almost holding my breath as she carefully opens the box and pulls out the gold chain with the pineapple pendant hanging.

With downcast eyes and quivering lips, she remains quiet while removing the chain from the box.

"Drew," she murmurs. "It's . . . it's *perfect.*"

She closes her eyes, clutching the necklace and holding it close to her heart.

And then it clicks. It would have been perfect.

If she wasn't moving to London.

"I have to go," I stammer, clutching the door handle and motioning for her to back away.

"Let me come with you. I'll just tell Gigi and Mia . . ."

"No," I interrupt. "I need to be alone."

She doesn't say a word, and backs off. Placing my keys in the ignition, the engine roars. I could easily turn it off, walk towards her, and tell her I'm sorry.

But everything about tonight just hurts. Real fucking bad.

I drive straight to the apartment and throw some stuff into my bag. I don't want to go back to Dad's, but have nowhere else to go. I pull out my cell and dial Kristy's number, asking her if I can crash at her place for a couple of days. It works out perfect since she's heading out of town till the end of the week, so I will have the place to myself.

For once, Zoey doesn't bother me. Not a single text or call to ask where I am or how I am. I don't blame her. I made

myself pretty clear.

I'm done.

For the next few days, work keeps me occupied, and by Tuesday, I make my way back home, facing the inevitable.

Opening the door, it dawns on me that soon I will open this door to an empty apartment. That no one will greet me, hopelessly throw their keys onto the nightstand, and miss every time, only to leave them sitting on the floor.

"You're here." She offers a faint smile, returning her focus back to the television. The movie playing is *Dirty Dancing*—her favorite.

On the coffee table sits a bag of low-fat chips and a can of Diet Coke. I want to laugh, and normally, I would. I'd tell her that when it says low fat, it means it still contains fat.

Chips and Diet Coke are still junk food.

"I'm here." It's all I manage to say.

"Can we please talk, Drew? I gave you some time but I really need to talk to you."

I sit on the sofa, purposely keeping my distance. She pauses the movie, right before Johnny teaches Baby to dance in the studio. *My God . . . I have seen this movie way too many times. Someone please hand me my balls back.*

"I wanted to tell you. I really did," she explains. "But Mr. Becker only sprung it on me a couple of weeks back and so much has been going on."

She shifts around uncomfortably, twitching as she talks fast. "It's not an excuse. I just want you to understand that I didn't mean to spring it on you. I only accepted his offer last week and things between you and I have been so difficult lately. I just wanted you to be proud of me for taking the offer."

"I am proud of you . . ." I soften.

"It doesn't feel like it. You're angry with me. Your eyes keep doing that whirly thing like a cyclone about to hit."

"What do you expect?" I try not to lash out, keeping my tone low. "What about rent?"

I don't care about rent. I have nothing to say except that I don't want her to leave, and all for my own selfish reasons.

"I've already paid my share for three months. I figured that should cover you until you find a new roommate."

"And what about all your stuff? And your family?"

What about me . . . that's what I wanted to say.

"I'm only taking a few things, the rest I've already gotten rid of or packed up and sent to Mom and Dad's. As for my parents, they're sad I'm going but promise to visit."

"And you think you'll get on that plane on your own. With all the plane disappearances of late?"

The nerves are etched all over her face. Shifting her focus towards the ceiling, her eyes begin to fill with tears. I'm a jerk. I knew how much flying terrified her, yet I had to open my big fat mouth and question her ability to conquer her fears.

"I have no choice, Drew. I need to do this. For me."

"For you . . . right."

"Will you be okay? Maybe you could come visit? We could make a schedule of some sort. Look . . ." She fidgets nervously with her cell, then shows me some scheduling travel app. "The traveler's guide highly recommended it. It could be so much fun. You and I in a foreign city."

I grab the remote from where it sits beside her and give her a small smile. "I'll be fine. And I'm sure you don't need me to cramp your style."

"You wouldn't be cramping my style . . ." she mentions softly. "In fact, I would—"

I interrupt her. "How about we just enjoy the rest of the movie? You're leaving tomorrow, right?"

"Yes." Her voice croaks while staring back at me with wide eyes. She's struggling not to blink or show any more

emotions in front of me. I desperately want to reach out, hold her in my arms, and tell her everything will be okay. But my pride won't allow it.

I don't want to talk about it anymore, and welcome the distraction of turning the movie back on. The scene restarts as Johnny and Baby dance to "Hungry Eyes." The entire time I sit here, I'm becoming more miserable as each minute passes. There's this tight feeling in my chest, constricting my airways and interrupting my steady breathing. My palms are sweaty, and all of a sudden, I'm struck down with an awful headache.

I stretch my neck to the side, trying to release the tension. "I'm heading to bed. You have an early flight, right?"

"Crack-of-dawn early," she says plainly.

"Goodnight, Zoey."

I walk away until she stops me, wrapping her arms from behind and hugging me *really* tight. I don't want to pull away, and any resistance that I feel, I let go of, if only for this moment.

We stand there, quietly, without saying a word, until she finally pulls away and walks directly to her room, shutting the door behind her.

I lie awake, and with my hands resting behind my head, I think about her being in the next room. How for all these years she was just next door. Behind these thin walls. Never once did I think about us not being roomies. Even when she was with Jess, I always had this feeling that she wasn't ready to move out with him. I never worried about it and took for granted all the times we shared, the fun we had, and even the petty arguments that would arise every so often.

It's too soon . . . this isn't meant to happen yet.

The door to my bedroom opens slowly, making a slight creak. The light from the hallway filters through the crack, enough for me to see Zoey tiptoe into my room. The bed moves to one side, and her body, warm and delicate, lies beside mine.

"Drew," she whispers, placing her hand on my chest.

Gently, I place my finger on her lips, turning to the side to face her.

"Shh," I hush.

The heat between our bodies lingers, my heart beating erratically as my finger traces the tips of her shoulders. Silence falls over the room, and if I listen carefully, I can hear her beats mirror mine.

Rapid, accelerated beats. Echoing like the sound of a drum.

She whispers my name again, almost chanting it in tune with her breathing. "Tonight, let me have tonight. I don't want to ask you for anything more."

One night. That's all she wants. A night to remember. An unforgettable moment that will stay with her forever and follow her to London.

Or maybe, a night to make her stay here with me.

There's so many words left, so much more that needs to be said, but for now, our words lie here mute.

I tilt my head and bend just enough that my lips graze hers. They're soft and taste like Fanta. Our lips move in sync with each other, holding back slightly, while our bodies move closer until they are touching.

With her tits pressed against my chest, I distract myself from my raging hard-on that she's giving me from a simple kiss. *A kiss with no tongue.*

My hand slides towards her back, sneaking in underneath her tank, gliding along her delicate skin. I can feel the heat bouncing off her. It follows with goosebumps as my hands move further up until I'm cupping the back of her neck. It allows me to move her closer and angle her head so our mouths are positioned perfectly, enabling me to slide my tongue inside, gently and without too much force.

Her soft moans melt within our kiss, and as her lips press harder, her body shifts as she climbs on top and straddles me.

Fuck. Don't lose control now. It's too early.

Pulling away, allowing the air to flow between us, she sits up and watches me. In the darkness, with barely any light, I can still see her. All of her. Inside and out.

I concentrate on her face, the lust, desire, and bite of the lip that's driving me insane. Does she know what she's doing to me? Just this one stare, how animalistic and dangerous this could get. All sense of control is disabled; I'm drowning without a life jacket to save me.

Her hands move to the bottom of her tank as she slides it up and pulls it over her head.

She's wearing no bra.

Fuck . . . she's wearing no bra.

I'm mesmerized by the sight of her tits. They're so full, delicately round, and perky. My mouth is gravitating towards them, and the second my lips touch her erect nipples, she moans out loud, burying them in my face.

I want to lose myself in them, rubbing my cock against her with more force, the pleasure consuming all of me. How could this sexy woman be living in the room next door to me for four years? To think of the amount of times I could have taken her, buried myself deep inside her while we both screamed in delight.

My hands lace around her back, moving her with ease and positioning myself on top of her body. Pinned to my bed, I don't hold back, pulling her shorts down until she's bare underneath me.

She's a fucking goddess; I want to worship every inch of her, but my body has different ideas. It wants to take her, here and now. No more holding back, ignoring the foreplay. I need her whole. I'm fucking selfish, I know. I want to *fuck* her.

The frenzy within me doesn't allow her time to get comfortable, finding its way inside her till I'm all in and she moans loudly, arching her back into the mattress.

She murmurs my name, and I follow her lead. Thrusting harder, losing myself completely to her whims. Biting my lip hard, I'm struggling to hold back, wanting her to reach breaking point until she can no longer take it, exploding all over me.

"Drew, wait." She stops me, catching her breath. "We need protection."

I had completely forgotten. *I've never forgotten in my life.* After the lecture I gave her, it would be hypocritical of me to continue on bareback.

But she feels like fucking heaven. Soft, wet, and tight. *So nice and fucking tight.*

I lean over to my nightstand, opening the draw and grabbing a spare condom I had lying around. Removing myself from inside her, I quickly put it on and resume position, not wanting any more time to pass. Scared that she will change her mind at any moment.

This time, I'm going in guns blazing. Giving my body full control to do whatever it pleases. Her moans become louder, sweet beautiful music to my ears as I bury myself deeper inside. Picking up the speed, I listen to her body, from the way she's arching her back to her tight grip on my forearms. I want to hear her say it . . . I *need* her to say it . . .

"Drew . . ." she moans, moving her arms around to my back and digging her nails deep into my skin.

The pain is mixed with pleasure, and with one violent thrust, she releases a deep grunt as her pussy contracts around my cock. Every inch of my skin is tingling, and not even a minute later, I follow in delight. Throwing my head into the crook of her neck, releasing myself into her.

I can't breathe, seeing only stars and bright fucking lights. The weight of my body feels heavy, and careful not to crush

her, my weak limbs move enough that I'm lying beside her.

Can I tell her now that I love her? To not go and stay here with me? I'm trying to find the courage, but this euphoric feeling has exhausted me, and for some reason, I'm enjoying the silence. Time to reflect on how perfect that moment was.

Moving my hand towards hers, I pick it up and place it against my lips, kissing it gently. My eyelids become heavy, struggling to stay open until I lose the battle, drifting off.

In the morning I wake, a smile in tow, until I turn over and see the bed empty. The heavy rain is tapping against the window. The weather bureau predicted correctly again. I jump out of bed in only my boxers, noticing the gold foil packet and used rubber sitting on top.

Thank god—it wasn't a dream.

I rush straight for her room, expecting to find her lying in bed. *Its empty.* The walls are bare, and desk cleared. The bed has been stripped and the only thing that remains is a box labelled *Zoey's fragile items—Mom & Dad to collect.*

Agitated and alarmed, I run to the living room and see everything turned off. Turning back around, I make my way to the kitchen. She's nowhere to be found, and in the corner of my eye sits an envelope against the coffee machine. I move closer towards it; my name is scribbled on the front.

I pick it up and stare at my name. The envelope shakes in my hand. My temper is out of control, grabbing the mug beside me and throwing it against the wall. It smashes into a dozen pieces, mimicking my *fucking* heart.

She chose to leave me.

And last night should have made her stay.

We are done.

And this time, it's official.

CHAPTER Nineteen

Zoey

T HEY SAY TIME FLIES WHEN you're having fun, or maybe time flies when you refuse to acknowledge you have a past, and part of you admits you ran away from it.

Denial—the easiest way to pass time and move on with your life.

After spending six months in London, the company I worked for won a tender for a new project in Dubai. Considering I was fairly new to the business, and was yet to really learn the ropes, the invitation to move to Dubai and assist on this important project came as a surprise. Mr. Becker's brother, Peter, was a great mentor and believed that I had the intelligence and capability to work with the business in a fast-paced environment.

I was reluctant to move again, having just settled in London and adjusting to the awful cold weather. But I couldn't and wouldn't allow an opportunity to pass by because I was stuck in some comfort zone. Despite only being in London for such a short time, I had grown fond of the 'Poms' and their overuse of the word 'bollocks.'

Dubai is known for its architecture, from its ridiculously

tall buildings to lavish hotels that accommodated the wealthiest people. It's bustling with tourists, and the hip place to be right now.

Packing my bags and saying goodbye to the friends I had made over the past six months was difficult, but Dubai is so fast-paced that from the moment I landed, I hit the ground running. The company put me up in a great apartment overlooking the city, and with long hours, I didn't have much time to socialize.

I'd wake up at the crack of dawn, as I hadn't adjusted to the time difference, and before I knew it, I'd stumble into my apartment, face-planting the bed in exhaustion. Long days on site, dining clients, to launch party after launch party.

The heat . . . well, that was another thing.

Dressing up in designer work attire was a nice change, but the sweltering heat made me sweat like crazy, and the weight began to fall off. I had the glow and physique of someone who worked out at the gym, without having to attend every day. Occasionally, when I had some time, I would hit the communal gym in my building just to build stamina. The only way to survive in Dubai is to be on top of your game, and endless amounts of coffee.

Dubai is the fashion capital of the world, countless shopping malls—extravagant and spacious—with people spending big everywhere you turn. It was easy to fall into that trap, but I had tried my best to save some extra money so I could buy my own place real soon.

A home.

Wherever that was.

I had even met someone. His name was Josh. He was from Ireland, on a worker visa with a big firm that specialized in IT communications. We got along well, having a lot in common. It wasn't a serious relationship; he was simply a nice guy who I enjoyed spending time with. Josh was far from being a complicated person. If anything, he is the least

complicated person I have ever met.

He had Mom's approval because apparently I needed it. Mom and Dad came out to visit but lasted only four days. Dad complained about the heat the entire time, and Mom maxed out three credit cards, much to Dad's disapproval. As much as they loved me, they couldn't wait to go back home. Well, those were Dad's words. Mom already arranged a trip back for just us girls.

Life in general is going well, until one Saturday morning, it's thrown a massive twist. A curveball, or shitty stick of epic proportions. Something I wasn't expecting. I should know when the phone begins ringing at four am, and reaching to find it, I knock my golden pineapple over. *A bad sign.*

I glance up at the clock beside my bed and answer with a croaky voice, "Hello?"

"Zoey? It's Gigi."

"Gigi?" I sit up, in shock to hear her voice. I hadn't spoken to her in a couple of months since she had been travelling to New Zealand and had limited cell coverage on the mountain range.

"Yes, it's me, doll. I'm sorry to call you so early."

"It's fine." My eyes are wide open, worried at the tone of her voice. "Is something wrong?"

"I've got some bad news," she mentions sadly. "Drew's father passed away."

The second she says the words, the pit of my stomach swirls into a massive knot, threatening me with the urge to vomit. *"Drew's dad passed away?"*

"I'm afraid so."

"When? How?"

"Two days ago. I just flew back in an hour ago and Mrs. Porter from down the hall informed me." Letting out a sigh, she continues, "It was an accident. He was working on a car when his arm got trapped in a cavity. He tried to pull himself free, but suffered a heart attack when doing so."

"Oh my god," I cry out loud, momentarily beyond words.

The tears fall down, past my lips and onto my lap. My heart is in pain thinking about how much Drew must be hurting right now. His dad was his hero. He was never shy of telling anyone that. I can't even begin to put myself in his shoes, and to think, he's going through this all alone. "And Drew. How is he taking it?"

"Not well, doll. Drew was the one who found him."

Dropping the phone, I race to the bathroom and vomit profusely into the sink, not making the toilet. I manage to compose myself for a few moments, retreating back to the bedroom and picking up the phone. I sob into the receiver, Gigi trying her best to calm me from her end. I listen intently as she fills me in with all the details. The funeral would be in three days, and without a question, I book the next flight back home.

The long flight gave me plenty of time to think. I'd been so caught up in my new life that I never allowed myself to stop and think about the past. Scared that if I did, I would run back and reverse all the positivity that's been happening.

The night before I left for London was *the* best night of life, spending those last moments with Drew. Sometimes, without notice and in the most highly inappropriate situations, a memory of the way he kissed me, the way he was inside me, flashes before my eyes. And every time it happens, I have to break away from the fantasy, reminding myself that it was never meant to be. Chasing a dream that wasn't attainable.

But I can't forget the image, the moment. The look in Drew's eye's as he touched me. Fueled by lust, desire, and the fact that what we were doing was forbidden. *We had*

broken all codes.

I wanted so much for him to follow me to London, suggesting the idea and hoping he would read between the lines without me having to lay my heart on the table. But he wasn't interested. That last night between us meant more to me than it did to him. I guess all it was for him was a chance to screw his roomie.

Although it hurt that the feeling wasn't mutual, leaving Drew was the hardest thing I had ever done. I knew that if I didn't take the opportunity, I would regret it for the rest of my life.

And I was sick of living in regret.

I was completely done with Jess. According to Mia, he had knocked up some woman that already had four kids to different men and was chasing him for child support. Serves him right. His wandering dick finally got bitten in the ass.

Callie and I restored our friendship—via email. It was really nice to have her back in my life. We had both moved on from the past, chatted every now and then, hoping to catch up when I returned home one day.

My biggest regret of all is losing Drew. We promised to remain friends, stay in touch, but that never happened. That night was the last night I spoke to Drew.

He deactivated all his social media accounts, changed his cell number, and the only thing left was his address. Or so I thought.

According to Gigi, he had moved closer to the hospital. Only Gigi and Mrs. Porter from down the hall remained in contact with him. It was evident that he didn't want anything to do with me, and so, I gave up trying to hold on to something I never had.

Then this happens.

Life.

The exhaustion of the flight consumes me, my overtired brain barely able to sleep amidst the noise that the other passengers make. There's a kid crying a couple of rows down, and feeling sorry for the little guy, I assume his ears are popping from the altitude. Turns out Mommy dearest thought little Johnny needed to sleep, removing his iPad. The kid has lost it, and so I have lost my will to live.

The couple beside me are nice enough. Married and middle-aged. They kept to themselves, not forcing me into any awkward plane talk. Somewhere during the night, the wife leans over and whispers to her husband, who then returns a big smile. He stretches his arms, unbuckles his seatbelt, then heads towards the restroom.

A minute later, she follows.

The frequent mile-high clubbers.

I'm grossed out, wanting to ask the flight attendant if I could switch seats. When they return, their faces are flushed and I swear on my grandmother's grave—something I rarely do—they smell of *sex.*

When the captain announces our descent into the airport, I couldn't be any happier. *I think I just aged ten years.*

I check into the hotel closest to the airport to have a quick shower and change into my black dress. I know I've missed the ceremony, but if the cabbie sped up a little, I would just make the burial.

The cemetery is in sight, small with luscious green lawns and well-kept tombstones.

I point out to the cab driver where people are gathered near the plot. Drew didn't have much family, so it was mainly his dad's friends paying their respects.

I pay the cabbie a twenty and step out. Taking a deep breath, I walk over to the crowd as my heels dig into the grass. Ballet flats would have been optimal, the ground a little damp from some overnight rain.

The closer I get, the tighter the knot forms in my stomach.

And then, I see him.

His back is facing me, and his posture is fallen over with his head down. I try my hardest to hold back the tears, dabbing the bottom of my lids to not smudge my eye makeup. Around me stand guests. Women crying softly into their handkerchiefs. Men holding on to them, trying their darndest to be strong. It's a sad day, one that I wish Drew wouldn't haven't to go through alone.

You're here.

Be here for your friend.

No matter what happened between us, my friend needs me, and I'm not going to let him down. With every strength I have in me, I walk towards him, excusing myself as quietly as possible through the crowd until I am by his side.

In a bold move, I drop my hand and entwine my fingers into his. He doesn't look up to face me, his eyes slowly moving towards my hand. I don't allow him to let go, trying to warm up his ice-cold skin.

And just before the priest says a prayer, he gently squeezes my hand.

He's alive.

He has acknowledged my presence, and that is the first step. A small part of me is terrified that this will kill him, which I'm sure it is, but in a way that he can move on from and continue his life.

Not in the way of losing all will to live.

Simon & Garfunkel's "Bridge Over Troubled Water" plays as the coffin is lowered into the ground. It was his dad's favorite song; I remember him telling me that he would sing it to Drew back home in Australia when he was just a baby.

While the song plays, I can't hold back any longer, a single tear falling down my cheek as I keep my sniffs as silent as possible. It's futile. Drew's grip tightens and his body begins to shudder. I wrap my arms around him, wanting to shield him from the pain of watching his dad being buried. I don't let go, not even when the music stops and only silence surrounds us. People begin to move forward, patting Drew on the back, and some others throw roses into the plot.

I wait patiently, without a word, and give Drew the time he needs. His persistent, dark stare at the tombstone begins to frighten me. With everyone almost gone, besides a woman hovering, I open my mouth before quickly shutting back up as the woman walks over and calls his name. It seems to catch his attention, and judging by the way she looks at me and then him, I'm guessing it's his latest squeeze.

"Drew," she says calmly. "Are you ready to go now?"

My hand begins to slide away, not wanting to cause an argument between them, but Drew latches on even harder. Squeezing it so tight that it begins to hurt.

"No" is all he responds.

She appears persistent, resting her hand on his shoulder, still watching me with a curious eye. "I think it would be best to go. Everyone will be waiting."

"Then go!" he yells back. "They can fucking wait for me."

Backing off, and offended, she walks towards the cars and leaves us alone. I didn't get a chance to have a proper look at her, leggy with brown curly hair. *Drew's type. No need to get jealous, especially at a time like this.*

It's just us, alone, and stumped on how to talk to him, I continue to sit quietly, allowing the chirping birds to sing.

"I'm sorry, Drew," I cry.

He squeezes my hand again tight, trying to comfort me.

"You know what's ironic?" he says, without looking my way. "When I found him, "Cat's in the Cradle" was playing on the radio. I mean, is that fucked up?" A sinister laugh follows, scaring me a little as we sit alone in the cemetery.

"Drew," I whisper, composing myself enough to be a good friend. "Maybe it was his time."

"He was only fifty-five. It's too soon," he adds, bitterly. "He *begged* me to visit but I'd been so caught up with work. There

was always an excuse."

"You didn't intentionally not visit him, Drew," I tell him.

"You're skinny."

I'm confused by the change of topic. "Excuse me?"

"You're skinny, like stick-skinny. Why?"

Do I answer him? This is odd.

"Uh, the heat in Dubai is like being in a sauna every day with like a thousand Arab men and women. All dressed, of course."

He doesn't say anything else, letting out a breath. "Are you coming to this lunch thing? I mean, what's the point? Why the fuck do we need to celebrate burying my dad?"

"Maybe look at it as celebrating his life," I say, smiling.

"Let's go somewhere else. Just you and me."

"Uh sure, but what about everyone else?"

"Fuck everyone else." He laughs, removing a flask from his jacket and taking a long swig.

"Okay, but how about you hand me the flask? Where do you want to go?"

He pulls my hand along to his car, not turning around to say goodbye to his dad again. From where I'm standing, I can smell the potent scotch on his breath. "How about I drive?"

He tosses me the keys. I climb into the car and put the keys in the ignition. "Where do you want to go?"

"Just follow my lead."

It's beautiful—a small piece of parkland that overlooks the ocean. We sit on a small rock, wedged between two larger rocks. It's pretty secluded; only an old couple walking their dogs are nearby.

"I come here a lot, just to think."

"It's beautiful." I smile.

"I bet you don't have views like this in Dubai."

"No." I laugh. "Skyscrapers and desert."

Staring at the ocean, the calming blue water and salty sea air ease my worries. And maybe it's not just where we are, but who I'm with.

Drew picks up a daisy from the small shrubbery beside the rocks and tears the pretty white petals apart. "I'm sorry I cut you out."

"I shouldn't have left without saying goodbye," I admit truthfully.

"You did what you had to do. And now look at you, you're all grown up."

"Am I?" With a playful smirk, I pull my sleeve up and show him my wrist.

Pulling my arm closer to him, he examines the tattoo, blinking repeatedly. He's wearing his contacts, and I know how much they irritate him outdoors when the wind is strong.

"You got yourself a Rainbow Brite tattoo?"

I nod, grinning back at him. "I needed a reminder that wherever I go, whatever I do, it's okay to be me. Flaws and all." I look down at my wrist, remembering the moment I got it. There was this small tattoo parlor in the heart of London. It had been a stressful day at work and I was extremely homesick. After speaking to my brother for a solid hour, I stumbled upon this place. I remember looking at the window and seeing my reflection. It dawned on me that the person staring back was someone new. I had no clue who she was. She wore fancy clothes, ate salads for lunch, and went to art shows with colleagues because that was the latest trend.

I was thoroughly enjoying my new role, but every so often, I missed the old me. Carefree, sweats-wearing Zoey who lounged on the couch for endless hours, watching reruns of *Different Strokes* while eating a bag of Cheetos.

And so, I walked in and asked the cute guy to ink me.

"There's no doubt that you're unique. Quirky, I'll admit, and a tad neurotic when it comes to your music."

I punch his arm softly, easing the tension between us. "I went to a Foreigner concert in London. It was *so* good. I even managed to get my t-shirt signed," I tell him excitedly.

"Did you tell him that you want to know what love is?"

I chuckle softly, then turn my head curiously. "Wait, how do you know that Foreigner sings that song?"

"Mmm . . . would you believe that I've been listening to music released before the year nineteen ninety?" He shuffles awkwardly, kicking his foot against the rock. "Joanna, my girlfriend, likes that type of music."

Oh. There it is. The giant elephant in the room. Not so much an elephant, rather a skinny giraffe. It was bound to happen. I'm not allowed to be angry or jealous. I chose to leave here. I ran off. Embrace his happiness, move on, then cry about it later after a few shots of tequila and some bad karaoke of "My Heart Will Go On."

"Joanna. She seems nice."

"Yeah, she is," he says plainly.

"Been together long?"

"Four months."

"That's nice. She's really pretty."

"She is."

I'm grasping at straws. "Okay, you gotta give me something here."

He's awfully fidgety, probably from the scotch wearing off. "I met her in the ER. She had a pencil stuck in her hand."

"What? Are you kidding me?"

"Nope."

"Ouch! How did that end up being a relationship?"

"When we were removing the pencil, I asked her out to distract her."

We laugh in unison, our shoulders colliding. "So a sympathy date?"

"It was. She's nice. A middle-school teacher."

"I'm happy for you." It's genuine, coming from a good place in my heart. The bad place, the small area called *Jealousville,* is rocking itself in the corner with a voodoo doll with Joanna's face on it.

"Are you seeing anyone?" he's quick to ask.

"Uh, kind of. It's nothing serious. Just someone I met in Dubai. He's from Ireland and . . . he's really nice."

How many times could the both of us use the word 'nice'?

"Does he make you happy, Zoey?" He's watching me intently, making me self-conscious. What is he thinking? *Oh, to be a fly on the wall of his brain right now.*

"He's the most uncomplicated person I've ever met. It's refreshing."

"And boring?"

"Hey." I nudge him with my arm. "It's nice to date a guy that has no baggage."

There's that word again. *Nice.*

The wind begins to pick up, the sun setting in the horizon. The elderly couple have left, and with the darkness upon us, we should both be heading home. Or to the hotel, in my case.

"It's late, we should probably head back," I suggest.

He nods his head in agreement, standing up and extending his hand for me to latch on to. "How long are you here for?"

"I leave tomorrow night."

I can tell that something is bothering him. With a frown, his forehead creases and his smile disappears.

"I have to go to dad's place tomorrow to get some paperwork . . ." Clutching the back of his neck, he rubs it nervously. "I don't want to go—"

"I'll be there, Drew." I smile, holding his hand to calm his nerves. "You don't even have to ask."

Stepping into his dad's house brings back a lot of memories. I have been here numerous times, and suddenly, the sadness of him being gone creeps in. *Don't cry.* Be strong for Drew.

The musky scent inside the living room smells just like him, and everywhere you look, there is something that has a story to tell. The stuffed fox fighting the rattlesnake that sits next to the TV, something that always creeped me out. The large photo frame with a picture of him feeding a crocodile back home in Australia.

And then, there's a picture of Drew. Four years old, sitting on a bike next to his mother. The photo is old, sepia with corners fraying. I haven't seen this picture before, and upon closer inspection, I look at the face that belonged to his mother. *She was beautiful.* Same color hair as Drew, and the lips did the same pose, curving to the left slightly when they smiled.

"I've got the papers." Drew stops just shy of where I'm standing.

"That's my mother."

"I kinda figured that. She's beautiful and you're the spitting image of her."

My skin begins to tingle, goosebumps appearing up and down my arm. I can't see him standing behind me, but I feel it. All over. Every inch of me senses the warmth of his body right behind me. So close that his shallow, uneven breaths warm the tips of my shoulder blades.

And this, right here, is everything I was afraid of.

The sole reason that for the past year, I'd blocked out everything about him. I can't deny it anymore: I love him. I've loved him for such a long time, long before that night.

But is love enough? Can I honestly give up everything I've

worked so hard for because I love a guy? Just because you love someone doesn't mean it'll end up with a 'happily ever after.'

"Stay," he says, barely above a whisper.

"Drew."

"No." Gripping my arm, he turns me around so we're facing each other. "I should have asked you to stay that night. Maybe if I did, things would be different between us. Maybe Dad would still be here."

I stroke his cheek with the palm of my hand, wiping away the single tear that has fallen. He missed his dad, but no matter what happened between us, it wouldn't change the fact that it was his time to go. *He's hurting.* So much of me wants to protect him, wrap him up in a cotton-wool blanket and sprinkle happy dust on him.

But deep down inside I know I can only do so much. I'm not God.

"I . . . I can't stay."

He pulls away, my hand falling abruptly. "Of course you can't."

"I want to. I really do," I quickly add. "But what I'm doing, it's for me. I don't want to resent you because I stay here."

"I get it."

"Do you?" I ask, reaching for his hand again.

Tilting his head towards the ground, he ignores my gesture and doesn't make eye contact. "It's never been right, us. We're just not meant to be."

"I don't think it's not meant to be. It's the timing, Drew. We're both at different stages of our lives. If we're meant to be, it'll happen. It won't be forced, and neither one of us will have to make a sacrifice."

When did I become a relationship expert? I know nothing about love or relationships, for that matter. I know one thing and one thing only: I have to take care of myself first.

My voice croaks, holding back my emotions. "My flight . . . I have to go."

His body remains the same, and then out of the blue, he raises his eyes to meet mine with a genuine smile on his face. "Go, Zoey. Finish doing what you need to do."

"Can we stay in touch this time? Don't pull a girl tantrum on me and change your number," I say, deadpan.

"Were you stalking me?"

"If I admit that I was, would that make you happy?"

His lips curve upwards, eyes dancing in delight, grinning hopelessly back at me. "Surprisingly, yes."

"Then yes, I stalked your ass big time," I laugh. "Now, I really have to go."

Pulling my body close to his, he places his hands on the sides of my neck, leaning in and kissing my forehead. "Bye, Zoey Richards, till we meet again."

The scent of his cologne lingers, and the memories of us flood back. Our laughter on the couch while I made him watch chick-flicks, to our arguments in the kitchen over my lack of cleaning the dishes.

And the one memory I will cherish forever.

The way his eyes fluttered when he fell asleep beside me. How peaceful and content he looked after we made love.

Love. That's what happened between us that night.

We don't need to say the words right now, or maybe even ever. It's there, and there's no denying it.

I whisper softly into his chest as we hold onto each other, "Till we meet again, Drew Baldwin."

And there, in front of his dad's house, we say our goodbyes. It should hurt more, I should be crying, but I'm not.

Drew, my best friend, did what all best friends do. He encouraged me to follow my dreams. Best friends don't allow you to settle for anything less. They fight to build you up, not bring you down. They see you through your darkness moments, and hold your hand to guide you into the light.

I couldn't have asked for a better friend, roomie, and maybe one day, soulmate.

I throw my bag into the trunk and get into the car. I open the window and see Drew outside, his gaze fixated on me. A mixture of sadness and pride.

And right then, I know there will be a time and place for us.

It wasn't last year, and it's not today.

But sometime, in the future, our cosmos will align and everything will just fall into place.

EPILOGUE
Drew

*H*E SAID WHAT?

I read the printed email that Gigi had sent me. Male, forty-six, professional molder. Perhaps we had our wires crossed. A molder was someone who molded, right? *Molded what?*

"So Karl, when you just said you worked for Adults Delicious Entertainment, you meant . . ."

"I'm a penis model," he says, proudly.

I choke on my own saliva, trying to cover it up with a cough. What the hell did a penis model do? Wrap it up in a bow and walk down a runway? This is uncomfortable, to say the least.

I don't know why I ask, but my curiosity gets the better of me. "I'm curious. What exactly does a penis model do?"

"They use my penis to create molds for dildos."

He takes out a box, handing it over to me. My instant reaction is to throw it across the room. I *really* don't need to see a rubber dick sitting inside a box. I have my own dick—a perfectly sized one, according to the women I've slept with.

Karl is dressed in a sky-blue suit and white collared shirt that's buttoned down too low, exposing his tan yet hairy chest. He seems to enjoy his jewelry; a thick gold bracelet sits on his wrist, accompanied by an oversized ring on his pinky finger. All he needed was a manicured moustache and he'd mirror Robin Williams from the movie *The Birdcage.*

Walking around the room, he admires the ocean view and comments on the beautiful shade of the drapes. Winterberry, according to him. They're fucking pink. *Like the big giant dildo sitting on my coffee table.*

"So listen, a bunch of other models would come by from time to time. Just to test the products."

Test the products . . . on each other? I'm mentally strangling Gigi. What the hell was she smoking when she sent me this application? Or worse yet, maybe he's one of her many ex-lovers. *Erase the image . . . erase the image.*

"You mean there's more of you?" I hesitate.

I'm living in a bubble, one that's void of giant dildos. Who would have thought that there's a whole army of penis models just frolicking around like it's no big deal. 'Professional molder' is so misleading.

When I told Gigi I was looking for a roommate, I specifically said male. No more living with women and all the drama that comes along with it.

But this . . . is he gay?

I'm not opposed to having a gay roommate, but I don't exactly want a tribe of them in my living room whipping their dicks out and comparing sizes, hashing out marketing plans for whose dick will have the largest profit.

Next.

I tell him that I'll call him and send him on his merry way, but not without him offering to leave a sample of his product for any lady friend or male who might be interested.

I smile politely and close the door behind him. Gigi is going to get an earful from me when I see her tomorrow for our weekly lunch date. That, and I'll offload Karl's parting gift onto her with the promise to not tell me what she does with it.

It was about three months ago that I bought this fantastic,

albeit rundown apartment near the beach. It's a two-bedroom, decent-size living area with a dining room and a massive functional kitchen. My favorite area is the huge balcony that overlooks the ocean. With my hectic schedule at the hospital, I haven't decorated or changed anything. The previous owner is one of Gigi's friends, a retired lady that had let the place go and needed to move to a more manageable unit. She's the reason behind the 'winterberry' drapes and doilies scattered everywhere you turn.

For now, it would do. Finding a roommate would ease the burden of paying the mortgage, with some extra change to start fixing up the place. Many of dad's friends suggested I sell his place to renovate here, but I just couldn't do it. I wanted to keep his memory alive, and when I needed a break or some downtime with Betty, I'd stay there for a couple of days.

Heading to the kitchen and grabbing myself a beer, I hear a knock on the door. It's the next applicant. *Shit.* I quickly look at the paper, searching for his name. It's nowhere to be found. A bad omen; stupidity is not something I look for in a roommate.

"So, I hear you have a room available?"

I hear her voice, a sound that is forever ingrained in my memory. It's like a thousand butterflies fluttering around you in an empty room. Oh, wait, inside my stomach. *That's how she makes me feel.* I haven't even laid eyes on her, yet my excitement is paralyzing my ability to respond to her.

"Zoey, what are you doing here?"

Her back is facing me, and closing the door behind her, she finally turns around.

"I hear you have a room available?"

And there she is. Standing in front of me, no longer a figment of my imagination.

She's more *beautiful* than I remember. Matured, yet still has her cute cheeky smile that lights up her entire face.

She's wearing a dress, strapless, that sits just above her knees. It's very summery with little pineapples all over it. *Pineapples* . . . I smile at the thought. I notice her hair; it's cut short, sitting just above her shoulders.

"I do have a room available but . . ." I trail off, mesmerized by how radiant she looks. Then, I spot it. The gold pineapple pendant that sits on her delicate pale skin. *She still has it.*

"Well, aren't you going to interview me?" she asks, trying her best to keep a straight face.

I play along with whatever game she is playing, also trying to keep a straight face.

She walks further into the room, and stops at the coffee table. Arching her brow, with a slight scowl, she lifts the box that Karl left behind. "Interesting choice of coffee table decoration."

"Oh, it's not mine," I quickly say. "The guy who just left is a penis model. It's bizarre, I know."

The green in her eyes brightens, twinkling with amusement. "I'm glad it's not yours, but then again, that's kind of kinky. Huh, interesting profession."

I want to kiss that smirk off her face. Tell her to stop being a smartass and get over here so I can show her what a real dick looks like, not some rubber bullshit. But that would be rude of me; just because I haven't fucked anyone since the day she left doesn't mean I should be so brazen. *Stop thinking with your blue balls.*

"So, are you going to ask me to sit down?"

"Yes." I smile, extending my hand towards the couch.

"Where's your interviewing etiquette? It's almost like you've never had a roommate before," she says, deadpan.

"I had a roomie once," I play along. "You left your name off the form."

"Did I?" she says plainly. "Zoey. Zoey Richards. And you?"

I take a seat beside her, keeping the distance to avoid my

blue balls mauling her in the heat of the moment. "Drew. Drew Baldwin. Some like to call me Dr. Drew."

"Like Alec, Stephen, Daniel, and what's the one that no one remembers?"

"Billy. And no, I'm not related."

Bowing her head, and hiding her mischievous smirk, she fiddles with the hem of her dress before moving her attention back to me. "So, you're a doctor?"

"Training to be a surgeon. I specialize in cardiology."

"The heart. An interesting choice."

"Mending broken hearts. It's kinda my thing," I murmur, fixing my gaze on her lips. I missed them. *I missed her.*

"So, tell me about you, Zoey."

"I'm an architect. I just started my own business the next town over so this location is perfect." With a sly grin, she slides closer to me, lowering her voice as if she's going to reveal a secret. "In my spare time, I like to cyberstalk my ex-roomie and see what he's been doing with his life."

I struggle to hold back my smile. "And how is he?"

"You tell me?"

"Zoey."

"Drew," she whispers back.

Our bodies are close enough that I could lean over and take what's mine. But instead, I want to show her how much she means to me. That even after all this time, I have faith in us.

"I want to show you something." I pull up my sleeve, and there on my forearm is my tattoo.

"You got a tattoo?" she exclaims. *"And it's a pineapple?"*

I place my hand on top of hers, shocked at the jolt of electricity that runs through my veins the moment we touch. I know she felt it too; her body jumped the moment mine did.

"See. There's this woman and I'm kind of in love with her."

I smile, continuing, "I realized that our timing was just off and she has this thing for pineapples. Apparently they're good luck or something. So I inked it on my skin, because I knew one day she'd be back."

Moving her hand on top of mine, she squeezes it tight. My eyes meet hers, full of content and joy that she's returned. "Oh, and she's a real pain in the ass."

"Drew, I love you," she blurts out. "It's always been you. I should have known all along, the day you walked into the apartment wearing that gross SpongeBob shirt of yours. It was a sign . . . SpongeBob lives in a pineapple under the sea."

I smile hopelessly back at her, touching her cheek with the tip of my finger, calming her nervous energy. *"I love you too, Zoey."*

"Is this it, are we done with being done?" she asks, almost begging.

"We're done with being done," I repeat. *"Stay with me?"*

"I'm home, Drew. There's nowhere else I want to be. You had me at 'she's a real pain in the ass.'" She smiles.

I close the gap between us and bring my lips towards hers. They're soft and taste like Coca Cola, just how I remembered them. I want to savor this kiss, and all of her. Then it dawns on me: I'm never going to let her go. This is just the beginning. I've never wanted anything or anyone more than I want her.

Pulling away, but keeping close, she reminds me, "You know, if we're going to live together we need to establish rules."

"Hmm, okay. I'll start." I think for a moment, then it hits me. "I don't like wasting water. So we should shower together every day."

"Deal." She grins.

Raising her index finger to the corner of her mouth, she adds, "I don't like doing laundry, so don't wear anything to bed."

"Deal." Unable to contain my joy, I pull her back, kissing her feverishly, allowing her to moan while our tongues slide, battling each other.

"Wait." She stops me, pulling her cell out of her purse and typing quickly. My cell beeps and she nods for me to check it. I lean over to where it's sitting on the coffee table and open the text on the screen.

Code Red.

I shake my head, grinning from ear to ear, and throw my cell back onto the sofa, scooping her up and wrapping her legs around my waist. I drop my head to meet hers and plant a soft kiss on her lips, lingering as I allow it to sink in. *She's here, with me.*

"One more rule." I kiss her lips again, and withdraw with a devilish smile. "This apartment is environmentally friendly . . . so no condoms on the premises."

She laughs, wrapping her arms tighter around my neck. "Wait, do you hear that?"

"Hear what?" I ask, listening to the sound of nothing, aside from the ocean.

"It's my ovaries. They're dancing. Some sort of celebration, and they're all jumping up and yelling, 'Yippee' . . ."

"You know what?" I grin, keeping my voice to just above a whisper. "I do hear that."

I had never pictured myself having a family with anyone, nor being married, and just in one heartbeat, it's all I want with the girl wrapped up in my arms.

Lifting her higher, I steal a kiss, lingering as she moans softly against my lips.

"Wait." She stops me again. "We need a song for this moment."

"A song for this moment?"

"Yes. It'll be our song . . . at least, one of our songs. Something to remember this moment by, and if ever we hear it on the radio we'll be like, 'Oh hey, our song!'"

I think about it, the perfect song coming to mind. That, and I've had it on repeat for the past week. "I've got the perfect song."

Carrying her in my arms, I make my way to the shelf near the television and turn on my iPod. Shuffling quickly, I hit play.

"I love this song." She beams, resting her head on my shoulder while Bryan Adams's "Heaven" plays in the background.

"I'll be honest," I tell her. "I'm not a fan of the eighties . . . but we could meet halfway perhaps? The nineties?"

"The nineties," she acknowledges, nodding. "I'm down for some Vanilla Ice, MC Hammer . . . oh wait, what about Wilson Phillips?"

She breaks out laughing, and it's so contagious, I laugh along with her as we make our way to *our* bedroom.

Finally, my girl came home.

Keep reading for a preview of

BESTSELLING AUTHOR
KAT T. MASEN

CHAPTER One

Drew

Son of a bitch.

My big toe hits the metal bar. It's followed by empty threats and loud swearing as the pain ricochets throughout my body, making me see nothing but stars. Leaning over to the table, I manage to switch the lamp on to see what I ran into: a thigh master.

A growl escapes my throat. The urge to grab the useless piece of crap and throw it off the balcony is difficult to control. This isn't the first time this has happened and probably not the last.

Remember why you love her.

The irony—which strikes me as I writhe in pain—is that Zoey has fantastic thighs. And trust me, I should know. I've spent countless hours between them. Yet, her fascination with fitness gimmicks such as the thigh master is bordering obsessive.

With my hands full of pizza boxes, I hobble through the narrow hall and into the living room to be met with dead silence. Zoey had a work dinner that would end in an hour and this is the only night I could schedule off that coincided with her staying out late.

Why?

I had a plan.

See, Zoey and I had been living together for just over a year. The moment she walked back into my life after living in London and Dubai, I knew I couldn't let her go.

Everything just fell back to normal between us. Almost as if no time had passed. The only thing that changed: the insanely hot sex that happened whenever we were in arm's reach of each other.

It blows my mind to this day how we were roomies for four years and wasted our time screwing other people rather than each other. But I guess, like everything in life, things happen for a reason.

I love her. No more wasting time on boyfriend/girlfriend bullshit. I had to make it official. *Seal the deal.* Though I know she'll argue about taking on my name. Yeah, she's one of those women. Fights for her own rights but it's just a charade. She does it to appear 'cool' and is quick to complain about how draining it all is and would rather be on the couch watching *The Love Boat* with a bag of popcorn.

And that's if she says yes.

Don't get ahead of yourself. What if she tells me she needs more time, which, in turn will bruise my ego, making me doubt our relationship and cause another fight between us?

Then again, she's not one to disguise her desperation to get married. Especially after she made me watch three movies last week that all revolved around weddings. I stopped counting after the tenth time she began a sentence with *"When I get married . . ."*

Impatient. Obnoxious. Pain in my ass.

That's Zoey Richards.

I'd been sitting on this idea for a while. *A long while.* It was never a question of whether or not I would do it. I just needed the right time, place, and way of asking her to be my wife. After all, this is supposed to be one of the biggest moments in a couple's relationship.

Fuck. Talk about pressure.

I continue to carry the eight pizza boxes to the kitchen. Despite my healthy eating habits, I'm not immune to the glorious smell of melted cheese. I just have more self-control

than Zoey. Placing the boxes down on the kitchen table—careful not to tip the stack—I glance at my watch to check how many minutes I have left. There isn't much time to execute this plan before she comes home.

In a mad rush, I reach for the top kitchen cupboard where I keep a box of candles. Pulling the box down, I quickly take them outside to the balcony and scatter them somewhat evenly on the ground. There is a strong breeze from the ocean, which I knew would hinder my plan to get all romantic hence using battery-operated candles that look like the real deal. Seriously, whoever invented this is *genius.*

Rushing to the spare bedroom, I remove the brown box from the closet. Zoey never checked in here so it became the perfect spot to hide my treasure—eight gold pineapples.

Eight is considered a lucky number, and pineapples, because Zoey was obsessed with them. She kept that gold pineapple on the bedside table. Another one of her quirky traits that I had grown accustomed too.

Carrying the box with the utmost of care, I take them outside and place them exactly where I imagined them to be, positioned with the correct lighting so they can easily be seen. With the sun almost setting and the breeze calming down, it's a perfect night to propose to the woman I love.

I scurry back into the kitchen grabbing the seven empty pizza boxes and moving through the apartment, creating a trail to the balcony. I know it sounds like a crazy idea, but if anyone would follow a trail of empty pizza boxes, it's Zoey.

I'm almost done. All I need to do is take a quick shower and get dressed. I really wanted this moment to be perfect, torn as to what to wear. I finally decided on wearing my navy suit—her favorite. With my hair styled, I spray the bottle of aftershave against my neck. It leaves a sting; the cut skin from yesterday's rushed shaving job is still slightly open.

Walking back to the balcony with a portable speaker in my hand, the song is ready to go at the touch of the play button, the moment she walks through that door.

Annoying as it usually seems, Zoey had the tendency to over-text me after work. Usually she's complaining about traffic, and sometimes she'll go on and on about the growls her stomach makes believing it sounds like the tune of a song. Once, she actually put the speaker to her belly and claimed that it sounded like "Livin' on a Prayer." Funnily enough, it did. Just goes to show how my brain has been warped by her.

On cue, and just like I said she would, a text comes thru.

> Do you think there is some radio god that purposely plays a good song just as you're about to exit the car? I'm seriously sitting outside our apartment because Heart came on.

I shake my head, holding my laugh and easily breaking into a smile. I had no clue who Heart was, but no doubt, it was some eighties group.

C'mon, it's Zoey after all.

I should respond, but can't think of anything witty as the nerves begin to consume me. She thinks I'm at work. So perhaps a little white lie wouldn't hurt for the greater good. At least, to calm me down.

> I think you're right. When someone dies on the operating table, I swear Knockin' on Heaven's door is blaring through the speakers.

I wait for her response, and knowing Zo, she'll have an opinion on my morbid text.

> Way to ruin my Heart buzz.

Deeps breaths—she's here. Amid the excitement and bundled nerves, I forget the most important thing: the ring. Running back into the kitchen, I find the last pizza box sitting on the table where I had left it. It contained a freshly cooked pepperoni pizza in the shape of a pineapple. The lengths I had to go through to get this pizza made. Pepe— our local pizza guy—was not the most creative and easiest

person to work with. Firstly, his strong Italian accent made it difficult to understand in the easiest of circumstances.

Try explaining to him that I needed a pineapple-shaped pizza.

The look on his face was priceless. Then he proceeded to give me a history lesson on the origin of pizza. I Googled some pictures of different-shaped pizzas, which piqued his interest. I wasn't sure what intrigued him more, the endless number of pictures or the fact he had never heard of Google.

In the end, he made it work. And it looked damn good.

All I had to do was grab the ring from the vegetable drawer in the refrigerator. A place Zoey never ever ventured to. My idea had been to set the navy box in the center of the pizza. A gesture that seemed very personal. *Very Zoey.*

I've got a minute at the most to spare, rushing back to the balcony and waiting for her to enter the apartment. My anxiety is really clouding this moment. I'm sure this is normal. I'm doing the right thing. It's just jitters . . . cold feet. This moment could be the biggest moment of our lives, and I have to deliver my speech with the utmost care.

Fuck me dead.

I rarely drink, but a bottle of hard liquor would be fantastic right now.

Closing my eyes while taking a deep breath, I drown out all the fear and envision her face. I never expected her to be my soulmate. We were polar opposites. She hated to eat healthy, and I only ate organic. I love modern music, she's happy to remain in her nineteen-eighties bubble. She loves to be on top, and I love to fuck her from behind.

Maybe that last one wasn't such a big deal.

The sound of the door banging shut echoes through our small apartment.

A sea of anxiety swirls in the pit of my stomach as I swallow the giant lump in my throat, wringing my hands nervously. *You can do this.* Why the fuck is this tripping me out so much?

Her pumps—the camel-colored ones with the strap around the ankle—click against the beaten old floorboards. Then, all I hear is silence.

I straighten my posture and wait for her to find me, remembering mid-thought to press play on the speaker. With sweaty palms, I almost knock the speaker off the table. *Calm the fuck down, will you? When it comes to operating on an almost-dying patient, you've got no problem whatsoever.*

The instrumental intro of "Take My Breath Away" plays, soothing my panicked state. She loved this song, and I had to admit that I somewhat did too.

My eyes are fixated on the doorway, heart thumping loud mirroring the beats of the song. The shadow of her body moves closer, and her head is carefully following the trail of pizza boxes creating a path to where I stand. It only takes a split second for her to be in full view, and when her beautiful green eyes meet mine, my heart stops the mad rush and slows down, calming itself.

It's time.

Eyes wide and with a confused expression, I can almost see the wheels turning inside her head. Then, as the wind slowly brushes past us, her gaze meets mine.

"Drew, what is all this?" Her voice is shaking. It's cute. Shouldn't I be the nervous one here? Yet suddenly, I am the calmest I have been in my entire life.

Zoey enjoyed rambling most of the time, but now, she's completely speechless, leaving me even more in love with her. Her eyes scan the balcony, her mouth quietly counting the gold pineapples. With her soft, delicate hand within reach, I extend my hand forward, motioning for her to come closer while still balancing the pizza box with my other hand. Our skin touches and instantly I see her eyes close with her chest rising and falling. I love watching her like this—dead

silent. Taking in the moment with every expression easily readable on her beautiful face.

"Zoey." I smile, grazing her cheek with the tip of my finger. "Six years ago I had pictured a very different life. A life you weren't part of yet."

Her big green eyes are boring into me; etched with anticipation and curiosity. She doesn't realize that when lost in thought, she parts her lips slightly with her tongue resting comfortably between her teeth. My gaze moves away from her mouth and focuses back on her eyes.

I tell her slowly, "While that life would have taken me on a different road, it would have been lonely without you by my side."

"You are the most frustrating person I have ever met," I continue, "and we couldn't be more opposite. I mean, seriously, why would you enjoy listening to songs sung by a daggy redhead that looks like a goddamn geek?"

"*Rick Astley,*" she interrupts, finding her voice, "had women *falling* at his feet. He was never going to give you up, or break your heart. And, he was never going to run around or desert you. Hello, why wouldn't you want a man like that?"

I place my finger on her lips, quieting her rambling.

"I love you," I state, bending down on one knee. I open the pizza box, raising my eyes to meet hers. "Zoey Richards, will you marry me?"

A small breath escapes her mouth, her eyes dancing in delight with clouded vision. I can only assume they are happy tears, but each second that passes in silence tightens my chest. For someone who was born with the verbal diarrhea gene, I begged silently for her to say something. *Anything.*

The corners of her lips curve in a delicious smile, and she follows with on-the-spot jumping. It could be a reaction to the pizza itself, but then she follows with a "YES!"

I allow the tight breath to release, steadily removing the ring from the box. Placing the pizza aside, her eyes follow, and then I do what I've been wanting to do for such a long time—I slide the ring along her petite finger. Her cute squeals and excited jumps make it hard for me to get it on. But when I do, it looks perfect.

"It's so beautiful!" she exclaims, staring at it with awe. "Canary diamond. Just like a pineapple. I can't believe you did this. Oh my gosh, we're getting married!"

For a split second, it almost seems like she's having a panic attack. Her breathing is out of control, her body shaking unpleasantly. And just as I am about to ask her if she is okay, she continues.

"That proposal was more intense than when Emmy was thrown onto the conveyer belt thingy to be shredded into nothing. I mean, yeah okay, I kinda knew that Jonathan would save the day but still. I was on edge the *entire* time."

I stand in confusion like I'm being quizzed. Then the light bulb goes off in my brain. "Are you talking about that movie you made me watch with the mannequin coming to
life?"

She slaps her hand against my chest, distracted by her ring, then follows with a sarcastic laugh. "How quickly you remember the blonde with the lean legs."

"The most ridiculous concept for a movie. Mannequins coming to life, give me a break."

She shakes her head left to right, grinning like crazy. Staring back at me is this beautiful woman who just agreed to be my wife. Wrapping her arms around my neck, I settle my hands on her hips and bring her in for a long-awaited kiss.

She said yes.

Zoey Richards is going to be my wife.

ABOUT *the Author*

Born and bred in Sydney, Australia, Kat T. Masen is a mother to four crazy boys and wife to one sane husband. Growing up in a generation where social media and fancy gadgets didn't exist, she enjoyed reading from an early age and found herself immersed in these stories. After meeting friends on Twitter who loved to read as much as she did, her passion to write began and the friendships continued on despite the distance.

"I'm known to be crazy and humorous. Show me the most random picture of a dog in a wig and I'll be laughing for days."

Where to find me:
Facebook: www.facebook.com/authorkattmasen
Twitter: @authorkattmasen
Instagram: @authorkattmasen
Website: www.kattmasen.com

Printed in Great Britain
by Amazon